# BRUGES BLOOD

## MIKE DONALD

Published by Bonny May Publishing, Oxford, United Kingdom
www.touchwoodpictures.com

ISBN 978-1-9161065-0-5
e-ISB 978-1-9161065-1-2

First Edition

Printed in the United Kingdom

For Dorrie.

# ONE

HE WAITED UNTIL dark. The water from the canal slapped against the stone arch outside the wrought iron bars, the lights from the buildings opposite reflecting off its surface. The tour boats and their amplified spiel on historic Bruges had finished for the day and the canal was quiet. He looked over at the dark shape hunched in the corner of the basement, and shivered in the dank atmosphere.

It was going to be a struggle getting it under the bars, but once it was beneath the water natural buoyancy would lighten the load. He slid into the clammy neoprene of his wet suit, strapped on his tank, checked his regulator and ran through his pre-dive ritual. He wasn't exactly diving the Mariana trench, but it didn't take much water to drown a man, and he'd learned recently that if a thing could go wrong, it usually did.

He wasn't going far, it was a journey of less than half an hour. Once he'd reached his destination and finished the job, he would make his way further along the Dijver canal passing under the Bonifacius bridge next to the Arentshuis garden.

He'd checked the CCTV coverage and located a blind spot encompassing a drainage conduit that gave access up into the garden hidden by overhanging trees. He would be able to make his way from there to where his van was parked in the building site in front of the Gruuthusemus

The museum had been undergoing a massive refurbishment for years and it had been easy enough to gain access to the site earlier in the day. Once there he would change out of his diving gear, stow it in the van and drive away. He strapped his facemask on, took a few breaths through the regulator and began work. As he'd expected it was an awkward maneuver to gain access to the canal beneath the iron bars.

Once he was underwater things got a lot easier and he used the sealed UWIS, an Under-Water-Information-System, like GPS for divers, to guide him down the Groenerei, towing his load behind him.

Ten minutes later he was moving under Peerdenstraat bridge, and then beneath Meestraat, passing the fish market on his left-hand side before swinging left and then right under Woolestraat and on into the Dijver canal. Fifteen minutes later he was in position opposite the old police station in Kartuizerinnenstraat.

His underwater flashlight revealed the murky shape of the concrete stanchion that supported the beer pipe on the bed of the canal. The pipe ran beneath the canal for over three Kilometers, pumping the beer from the brewery to the bottling depot across town. He'd brought the rope and used it to tie the special knot. He'd practiced tying it underwater, and with his eyes closed. He knew how important it was that the system he was putting in place functioned flawlessly. She'd been very clear. If he let her down then things would not go well for him. He 'd seen what that meant while working for her. The power she wielded, and the way she punished failure was beyond belief. She hadn't told him any of the real details, he'd just followed her instructions to the letter. But he wasn't stupid. A lot of resources were being employed to ensure her plan would succeed.

He knew one thing for sure. If she was settling a score then God help the person she was settling it with.

He checked the knot for the third time and slowed his breathing before looking around. His flashlight illuminated the dark shape in its powerful beam. The reason for his journey. He'd been responsible for many deaths in his time, but this wasn't one of them. He turned away, and headed back up the canal towards the Bonifacius bridge, leaving his grotesque cargo further behind him with every stroke.

# TWO

## LONDON, ENGLAND

"HEY, SLEEPYHEAD!"

Chandler jerked awake. He'd been sitting on a park bench in the heat of the sun and nodded off. Roxie was throwing pieces of bread to a gaggle of ducks squabbling over the spoils.

"Sorry. The heat of the sun," he said.

"You were muttering to yourself. Didn't sound like the dream was a pleasant one."

"It wasn't too bad."

Chandler had suffered from PTSD, post -traumatic stress disorder when his wife was killed during London 's 7/7 terrorist attack on the bus in Tavistock Square. His symptoms had reappeared during the traumatic events out in Louisiana but had soon passed, and now he just had the occasional bad dream.

Roxie came over to him and gave him a kiss. "Was it the sisters?"

He nodded. "Yes, but they didn't get to me this time." He gave her a kiss back.

"Well, that's good to know. Maybe you should keep out of the sun.

4

"You obviously don't know how rare a commodity sun is to an Englishman."

Roxie smiled and threw some more bread to the ducks. "I can imagine."

They'd been in England for nearly a month now, and she'd been helping him to clear out his father's flat. There was no need to keep the piles of research material, or any of his father's belongings that didn't have sentimental value. Her presence in his life was a good enough reason to move on and start the cleanup he'd been putting off since his wife died. Even though Duke had joked about him tiring of swamps, it wasn't for that reason he was back home. Roxie was fascinated by history. It's what made her such a good investigator. In between cleaning up the flat and dropping things into various charity shops, he'd shown her parts of London that he'd either taken for granted or seen as tacky tourist destinations. Needless to say, she loved them all.

London's Tower Bridge had proved a big hit. It was a subject he knew a lot about and was able to entertain her with all sorts of arcane facts and anecdotes. She listened, spellbound as he recanted its history, and was intrigued to discover that the high-level walkways between the towers were a favorite haunt for prostitutes up until it was closed in 1910. He got up from the bench and moved behind her, stroking her neck as she threw her last piece of bread to a particularly insistent duck.

"You know there's a law against overfeeding wildlife don't you." Roxie dusted the crumbs from her hands and turned around. "There's a law against everything in England, but I'm sure you just made that one up."

"You're probably right."

They looked across the still waters of the park, the sun high in the sky, while white clouds drifted aimlessly above them.

"You must be missing them," Roxie said. Chandler looked at her. "Missing who?"

"The swamps." Chandler smiled. As usual, she was right.

"Not so much the swamps, but I'll admit that being around Duke and Chilly was never dull."

"Don't tell me you find feeding ducks dull?" "Of course not."

Though he'd been in contact with Duke and Chilly via Skype, it wasn't the same. While investigating the case out in Louisiana, he'd dodged alligators, been shot at by corrupt officials and met Roxie, who had become the love of his life. Maybe compared to that, feeding ducks in a park could be seen as a touch prosaic.

"I've seen that look before." Roxie's voice snapped him out of his reverie.

"Sorry, I was miles away."

"Back in the swamps?"

"Sort of."

Roxie gave him a kiss. "We can always go back to the flat, and I can try and snap you out of it."

"That's sweet. But I promised you a special trip, and that's what you're going to get."

Roxie smiled. "Well, I'm not going to argue with that, but…if you want to go visit the land of the swamps you're more than welcome." Chandler hugged her. Part of her trip back to London with him was to give her a break. Having lost her mother shortly after the investigation, they'd both felt it would be beneficial for her to have a change of scenery. Together they had helped each other to move on from the past. "The thing that made those swamps so interesting was that I was there with you."

"I remember. The only problem with that was all the mad people and alligators that came along for the ride," Roxie said.

"Well, speaking of rides. Follow me." Chandler said.

He took Roxie by the hand, and they headed toward the exit.

# THREE

**IBERVILLE, LOUISIANA – Present day**

SHERIFF DUKE LANOIX took a last, deep sip of his iced coffee and looked nervously at the door that led into the Iberville Parish Library. The scrape of chairs and the muted chatter of the people bled through the door and into the room. Though it was over a month since the excitement of the torso case and the exposure of the multiple conspiracies surrounding Governor Roman Blackburn's ancestors, interest in the controversial investigation and its links to Jack the Ripper was still high. And in the light of this, the mayor thought it would be an excellent opportunity to have an open press evening to appease the press's appetite. Duke, along with Roxie and Chilly, had done numerous interviews, while the college student's thesis on the conspiracy behind Jack the Ripper had become a best seller. Duke wished that Chandler and Roxie were there to give him support. The intellectual insight that the Englishman had brought to the investigation with his quirky sense of humor and his strange loping gait was something he sorely missed. Chandler and Roxie had been a formidable unit. It was an investigative team that had turned into a romantic partnership by the end of their adventure.

But after Roxie's mother had succumbed to her illness, and once her affairs had been taken care of, she and Chandler had headed across the water to London for a well-earned break. There was a knock on the door, and Chilly stuck his head in. "You good to go?"

"As good as I'll ever be, is Jonas there?"

Jonas was the taciturn local coroner that had played a large part in piecing together the connection between the bodies in the swamp and their relation to the Jack the Ripper case. Unlike Duke and Chilly's dislike of public exposure, Jonas seemed to relish in the attention of the media. All those years spent with his silent customers had obviously stored up an ocean of unused conversation, and he was wasting no time catching up.

"Oh yeah, he's already doing some pieces to camera for the local news. I think he's hoping to write a book and retire. Looks like we're the only folk not making a buck out of this."

"The way I look at it," Duke said, "we get some fame, and skip all the hullabaloo. Chandler made the right decision letting the college kids get on with their thesis and book." He put his glass down and straightened his clothing. "How do I look?"

Chilly looked him up and down. Duke wore a new pair of leather cowboy boots and a leather belt with a silver buckle. Duke hated public appearances, and his dress code reflected that.

"Like you've lost your horse," Chilly said with a smile.

Duke headed toward the door. "I can see my new-found fame has gained an enormous amount of respect from you."

"You got it," Chilly said as they walked out into the library.

There was a lightning storm of camera flashes and a sea of waving hands within the posse of news cameras. Duke spotted Jonas standing to one side of the reporters and gave him a nod. After all this time, he couldn't imagine that the press could have anything more to ask.

# FOUR

**LONDON, ENGLAND**

CHANDLER LOOKED OUT the window of the cable car pod. The sun sparkled off the gray surface of the Thames far below them. The Emirates Air Line car gave breathtaking views of London, including Greenwich, the Thames Barrier, and the Royal Docks, during its round trip. It was a crisp winter 's day, and the bright blue sky framed streaks of cloud above the London skyline. It was a very different view to that of the Louisiana swamps he had recently left. He'd stayed on after the investigation, and remained until the media frenzy had died down.

There had been an enormous amount of interest in the details of the case. Roxie and the students had more than enough intellect and stamina to handle the blizzard of tweets, social media posts, and newspaper interviews triggered by the revelations concerning Jack the Ripper. After the final confrontation, during which Blackburn and his sidekick, Kale, had met their ends out in the swamp, Chandler and Roxie had taken a while to get over the trauma of their experience. During his stay in Louisiana, their feelings for each other had only grown deeper. And as the weeks passed, Chandler was convinced it wasn't just a bond formed by the adrenaline rush of their near-death experiences. Looking across the historic river Thames with Roxie by his side he couldn't imagine his life getting any better than it was right then.

# FIVE

## IBERVILLE, LOUISIANA

A HALF-HOUR into the press conference, Dukes throat was like a bullfrog after a night of courting. The questions had come thick and fast. Was it true that Detective Chandler was related to the Ripper? Was Duke planning on performing a new version of "Mack the Knife" with his band? That got some laughs.

A woman in an immaculate cream linen trouser suit with blond coiffured hair stood up. The room fell silent. "Aurora Tyler, *Texas Scientific*," she spoke with an Appalachian accent.

"First of all, I'd like to add my congratulations along with everyone else, on the way the investigation was handled. It couldn't have been easy given the complexity, and the dangers you faced." There was a ripple of clapping from the assembled reporters.

"Over the last few months, the case has been raked over like the embers of a much-used campfire. However, now that we have laid to rest the sensationalist side of the case. I think it might be time to focus on what was taking place out in Spirit's Swamp," she paused. "I'm talking about what was found beneath the ruins of the Rafetti house."

A journalist quipped from behind her. "It's alive!" Aurora shot him a steely look, and he shrugged.

"Despite the levity of my fellow journalists, I think the public has a right to be told exactly what Governor Blackburn and his accomplices were doing out there," she sat down.

Duke looked over as Jonas stood up to respond. "Your suggestion that the case has been more or less closed, that is far from true. The evidence we found beneath the house was proof that experiments had been carried out over a long period of time. Those experiments are still being investigated, but our initial findings point toward an attempt to extend life, and within certain genetic parameters take it to the ultimate level."

"Do you mean immortality?" Aurora asked.

"Yes. The evidence points in that direction," Jonas said.

Aurora nodded. She looked down at her iPad before continuing. "I believe you also found a separate line of experimentation had been carried out in an attempt to go back to the very building blocks of human life."

Duke looked at Jonas, glad he wasn't up to his neck in that particular vat of flatworms.

"You're talking about CRISPR?" Jonas asked.

Aurora replied. "Yes. Clustered Regular Interspaced Short Palindromic Repeats—for some of my colleagues who might not be as biologically savvy as your good self."

Jonas looked around the library. He doubted if there was anybody other than himself and Aurora who had a clue what CRISPR meant. "Thank you, I'm sure it's now as clear as swamp mud to everyone."

There was scattered laughter from the assembled journos.

Aurora smiled like a cat. "Maybe you'd like to put it in layman's terms for us."

Jonas looked at Duke as if offering him the chance to respond before smiling and turning to Aurora.

"Of course, it's simpler than it sounds."

"I doubt that," Aurora said.

Jonas launched in. "A palindrome, as I'm sure you know is a word that reads the same forward as backward. In this case, it was discovered that some clusters of DNA are palindromic repeats, separated by stretches of spacer DNA without any instructions for building proteins. Some bacteria use the CRISPR system to alter specific sections of DNA in a virus as a self-defense mechanism."

Aurora stood up. "Very impressive, perhaps you'd like to connect that explanation to what you found."

Jonas smiled. He'd rattled her by not fumbling the ball.
"Of course. As one of your colleagues put it so succinctly, they were trying to create a human being, unsuccessfully as it turns out, but they'd been trying for over a century, and who knows, they might have got there in the end. We believe they only got as far as a crude form of artificial meat, a hamburger without a soul as it were."

Aurora nodded and gave a tight smile. "With Blackburn and his sidekick, Kale, reduced to gator food along with the Rafetti sisters, it seems the only suspect unaccounted for is Governor Blackburn's business associate, Marsha Brochell. From all the evidence you found it looks like she may well have been the driving force behind these experiments, and therefore able to continue with the process wherever she is. Can you tell us whether your department has any idea where that might be?"

Duke breathed a sigh of relief. At least this was a question that didn't involve science. Over the course of the past week, they'd been pursuing a line of inquiry that they hoped would help track Marsha down. Despite Blackburn's personal and business accounts being frozen, along with Marsha's, there was always the possibility that she had cash stashed away somewhere, or a bank account under a different identity.

This would enable her to make her escape and lay low anywhere in the world until the hunt died down. But then they'd got a break. Duke's deputy, Chilly, had been checking newspaper archives and come up with a series of credit card thefts from passengers on board a transatlantic cruise liner traveling between New York and England shortly after the showdown out in the swamp. Someone had accessed their accounts and taken thousands of pounds out from cash machines on board and at the Southampton terminal building in England. Chilly had made some calls and tracked down the passengers who had been targeted. He'd sent a photo of Marsha to each of the victims and they'd all identified her as one of the passengers on the ship. Chilly had spoken to some of them and learned that she'd been very popular with her tarot card readings and fortune telling sessions. It was apparent that Marsha had used her talents well during the transatlantic crossing.

Duke leaned toward the cluster of microphones. "We're following a new line of inquiry concerning Marsha Brochell which may well reveal her whereabouts, and we are confident of making an arrest soon." He wasn't entirely convinced of that, but it seemed to satisfy the press gathered in the room, along with Aurora. The press filed out of the library while Duke slipped out the back way with Chilly and Jonas.

"That Texan hellcat is a pain in the ass," Duke said as the hot damp air hit them. Chilly mopped his face with a sleeve. "Damn right. She was just making a big splash to please her editor."

"She wants to start a magazine of her own. It'll be some pseudo-science rag all about aliens and poltergeists," Jonas said. "Well, we walked right into that." Duke rolled his shoulders and felt his neck click.

"We could have done with Roxie and Chandler in there. Roxie would have hung her out to dry," Jonas said.

"Yes, and Chandler would have buried her under a ton of quirky but unconnected facts."

They stood outside in the heat and watched as the journalists and television crews swarmed round Aurora, thrusting their microphones out at her for a sound bite.

"Roxie needed to get away. Her mom was a major part of her life," Chilly said.

"Yup. Her Mom was so proud that Roxie had helped bring Blackburn down. There was a lot of bad blood between her mom and the Blackburn's," Duke said as he scratched at the stubble he'd allowed to grow over the last few months and wondered if it was a last-ditch play to look younger.

"Well, I imagine Roxie will lap up all that old shit they have over there," Duke said.

Chilly looked at him. "You don't think Chandler would like to get involved in tracking Marsha down?"

"He probably would, but he's on holiday, and I don't want to ruin their break, they both went through a lot. And besides, Marsha could be anywhere."

Chilly nodded. "For sure." He'd checked the ship's passenger manifest and identified Marsha from a passport photo travelling under the name of Marja Nalangu, it was probably one of many aliases she had at her disposal.

Duke thought for a moment. "I guess it wouldn't hurt to keep him in the loop though. He might come up with something we've missed."

Chilly smiled. "He normally does."

# SIX

**CALAIS, FRANCE – One month earlier**

MARSHA BROCHELL DROVE the dark blue Range Rover out of the Eurotunnel Le Shuttle carriage, leaving the Calais docks behind her and headed for Bruges, Belgium. It had taken a week for the Queen Mary 2 cruise ship to travel from New York to England. And once they'd docked at Southampton, she'd collected the dogs from the kennel facilities on board and disembarked from the ship. She'd picked up her hired car and driven the three-hour journey to the Eurotunnel terminal at Folkestone. Her license plate was scanned, and the machine spat out a ticket, which she hung on her rear-view mirror before heading to passport control. There was a moment's hesitation as the man studied her picture and details. Satisfied, he moved on to check the pet passports. Marsha had assumed there would be an alert out for her and was using one of her backup identities and passports. The man handed back the passport and waved her through. She drove up to the parking area outside the terminal, and after feeding the dogs, took them to the small dog area and made sure they were comfortable for the short journey beneath the channel.

Marsha walked back to the car and gave them a chew bone each before heading into the terminal. Her train was boarding in twenty minutes. Ample time to freshen up, grab a coffee and a bite to eat.

Thirty-minutes later she was driving up the ramp and into the claustrophobic confines of the train carriage. As the carriage doors closed and the train gathered speed, she started to relax. The race to book and board the cruise ship at Manhattan, and the drive on unfamiliar roads between the terminals across England had been stressful. Luckily the hired car came with GPS, so all she really had to worry about was making sure she was on the right side of the road.

During her trip from New York to Southampton, she'd passed the time amusing her fellow passengers with palm and Tarot card readings in the various bars and restaurants. They had no idea she was soaking up their credit card and bank details as she smiled and dealt their cards along with tales of imaginary futures full of tall, dark strangers and knights in shining armor. By the time she disembarked at Southampton, her account held over a hundred thousand euros, and she had five thousand euros of cash in her bag.

She'd barely made it to the Manhattan cruise terminal in New York in time for her departure. The dogs were brother and sister and were called Argos and Laelaps after the mythological Greek dogs. Terrified by the storm and fires in the swamp out in Louisiana, they'd run away. Marsha had managed to avoid the police cordon around the Rafetti house and had found them cowering at the side of the causeway stretching across Spirit's Swamp. She'd eventually managed to coax them into her vehicle with pieces of raw meat. Marsha remembered the horrific events of that night with gut-wrenching clarity. Sheriff Duke Lanoix and the English detective Chandler Travis had confronted her partner, Louisiana governor Roman Blackburn, out at Spirit's Swamp with fatal consequences. She'd warned Roman of the possible future that awaited him, but he had chosen to ignore her pleas. Now she was on the road with his remains and his precious dogs.

Marsha traveled through the featureless countryside of France, while the GPS did the work, and was soon leaving Dunkirk behind and crossing the border into Belgium before picking up the E40 motorway to Bruges. An hour and a half later, she reached the ring road encircling Bruges known locally as the Egg, because of its shape formed by the canals surrounding the City. She peeled off the ring road, past Sint-Salvatorskathedraal before circling the Market Square and heading off toward the Groenerei Canal and her final destination. Argos and Laelaps sat in the back, sniffing at the insulated container that gleamed with moisture despite the fierce air conditioning that blasted out of the vents.

Marsha turned to look at them. "You won't be seeing him for a while yet, so you may as well settle down."

The dogs whimpered and pawed at the container, muzzles flecked with drool, their eyes glistening like dark mahogany. It was as if they knew the chest contained the essence of what would soon become their master once more. Marsha wondered if the reverse was true; that the spirit of Roman had some symbiotic connection with their souls. Maybe the dog's superior eyesight, speed, and sense of smell ran parallel to an elevated spiritual link. As if aware of her thoughts, the dogs settled down and stared mournfully at the container.

# SEVEN

**BRUGES, BELGIUM – Present day**

A LARGE WHITE van pulled up at the Market Square as the sunlight crept across the ancient cobbles beneath the looming octagonal tower of the Belfort. Gunter, the foreman, a large, florid-faced man with hands the size of saucepan lids, climbed down out of the driving seat and stretched. He opened the sliding door of the van, and four men stepped out into the morning light, clutching their coffee flasks like a talisman. Gunter walked over to the barriers surrounding the ice rink construction. The barrier material had already been laid over the cobbles, and plastic pipes crisscrossed the site. The 360-ton chiller truck was parked along one side of the barrier and had been run up the day before to check it.

Gunter had been erecting rinks throughout Europe for years and was familiar with the process. The first week was spent laying the white plastic sheeting across the cobbles. Once in place, that was followed by rolls containing kilometers of special plastic piping that were then connected to the chiller unit. They would be filled with glycol, a form of antifreeze. Once the chiller was switched on, the temperature of the glycol was reduced to−22°C in less than a minute. Thousands of liters of ionized water then had to be sprayed over the glycol filled grid, gradually building up the ice one and a half millimeters at a time, until after thirty separate layers, a final depth of five centimeters was achieved. Gunter walked carefully across the rink, the glycol filled pipes made a creaking noise beneath his feet with each step.

He was still fuming over an earlier incident when the driver of the chiller truck had managed to reverse over one of the drainage covers at the perimeter of the rink fracturing it. There was no time to get a replacement, so they'd had to fashion a template from ice to seal the hole and make it safe. He still had to check that there weren't any leaks and that the pipes weren't chafing against the other drainage covers. They would be using ionized water to ensure that the ice was clear and create the semblance of a snowy surface formed by the white plastic sheeting beneath it. One of his team came over and handed him a mug of steaming coffee. "How's it looking?" he asked, as Gunter took the drink.

"Pretty good. I think we'll be done by today."

His companion nodded. They were, as usual, up against the Christmas market schedule.

They drank their coffees and watched as the other men walked back across the pipes, spraying a fine mist of water over them, adding to the frozen layers already there. Gunter took another sip of coffee and headed over to the chiller truck.

***

Marsha waited as the electric gates of the archway leading into the courtyard hummed open. The Grande Maison still took her breath away with its magnificence. The gardens were kept immaculate, and the cathedral of trees provided welcome shade during the warmer months of the summer. But right now, they twinkled with a light covering of frost.

The ten-bedroom house looked out over the Groenerei, one of the many canals bisecting the ancient city. With its enclosed garden and expansive rooms, it was the perfect retreat in which to recover her energy and rebuild her powers. The dogs ran out of the French windows that led to the garden, barking frenziedly at imaginary intruders as they played with one another, glad to be free from their recent confinement.

Marsha went into the living room that occupied most of the ground floor and threw open the heavy wooden shutters. The evening sun hung low in the sky, reflecting off the canal and painting the ancient stone of the houses alongside it with a soft purple wash in its dying light.

She looked around the room at the antique furniture, and the walls festooned with oil paintings, drinking in the beauty of her settings. She sat on the gilded chaise longue that faced the window looking out over the canal. Roman liked to furnish his homes in the style of Louis XIV. Unlike his Louisiana home, where the décor had seemed tasteless, in the medieval surroundings of Bruges, it seemed perfectly natural.

Marsha drank a glass of champagne, fed the dogs, and had a light supper as she watched the last of the day's tourist boats ply their trade along the canal outside. There were fewer boat trips taking place as they headed towards Christmas, but more than enough for her purposes. Now she was back in Bruges, she felt as if her world had turned full circle. Centuries earlier Bruges had been the site of her own rebirth. Not in the physical sense, but with the bestowing of her powers from a dying sorcerer.

Now that Marsha was back, she had to prepare for challenges on many fronts. Roman's rebirth and adoption of his European identity would require her inherent abilities aided by the experiments they had been carrying out for generations.

Her skills as a seer had given her the knowledge that the Louisiana Sheriff and the English detective remained a threat to their existence. She needed to make sure that any future confrontation took place on her terms. Marsha had to have her companion back by her side, and for that, she required a victim. She'd manage to salvage the necessary biological samples along with his DNA, but the complete process required a living component. As darkness fell, she set off into town and made her way into the busy Market Square.

It was crowded with tourists and surrounded by stalls selling freshly cooked food and drinks. Tourists flooded to the market to sample the large selection of prawns, hamburgers, chips, and waffles that were available late into the night. Pop music blared out over the ice rink in the center of the square making conversation difficult. It was a popular venue to meet up for drinks with friends. Marsha looked at the teeming masses of people. Her senses reaching out like tentacles across the sea of humanity.

It didn't take her long to find him. His recent contact with violent death made it easy for her to find him amongst the crowds. She could taste his evil. He had come to Bruges to avoid paying for his sins, but that wasn't going to happen. Not now.

Three drinks, and an hour later, he was in thrall to her, and they were headed back to her house. The American claimed he was an orphan, free to travel the world and move from one casual job to another. She knew he was no more a tourist than her and was looking forward to slaking her carnal appetite before he served his real purpos

She threw open the doors to the elegant living room and smiled at his reaction.

"Wow! I would die to own this!" He gushed.

She took him by the hand and led him to the opulent bedroom with its massive four-poster bed. Turning to him with a smile, she said, "Didn't your mother ever tell you to be careful what you wish for?"

# EIGHT

**GENT-SINT-PIETERS, BELGIUM – Present day**

THE SQUEAL OF brakes jerked Detective Katja Blondell out of a dreamless sleep as she approached Gent-Sint-Pieters station. The track, "Saint Claude," by Christine and the Queens, washing through her ear buds, failed to surprise her with the aptness of its lyrics. Back in the day, the diminutive force behind Christine and the Queens had been on repeat on her iPhone. But that was years ago, and now her songs only surfaced when the music app on her phone was set to random.

She'd left Antwerp an hour earlier and been lulled into sleep by the rhythmic clatter from the wheels of the train. She pushed a lock of blond hair behind one ear, rubbed her eyes, and looked out of the window. The setting sun was streaked with gray clouds, and a sea of bicycles flooded the station parking lot. Ghent was a university town with over 60,000 students, and it seemed most of them owned a bike. Bruges, her final destination, was now only half an hour away. She wasn't due at the Kartuizerinnenstraat police station based alongside the Dijver canal until the morning, but she wanted to be well rested before then. The Christmas markets would be up and running, and she was looking forwards to walking through them that evening.

Katja slipped her rucksack on as the train pulled into Bruges station and was soon heading down the steps into the tunnel beneath the platforms. She passed the rows of shops and exited through the doors leading out to the area where the buses and taxis congregated. It was a crisp winter evening, and the short walk into the city center was just what she needed to clear her head. She walked past the snow and ice sculpture festival outside the station, crossed over the road, and continued through the park. She reached Zuidzandstraat which was crowded with shoppers and followed it past the Sint-Salvatorskathedraal into Steenstraat and down towards the ancient Belfort that overlooked the Market Square. The square was already packed with tourists lining up at the stalls selling freshly cooked food and novelty goods.

She walked toward the ice rink and its booming sound system. The intoxicating smell of freshly fried shrimps and the tartiflette savoyarde, a cheesy potato combo sizzling in a large open skillet filled her nostrils, and reminded her she hadn't eaten since lunch. She ordered half a dozen prawns, a scoop of the potato dish, and topped it off with a hot chocolate laced with rum. She leaned against the side of the ice rink and watched the crowd of skaters as they swooped, lurched, or glided across the ice depending on their skill. She remembered years back, when she and a group of off duty officers, after a few drinks too many, had decided to have a race around the rink. First to complete three laps without falling over would be declared the winner. It was a catastrophe. Within the first few minutes, only Katja and one other officer were left standing. After her victory, she was given the nickname Elsa, from the film *Frozen*, and like the Disney character she was named after, Katja also carried a secret. Back in the day she'd helped her college skating team to many victories against their rival teams, and thus had skills that far surpassed her hapless colleagues.

When she'd confessed to the other survivor of the race, Detective Jochum Van De Hoog, he'd laughed at the ridiculousness of the situation, and they joined the others for a celebratory drink.

The events of that night had started a friendship that had grown into a relationship that lasted until it burned itself out under the pressure of the job. And now, two years later, she was back where it all began.

She watched the skaters and drank the last of her rum chocolate. One of the skaters caught her eye. He had a mane of blond hair held in place by a festive bobble hat, broad shoulders, and powerful arms. On the ice, he had an almost preternatural skill, switching between gliding forward to facing backward seamlessly. He reminded her of the fairground operators and their death-defying leaps from one whirling car to another.

She wondered how she would fare on the ice today. Though she'd kept up her fitness and core strength with martial arts, yoga practice, and weights, one could never really regain the balance and reflexes of one's youth. She dropped her cup into a waste bin and headed away from the market along Woolestraat towards the apartment she'd been given the use of by a friend while she was in Bruges. But as she walked down the familiar streets, she was already starting to worry about how she would feel, meeting up with Jochum after the years apart.

# NINE

**BRUGES, BELGIUM**

AWAKENED BY THE deep thrum of a passing diesel engine, Detective Jochum Van De Hoog slowly opened his eyes. He yawned and lifted the edge of the curtain beside his bed. The receding rump of a grain barge was making its way down the canal. He picked up his phone. There were a couple of text messages and one missed call. He got up, walked down to the galley and switched the coffee machine on. He slid open the hatch above him to let some air in, and opened a small fridge; scooping out the croissants he'd bought the previous day. He put them on a plate, dialed thirty seconds on the microwave, and walked down into the dinette.

The barge was an old Euroship 1800 Luxe Motor seized by the police as part of a drug dealer's assets. After the dealer had been convicted, it had come up in a police auction, and Jochum had bought it for a song. But he wasn't singing for long. It was a money pit. Eventually, everything was fixed. Bad welds redone, leaky rivets replaced, and engine overhauled. He'd managed to secure a mooring along the Coupure Canal, opposite the Kruispoort gate, on the outskirts of the city. It was an easy fifteen-minute drive into work…less if he added the siren. But most mornings he chose to walk.

The microwave pinged in the kitchen. Hoog took the croissants out, pressed the button on the coffee machine, and watched as it spat out a large helping of dark black coffee into the waiting mug. He picked it up, went into the dinette and sat down at the small table in the seating area. His phone buzzed gently. He took a bite of croissant, and the butter and honey flooded his taste buds with sugar, the crack cocaine of modern life. He took another slug of coffee and watched the gulls swoop down over the water outside, angling for scraps floating on the surface of the canal. Eventually, after disposing of the croissants and the coffee, he picked up his phone and tapped the first text. It was an unwelcome reminder of the parlous state of his bank account. The second was from Chief Pieters.

The Chief was a man of few words. Gruff, but fair, most of his colleagues would say. Hoog scanned the text. The chief wanted to see him at the station that morning, nothing urgent. He'd already planned to spend time at the firing range beneath the station, so that was no big deal. But it always annoyed him when people left texts, or answer machine messages with no clue as to the reason for their call. In his experience, it usually meant they wanted something from you that you didn't want to give. Whatever news Pieters had waiting for him at the station he would face it on a full stomach and a well-caffeinated system.

Hoog jogged past the Kruispoort gate alongside the canal. Back in the fifteenth century, it had been a prominent entry point into Bruges and where the Scottish soldiers crossed into Bruges to liberate the city during WW11. Now it was mainly used as a meeting place for a historical reenactment society. It was a pleasant strip of greenery that he regularly used for his morning runs. He was soon passing the Bonne-Chièremolen, one of two windmills on his route. He waved at an old man with a stick accompanied by a ratty looking dog, making his way slowly along the path. The man's name was Dirk, his ancient dog, Snapper, was a mix of Jack Russell and dachshund.

27

When he'd been younger, Snapper had helped Hoog shave a few seconds off his circuit time, but that was a few years back, and Snapper was now more interested in scraps dropped by tourists than chasing joggers. "Nice day for it," Dirk called out.

"For sure." Hoog waved, and the dog looked up briefly then continued his quest for scraps.

The crisp winter morning was perfect for his jog, and he soon reached the red sails of the Sint-Janshuismolen windmill, circled around it, and headed back along the path toward Kruispoort. He was looking forward to his shower, and another coffee before heading off to the police station. And was starting to wonder why Pieters wanted to talk to him.

# TEN

KATJA STEPPED OUT into Woolestraat, sucked the crisp morning air into her lungs and set off towards the police station. It was in Kartuizerinnenstraat alongside the canal, a short walk from the Belfort and the Market Square. In 2013, the main bulk of the staff had been moved to a new glass and steel headquarters in Zeveneke, two kilometers outside the center of Bruges. The original station had since become a satellite office in Bruges.

Katja passed the old stone arches and through the glass doors into a small reception. It was manned by a grizzly, white- haired veteran. The name on the desk read Sergeant Rutger Hoffman. She smiled at him.

"Katja Blondell. I'm meeting Detective Jochum Van De Hoog."

The Sergeant mumbled something that sounded like 'dancer,' but before Katja could say anything, a young officer with a name tag that read Ward Verhoeven ran up to the desk. "He's about to start."

Katja looked from one to the other. "Who, where?"

The sergeant leaned on the desk. "Hoog. Once a month he hits the range..."

Katja nodded. The old police station still had something to offer that the new one didn't; a large targeting area in the catacombs below the station. It had initially been an old convent, and the catacombs beneath had been converted into a substantial firing range. Katja had done part of her training down there. It was equipped with all sorts of targets, stationary and moving, and provided an excellent facility for urban assault training. She followed Ward down a corridor and a flight of worn spiral stone steps leading to the dank lower floor. Small, grimy arched windows looked out across the canal outside. In front of her several other officers walked quickly toward the sound of distant music.

At the end of the passageway, it opened out into a dimly lit expanse of vaulted catacombs that ran the entire length of the convent above them. The area was shielded by a wall of bulletproof glass. The music grew louder. An old Dua Lipa hit, "Be the One." Behind the glass, Hoog stood in front of the targets, hands loose at his sides. Tall, and with a lithe frame corded with muscle. Dark hair edged with a spray of silver. In each hand, he held a Smith & Wesson M&P9 Pro series semiautomatic, LaserMax sights and seventeen-round magazines.

As Katja watched him, she was aware of something stirring within her. Feelings. Feelings she thought had been dead and buried a long time ago. It came as a complete surprise that he could still have that effect on her. She whispered to Ward who stood next to her. "What's with the music?"

He grinned. "It's his thing. He believes that rhythm is the key to accuracy. Some Zen shit where the world is put in balance by harmonics. If you ask him, he'll tell you his whole philosophy."

Katja nodded, her eyes distant for a moment.

"He would." "Whatever he does, it works. His speed and Accuracy are off the charts," Ward said. He paused as the tempo of the music changed, and the chorus kicked in.

"Here we go."

Hoog whipped up his guns. Following the targets as they ducked and weaved across the range. He fired a quick burst as he whirled and pirouetted like a marionette dancing to the beat, decimating the cutout figures, ejecting the first magazine, slamming in another and continuing his barrage of fire. The sound of the shots coalescing with the rhythm of the music. The laser sight cut through the smoke, a deadly light show tracking its cardboard victims. Hoog poured fire into the targets, mowing them down until only one was left standing. A man armed with a machine gun, holding a child in front of him as a shield. Hoog emptied both guns into the target scything its gun hand off. The music faded. A wave of applause and whoops from the watching officers echoed around the catacombs. The whole event had taken thirty seconds and consumed sixty-eight rounds.

Katja stared at the remains of the targets. "Still as humble as ever," she said.

The young officer smiled at her. "He must be off form. Normally he would have taken the head off that last target." Ward looked at Katja.

"Do you guys know each other?" Katja thought about that and wondered how much anybody knew about events between them all those years ago.

"Been a while."

Ward nodded. "I've only been here a year. Guy's a legend." "I'm sure," Katja said. She watched as Hoog stripped down the guns, reassembled them, and slid them back into their holsters on either side of his jacket. He came over.

"You coming down with something Jochum? You left his head on." Ward said.

Hoog said, "No, Ward, my friend. Current research shows that the nerves in the hand could still be triggered by muscle mirroring even if I took his head off. Best to play it safe, no finger on the trigger, no risk," he paused, staring at Katja.

Ward looked from one to the other, sensing the spokes of a third wheel spinning in front of him. "Right, well I'm sure there are things that need my attention out in the real world. See you later."

Hoog gave him a look. "For sure."

Ward headed down the passageway leaving them alone. Katja gestured at the range behind her and the remains of the cardboard targets. "Now I know why they called you dancer," she said.

"Don't worry; I don't do that out in the field. Not with the music anyway." Katja gave a small sigh. "Should I read anything into you using our song as the background to your cardboard massacre?"

Hoog spread his hands in a gesture of denial. "Not at all. I use different tracks all the time." Hoog indicated for her to head along the passageway.

"And the dancer nickname is to do with one of my hobbies. I learn a different dance every few months. Samba, Salsa, Marimba…you get the picture. Keeps me supple and also stretches the mind." "I can just about manage the Macarena if I've had enough beer," said Katja.

"How was Antwerp?"

"Doesn't have the character of this old place," she said, coming to a halt at the bottom of the stone stairway and looking at him.

"Are we good?"

"Pieters told me you were coming back. Asked me if I would be okay working with you. I told him we were both grown-ups," replied Hoog.

"Well one of us is, for sure. The other…" she wobbled her hand in the air.

Hoog smiled. "I've missed that sense of humor."

They walked past the desk Sergeant and out onto the cobbled streets. "So, you know what this is all about?" Hoog asked. "You're going to teach me all I need to know about dealing with the general public."

Hoog nodded. "Which means?"

Katja gave a rueful smile. "They weren't too impressed when I punched a Japanese tourist."

"That's about the size of it," he went on. "So, all we have to do is tick the boxes and dot the i's, and we can all go back to the important stuff."

Katja looked at him. "And what's that? Parking tickets, illegal buskers and drunks?"

"Bruges is a safe city, what can I say."

"Don't you ever wish it was a bit more...interesting?"

Hoog said, "I guess that's why you transferred to Antwerp?" "You know it wasn't." Katja said.

Hoog remembered when Katja had first arrived at the police station in Bruges, and they'd become involved. Hiding it from their colleagues had become part of the excitement. But things became complicated. Katja had her eye on promotion and had applied for a position in Antwerp. He'd been upset and wanted her to stay. She'd accused him of being too controlling. He'd seen it as overprotective, but it was worse than that. He was an addict, and Katja was his drug of choice. In the end, she'd forced him to go cold turkey by leaving.

Hoog had spent too much time eating waffles and junk food as he vacillated in the vacuum of his loss. Eventually, he'd broken out of his self-imposed emotional exile and discovered dance. A colleague had suggested it would improve his balance, reflexes, and coordination, and along with that came the benefit of endorphins. Like everything he took up, it became an obsession, and he was soon working his way through an eclectic mix of dances.

But it got him through a dark period, and no one could deny his marksmanship and reflexes were outstanding.

He turned back to Katja. "I don't mind my job being less interesting. Gives me more time for an exciting personal life."

"How many dances can you learn for Christ's sake?" Katja paused, "I'm sorry, I shouldn't give you a hard time; it wasn't you that punched the tourist, after all."

Hoog laughed. "No, I didn't. But it's something I imagined doing many times, back when I was patrolling the streets." Katja sighed. "He was just incredibly annoying. Taking pictures of women, getting in their faces. And when I told him to quit, he went all Kung Fu on me."

Hoog pursed his lips. "It was probably more likely to have been Yoseikan Budo—Kung Fu is Chinese."

Katja glared at him.

Hoog held up his hands. "Just saying."

"I was generalizing," Katja said. "I should have known you'd be an expert on stuff like that."

"I have an interest in most things that use rhythm to achieve a purpose."

"Well the only thing achieved was pissing me off," Katja said. "Which is why he spent a month in traction drinking food through a straw."

Katja pushed some hair over an ear. "I may have overreacted."

Hoog grinned. "I'm not saying he didn't deserve it. Just that the average tourist expects to be protected by the law. A police officer hospitalizing someone for taking pictures doesn't sit well with their beer and chocolates."

They reached Market Square and stood looking across at the Belfort and the crowds of visitors. The carillon was chiming, and horses clattered past with carriages full of tourists. With the sun high in a blue sky dotted with cotton wool clouds, it was picture perfect.

"I could do with a bagel," Katja said. "I guess Bruges can survive for half an hour without your martial art skills."

"Great. Follow me."

\*\*\*

34

Hoog and Katja sat in the Sanseveria Bagelsalon, in Predikherenstraat, a few minutes from the market across the Groenerei Canal. It was popular with students and tourists and had recently expanded into a back room to cope with demand. Katja had been a regular customer before her transfer to Antwerp and had come to know Bert, the owner, well. She always had the same thing, so never had to order. It was a Juliet. The staff named all the bagels, and the Juliet consisted of salmon and cream cheese, which she accompanied with an Americano coffee, and apple crumble and cream. In her mind, that covered all the main food groups. It also had the advantage of being a handheld snack if an emergency cropped up. Hoog looked around. He hadn't been to the Bagelsalon since it had been upgraded. Bert played jazz music, which, combined with the décor, gave the place a hipster vibe. He'd ordered a Leon, a breakfast bagel with scrambled egg and smoked salmon, and it was taking all of his skill to avoid dropping it on his shirt. He had another sip of his Mocha and a bite of the bagel.

"This is good," he said, between mouthfuls.

Katja nodded as she swallowed. "Yes. I tried to get him to open a Bagelsalon in Antwerp, but he already has one in Oostende. You have to come here when it's quiet if you want to get in. Though I imagine he'd always make space for me." She pointed to a square of plate glass that covered some stone steps leading down into darkness. "That used to be where the old place ended. If he gets any more popular, he'll have to expand into the cellar."

Hoog looked at her. "Bruges hasn't always been a fairytale city of beer and chocolates."

"What do you mean?" Katja said.

Hoog smiled. "Every city has another side. Its hidden depths…the darkness below the surface. Katja leaned forward, intrigued. "Tell me more."

# ELEVEN

**BRUGES, BELGIUM – 1634**

THE CAVERNOUS WATERHALLE, usually bustling with ships unloading, stood nearly empty. The massive storms sweeping the coast of Europe had killed over fifteen thousand people, devastated the trade routes, and halted the flow of ships along the estuary into Bruges. Europe was locked in a frozen winter that destroyed crops and created widespread famine. People believed the end was nigh. They saw the work of the devil in everything and began to hunt down those they thought were aligned with him. At 95 meters long and over 30 meters in height, the Waterhalle had been built over the River Reie in the Grande Place back in the thirteenth century. It enabled the ships to unload goods inside the covered dock and store their cargo on the floors above. On the market side were homes and shops, and a row of stone columns supported the roof above the quayside. But right now, the Waterhalle was eerily quiet. One forlorn ship sat hunched in the gloom. Its mooring ropes creaking as it shifted against the quayside. The dim light from the candles burning inside the ship painted the shallow waters of the Reie a putrid yellow.

On one side of the ship, Cathelyne Verpoort wrapped her shawl tighter about her neck. Compared to outside it was cold and damp in the hall. But that wasn't the only reason she wore a shawl. She had a distinctive red mark on her neck in the shape of a sickle. With witchcraft mania sweeping Europe, she didn't need anybody thinking it denoted a connection with the devil. It was madness, but right now, madness was normal.

Trade had been slow, and it wasn't for want of trying. Her low rounded neckline showed her assets off to such an extent she was liable to catch a chill. But to no avail. She hadn't seen a customer for hours. She didn't like the Waterhalle. It had an atmosphere that kept her on edge, and her recent experience had left her uneasy. It had happened over a week ago now, and she'd only come back to the Waterhalle because she didn't have a guilder to her name. As she was preparing to go home, a man had approached her.

He wore a dark cloak, beneath which she caught a glimpse of fine clothes. She was used to the rich paying to abuse her. It reinforced the power that their wealth already gave them. But this man was different. He'd offered to pay her handsomely to sit for him, and told her his name was Count Brandt Van Zwart, and he was an artist. She'd been suspicious at first, but the feel of the two gold coins in her hand had quieted her worry.

He'd told her they were ducats from Venice. She didn't care where they were from, only that they were gold. She'd gone to his house, and he'd told her that he wanted to paint her sitting against the light in front of a window that looked out across the canal.

As she took up her position, the count shook his head. He wanted her to remove her clothes. Cathelyne was no stranger to that request, but usually, it was in the dark, and all they were interested in was getting under her skirts. In the bright sunlight, all her flaws would be exposed. These were dangerous times, and the elders were gripped by the persecution of witches sweeping Europe. Any woman with a deformity risked being burned at the stake.

No number of gold coins could save her from that fate. She told him she would only pose in her clothes. A look of rage instantly swept across his face like a storm cloud, and then, just as quick, it was gone. He gestured for her to sit. She wondered if maybe he would try to bend her to his will after the sitting was over.

As she took up her position, the count shook his head. He wanted her to remove her clothes. Cathelyne was no stranger to that request, but usually, it was in the dark, and all they were interested in was getting under her skirts. In the bright sunlight, all her flaws would be exposed. These were dangerous times, and the elders were gripped by the persecution of witches sweeping Europe. Any woman with a deformity risked being burned at the stake. No number of gold coins could save her from that fate. She told him she would only pose in her clothes. A look of rage instantly swept across his face like a storm cloud, and then, just as quick, it was gone. He gestured for her to sit. She wondered if maybe he would try to bend her to his will after the sitting was over.

Holding the pose had been difficult, but as the sun set on the waters of the canal behind her, he put his brushes down. As she'd been expecting, he tried to get her to disrobe. Once again, she refused. He tried to grab her, ripping the shawl from her neck. She ran from the house and was soon out in the streets again, darting through the crowds of people, casting looks behind in case he was following her. But he was nowhere to be seen. She'd waited for over a week before coming back to the Waterhalle, frightened that he might hunt her down and demand satisfaction for the ducats he'd given her. But she hadn't seen him since that night. She'd warned her friends about the man, but they just laughed and told her two golden ducats was worth taking your clothes off for. She had to agree that maybe she'd perhaps been too cautious. They said they'd be more than happy to make this artist's acquaintance.

As the weeks had passed, she'd lost touch with them and presumed that they no longer frequented this part of the city. Times were hard since the river had started to silt up. The days when the port bustled with crew and wealthy merchants were long gone. She shivered and looked around the Waterhalle. She saw shadowy figures moving around the dark edges of the hall…the occasional clink of coins and muttered conversation. And then it went quiet.

The rope fell slack against the prow of the ship. The river was a liquid mirror in the stillness of the night. Cathelyne stared across the water. She could just make out some dark shapes drifting towards her. Her eyes strained to see in the sulfurous light. As they came nearer, she saw what they were, and her blood froze. Bodies.

She counted five of them. From the skirts floating around them it was apparent they were women. But then her eye was caught by some smaller objects floating alongside the bodies. They were human organs, floating like offal from a butcher's slab. She felt her stomach contract and forced herself to be calm. A body drifted nearer, floating face down. The clothes reminded her of those she'd last seen on Hilda Cruucke. A stout, flaxen-haired girl in her twenties, and one of her missing friends.

The water around her glowed with a blood red sheen. Her clothes had been torn and sliced by something sharp. Her abdomen ripped open. Cathelyne looked around the hall; there was a faint scuffle, followed by a splash and the sound of footsteps in the gloom. She turned back to the floating body as it drifted past. And then it gave a shudder and rolled over like a barrel in the water. Her heart raced. It *was* Hilda. And as Cathelyne watched, Hilda's eyes opened, and she screamed.

# TWELVE

**BRUGES, BELGIUM – Present day**

HOOG AND KATJA were finishing off their second cup of coffee, and Hoog was deciding between apple crumble and cream or the carrot cake. The café was quieter now that the lunchtime rush was over. Katja's eyes sparkled with interest.

"So, somebody hacks five prostitutes…" she paused. "sorry, sex workers, to death, then dumps their bodies in the Waterhalle and Cathelyne Verpoort is accused of the crime and burnt as a witch?"

"Yes. Folklore has it that an artist called Count Brandt Van Zwart may have set her up in revenge when she refused to pose naked for him. She was also supposed to have had a sickle-shaped birthmark." Hoog said.

"That could have been enough to seal her fate in those days if they considered it to be the mark of the devil," Katja paused,

"I've never seen any paintings by Count Brandt Van Zwart."

"Me neither." Hoog took a sip of his coffee, "maybe your friend Erika at the Groeninge Museum can help? If you're intent on solving a 17$^{th}$ century murder that is."

"Well, it certainly offends my sensibilities that someone could get away with hacking five women to death and then set another one up for the crime. Besides, you know witches and me," replied Katja. "Yes, how many times did you drag me to Sint-Janshospitaal?" Katja thought back to how fixated she'd been when in 2017 an exhibition called "Bruegel's Witches" was held in the medieval attic of Sint-Janshospitaal. She'd found the whole thing fascinating.

"Yes, I remember." Katja took a sip of coffee. "I never understood why you couldn't except the possibility that witches might actually exist."

"Probably because I've never seen one…not in the real world anyway. Obviously, I was a big fan of The Craft."
"Nothing to do with Neve Campbell then?"
"Possibly. I was a teenager."
"Right. I imagine it's what defines a witch that's the problem, and of course the time frame."
Hoog shrugged. "Times change. If someone had predicted the weather back in the 17th century, they would have been burnt as a witch. Nowadays they have their own TV channel."
Katja nodded. "People spend more time in the online world than they do in the real one. Their exposure to infinite amounts of content should make them more open to different beliefs than ever. We have Wicca, pagan witchcraft and white witches that worship mother nature, and many other beliefs that people judge to be good or evil, depending on their views. Witches should be just easy to accept." Hoog smiled. "I guess I'm more of the doubting Thomas kind when it comes to witches. Part of it is the job we do, and the rest of it is probably my limited imagination." Katja smiled. "I always thought you had a pretty good imagination."
Hoog shot her a look. Was she flirting with him or just reminiscing? Though it had been over two years since they'd been an item, Katja wasn't a person easily forgotten. Their separation had been painful, but they hadn't split because of incompatibility. In the end pressure of work and their career ambitions had pulled them in opposite direction

Katja took a transfer to Antwerp, and he got on with his life. Having said that, now she was back he realized all he had done was fill his free time up with obsessive pursuits to blot out the pain of her absence. He looked at her. She was smiling. It was as if she could read his mind. Maybe she was the witch he'd never seen.

"Still thinking about Neve?" she asked.

"Naa, I've moved on."

"Good for you. Teenage boys are always lusting after unattainable women."

She took a sip of coffee. Eyes peering over the top of her cup like twin laser beams boring into him. He couldn't work her out.

"I guess you would know all about that," he blurted, cursing himself for joining in her game, if that's what it was.

"I admit I had the odd unsuitable admirer. But let's stick to the subject…unless you think I might be a witch?"

"Touché," Hoog said. The conversation was heading in a direction he didn't want to explore too deeply. Not until he knew where he stood. Katja looked at him, a mischievous grin on her face.

"So we're agreed. Your belief in witches is predicated between you actually seeing one with your own eyes, the prevalent beliefs of the day and a spectrum of perception somewhere between David Blane and the Salem witch trials." Hoog smiled. "Well, I imagine we can indulge your fascination in all things witch, after all you're not officially on duty until tomorrow."

"You say that, but witches are a bit like buses, you wait for centuries, and then three come along at once."

"Buses?" Hoog looked blank. "An English professor taught me art at Ghent. It was something he used to say all the time. It was something to do with their hopeless public transport system. I've paraphrased the expression a little to make it work with the witch vibe." Hoog nodded. "Right. Well, good luck with your search, and give Erika my love, and don't come back wearing a witch's hat."

"Why? You don't think I could carry it off?" she looked at Hoog's nervous expression and wondered if she was overdoing things. It was obvious they still had chemistry between them, and as far as she knew he wasn't seeing anybody. After hearing about how he was filling his free time that was obvious. "I'm sure you would suit one perfectly, but then I'd have to wear one, and as you know, I don't do hats."

"Yes, I remember. You couldn't wait to make detective and dump your cap."

Bert came over and served them with their apple crumbles and cream. "Enjoy," he said with a  smile.

Katja returned the smile. "My hero."

Bert drifted back behind the display cases.

"What are you going to do after we leave here?" Katja asked.

"I usually do a little drumming if I have time. Just an hour or so," Hoog said.

"Are you sure you aren't channeling Liese Meerhout from *Rough Justice*?"

Hoog gave her a smile. "Nah, I've always wanted to drum.

Just didn't have enough space."

"That's because you live in that money pit you call a boat." "Guilty as charged," Hoog replied.

Katja finished the last of her apple crumble and waved at Bert. Hoog reached into his pocket. "My treat."

"You can pay for the beers tonight."

Bert came over. "Everything all right?" "Even better than I remember," replied Katja.

Bert smiled and handed over a small cardboard box.

"Some gingerbread. It's a new recipe. I'd be happy to hear what you think of it."

Katja took the box. "You're a star."

They got up and headed back out into Predikherenstraat, continuing down into Meestraat and over the bridge, cutting through the Burg and into the Market. The square was full of people crowding around the Christmas market stalls.

Katja remembered how magical she had found it when she'd first worked at the station. But as the years passed, the constant rush of people bumping into her and the never-ending selfie requests had taken its toll. Spending some time in Antwerp had put some luster back into the ancient city of Bruges on her return.

"Okay, I'm heading off. Barring any serious crime like someone having their Christmas beanie stolen, we 'll catch up later."

"Enjoy your drumming."

"I always do," Hoog said as he strode off toward the exit into Breidelstraat and was soon swallowed up by the crowds.

# THIRTEEN

## BRUGES, BELGIUM

OFFICER WARD JOHANSSON made his way slowly down the dank stone stairs and into the dusty catacombs beneath the police station. The large box of files in his arms threatened to slip free with every cautious step. Ward nudged the light switch with his elbow and headed toward an old steel table that sat in the center of the first room. Some steel shelving units had been put in recently and held racks of A4 file boxes, which contained old paperwork still waiting to be scanned.

There had been a lot of rain during December and the lead up to Christmas, and the gray waters of the canal now lapped just below the dirt-encrusted windows. Dust motes swirled in the sun's pale light as he dropped the files onto the table. Ward looked around the dank space and rubbed his hands together to warm them against the chill. He 'd made the move from Brussels to Bruges in the hope of becoming a big fish in the smaller pond of the ancient city. Newly married, and with his wife Mari expecting, he needed to get on the promotion ladder, and fast. He'd promised Mari a night in, just the two of them while they still could. She was planning to cook a stoofvlees — his favorite dish. A traditional Flemish stew made with beef broth and beer. He looked at the time. The big fat G- SHOCK watch on his wrist had been a present from Mari when he 'd joined the police. She'd seen some Special Forces guys wearing them on patrol at Brussels railway station shortly after the terrorist attacks.

She told him he needed to look tough out on the streets and fumbling for his phone to tell the time

wasn't a good look.

He moved the files around, arranging them in chronological order. During the Procession of the Holy Blood, extra officers had been drafted in and space in the main office had been at a premium. But now the space in the catacombs had been freed up and allocated as a storage area for files, and somewhere he could work without interruption. He'd watched the Holy Blood procession as a child, and remembered his excitement at seeing the trumpets, the men waving fronds and of course, the donkey. He'd enjoyed the carnival atmosphere but had no idea of the significance of the parade until many years later. The belief that a sample of Christ's blood held in a reliquary became liquid on Ascension Day had seemed utter nonsense to him as a child, and nothing had changed his opinion since then. Even so, the ceremony pulled in thousands of tourists each year and was one of the most popular attractions of the ancient city. Looking back, he could still remember how annoyed his parents had been when he had demanded proof that the miracle actually took place. It was probably the first sign of a natural curiosity that would lead to him joining the police force.

He looked at the pile of files spread out in front of him. Chief Pieters had given him *an opportunity*. This turned out to be a massive pile of unsolved cold cases going back years. Ward had a feeling that this wasn't an altogether altruistic move on the Chief's part. The implication was that if he could clear up some of the backlogs, it would improve his chances of joining the fast-track detective program. Ward suspected that the chief had given him the task just to keep him quiet, but he was determined to prove Pieters wrong by finding something he could turn his advantage.

# FOURTEEN

DIETER AND ROLAND'S van was an old but reliable VW Transporter. It had been converted into a dive support vehicle and was fitted out with a compressor and racks loaded up with diving gear, suits, and tools. Dieter and Roland were old hands. They had served their time on the oil rigs of the North Sea before setting up their own small outfit. They'd worked the rigs together, drunk in the same bars, and maybe even slept with the same women when they'd hit port.

They'd settled in Bruges where they were kept busy troubleshooting the twenty kilometers of canals running through and around the old town. Today's job was to investigate a possible leak in a pipe that ran along the bottom of the Dijver Canal in the center of the city. The De Halve Maan Brewery had recently installed a second beer pipe stretching over five kilometers along the canals to pump beer from their brewery in Walplein to the bottling plant in Lievan Bauwensstraat. From there it would be bottled and delivered all over the world. The original pipeline through the town had been the first of its kind. It saved using heavy trucks, which would have had to travel through the narrow, cobbled streets of the city. But there had been various efforts to tap into the buried pipeline, and so a second one had been installed beneath the canal in an attempt to protect it against further attacks.

47

They pulled up at the side of the Dijver canal and turned off the engine. It was nine o'clock, and they had at least an hour before any boat trips were active. Across the water, sat the sixteenth-century convent that was now home to the police station in Kartuizerinnenstraat. Its dirt-encrusted windows looked out across the canal from the catacombs beneath the station. The sun glinted off the water's surface, reflecting the ancient beauty of the building. Alongside the entrance to the station, the new Bourgogne des Flandres Brewery did brisk business with tourists looking to try its tasting tours.

Dieter leaned forward and picked up a pair of binoculars from the top of the dashboard. They both climbed out of the van. Roland cricked his neck from side to side, easing his stiff joints. A lifetime of decompression hadn't done him favors.

Dieter leveled his binoculars at the canal, scanning the surface. "Over there," he grunted, handing the glasses to Roland. "Twenty feet in front of that bench, at three o' clock."

Roland looked through the glasses. "Could be something. There's been no change in the pipeline pressure between the plant and the delivery site, and the water readings from the canal came back clear,"

Dieter said, "Maybe. But the bubbles are right over the path of the pipeline." Roland shrugged. "Might be a dead swan, or rotting vegetation giving off methane gas…could even be some idiootheid trying to drill into the pipe and steal the beer." Dieter went over to the side of the van and pulled open the sliding door, which squealed in protest. Two diving suits hung from a rail inside. Below them, steel racks supported a pair of diving tanks. Dieter rummaged in his pocket and produced a coin. He flipped it into the air and caught it in one of his meaty hands. "Heads or tails."

"Tails," Roland said with a smile. Dieter opened his hand.

"Tails it is," Roland said with a grin. "I'll take topside."

Dieter reached into the van and lifted out his suit. "Let's hope it's a dead swan."

# FIFTEEN

TOMAS WATCHED AS the passengers clambered into the canal boat. The winter sun was warm against his face, and the trees alongside the banks of the Dijver were still an explosion of red and gold. It was getting to the end of the season for tours, and he only worked weekends as they headed towards Christmas. He 'd had to work hard to get the tourists on board, but it had been worth it. He looked around the boat. There was a sprinkling of different nationalities. As usual, the Japanese were well represented, a few Germans, a party of English girls, an old couple, and some Belgians visiting for the weekend. He made sure everyone was safely seated, then cast off the line and settled into his seat as they pulled away from the jetty at Boottochten Bridge.

The boat slid past the magnificent old houses that lined the banks of the canal, and the tourists snapped away at anything that moved or caught their interest. They headed toward Minnewater, past the swannery where the birds congregated on the bank. They passed a large house draped with ivy and shielded by trees. Tomas had never seen anybody living there, but recently he thought he'd glimpsed a couple of large dogs running behind the trees in front of the house. He pointed to the back of a large building.

"Over there is the Groeninge. This is not the sound your husband will make when you take him there, but rather a beautiful museum and exhibition showing many masterpieces by the Flemish primitives, neo-classicists, and expressionists."

All the cameras pointed toward the museum. They joined the Dijver canal and were soon passing behind the Basilica of the Holy Blood.

"Between the twelfth and fifteenth centuries, Bruges was a booming trade center and ships came in along the Reie as far as the Market Square. In 1218, they built a large covered hall, known as the Waterhalle, over the river. It had a bit of a shady reputation, like all ports back then, and when the river started to silt up, it became a popular haunt for a certain kind of woman. Does everyone know what I'm talking about?"

The group of English girls launched into a bump and grind routine while singing along to the tune of "The Stripper." Tomas smiled.

"Exactly. Women of the night, shady ladies, courtesans, call them what you will...anyway, with the absence of ships, the Waterhalle became their favorite hangout." Tomas paused for effect. "But Bruges was special for another reason back then. It was one of the cities with the highest number of witch burnings in Belgium."

There were squeals of excitement from the English girls. Tomas went on. "One of the supposed witches was a prostitute named Cathelyne Verpoort. She was accused of an act of witchcraft involving human evisceration. Do you want me to tell the story?" There was a clamor of agreement amongst the passengers. "Okay. Just for you, I will tell the tale. But I'm hoping that my reward in tips will enable me to save something toward buying at least a windowpane in one of those fine buildings we are passing." The tourists gave some cheers of encouragement.

"All right then. Please be aware this story contains witches, blood, and body parts. So, if you are of a sensitive nature, perhaps you had better move to a seat at the side of the boat."

# SIXTEEN

**BRUGES, BELGIUM – 1634**

CATHELYNE VERPOORT WAS numb with shock when the aldermen arrived at the Waterhalle. She could still hear the dying screams of Helga ringing in her ears. The aldermen's torches had revealed the full horror of the scene in the light from their flickering torches. They paid no heed to Cathelyne's protestations of innocence, and she soon found herself hanging naked from the strappado in the bowels of the jail. Throughout the night, masked men would enter her cell and pleasure themselves with her body. A roll of cloth was rammed into her mouth to stifle her screams of agony and only removed so they could carry out their most intimate perversions.

When morning came, she was taken down and laid spread-eagled across a table, her legs and wrists bound. Water was poured down her throat, her mouth forced open as she choked on her own vomit. Her fingernails were ripped off with pincers, and red-hot tongs were pressed against her flesh and used to rip at her most tender parts. With the smell of her own burning flesh in her nostrils, she would have confessed to anything just to stop the pain. After many hours, she was thrown back onto the stinking floor of her cell. But she knew there was much worse to come.

Her mind went back to the previous night in the Waterhalle as she'd stared at the mutilated and dying body of Helga floating face down in the dark waters. The elders had pulled five mutilated corpses out of the water that night including Helga. No weapon was found at the scene. But that didn't concern the Witch Finder. It merely added to the conviction that Cathelyne was a witch and had used her evil powers to carry out the barbaric and monstrous acts. That was the hideous beauty of the witch hunts. Neither proof nor witnesses were needed to persecute their helpless victims.

The rattle of the cell lock jerked her out of her tortured thoughts. Two men came in, dragged her across the floor, and down the passageway leading through the jail. She recognized one of the jailers from his twisted finger. He amongst others had violated her as she hung in agony during the night. It was a savage rape, but they justified it amongst themselves as they slapped and punched her during their base act...claiming they were impaling the devil that lived within her. They dragged her down more steps and along the passageway that led out into the courtyard. Her hands were bound, and she was thrown into the back of the rough wooden cart that was to carry her to the market. Once there, she was to be burnt at the stake.

She passed through the jeering crowds as the cart clattered down the cobbled streets. As she got nearer the pile of wood that formed the bonfire, she saw a Negress in the crowd. She was wearing colored beads, and her eyes blazed with an intensity Cathelyne had never seen before. She had rarely seen a Negress in the town, and when she had, they were always with their master. But this girl was on her own in a crowd of people, it was as if she was invisible. She watched in fascination as people streamed past, seemingly unaware of her presence. As they shared a look, Cathelyne's pain and fear faded away, and her head was filled with the Negress's voice.

*"You will feel no pain, but those that did you harm will*
*suffer terribly."*

And then she was past her, and the cart halted beside the bonfire. As they dragged her toward the stake, it was as if she was looking down at herself from high above the square. As if her corporeal twin had been released from within her flesh and become some kind of spiritual being. Her corporeal twin was smiling as they bound her to the stake and set fire to the kindling that surrounded her.

Cathelyne looked down in fascination as the flames roared across her earthbound twin's flesh. The crowd was cheering, their bloodlust fueled by the horrific vision of charred flesh. And then came the screaming. The jailers, including the man with the twisted finger, and some of the elders who had supervised her torture, were clutching their faces and beating at their clothing…as if trying to put out invisible flames.

And as she watched, their faces turned black, and the flesh fell away in smoking chunks as they collapsed to the ground. Then the voice came into Cathelyne's head again.

*"It is time for you to find a new vessel…"*

Cathelyne looked down at the crowd. The teeming masses, once excited by the burning of a helpless woman, were now terrified by the sight of the men who had perished as if by some invisible force. She found herself asking questions with her own thoughts.

*"How will I know where to go?"*

Once again, the Negress's thoughts came into her mind.

*"You will know, just look, and it will become clear."*

Cathelyne looked down. She studied the crowd but sensed nothing. Then she looked at the people of noble birth who had watched the spectacle from the comfort of their carriages or from horseback, not wishing to sully their senses by mingling with the stench of the poor. And then she saw him. He stepped down from his carriage. His fashionable clothes shone in the weak sunshine as the sun's rays caught the golden thread and rich brocade of his jacket. His hair was crow black, lustrous, and thick, and he was tall with dark eyes set deep in a cruel face. She remembered him well. It was the artist, Count Brandt Van Zwart.

53

She heard the Negress's voice again.

*"You know him as an artist, a cruel man of noble birth, and now he will be your new home. A vessel for your soul."*

Cathelyne would never forget the day she had run from his studio. And the horror that followed. Within that moment Cathelyne found herself looking at the world through the count's eyes as he climbed back into his carriage.

She smiled to herself, savoring her new surroundings. She'd always wondered what it was like to be a man with power, and now she would find out.

# SEVENTEEN

**GROENINGE MUSEUM, BRUGES – Present day**

THE SOFT CLACK of the old lady's stick echoed off the rough stone floor as she made her way slowly toward Katja. Even at eighty-five, whip-thin and bent over with age, she had a steely glint in her eye that suffered no fools, and a mind as sharp as a tack. Erika Houston Van Vinke had worked as curator of the museum for over fifty years. Back when the museum's computers had crashed, she was the only person who knew where everything was stored. She was a legend. Ruling her domain with an iron will, and an occasional prod from her stick. Her odd name came from her mother, who had helped a member of the American expeditionary forces escape from a POW camp in Germany. Erika was the result of his gratitude. Her mother never knew her lover's name, only that he came from Houston.

Erika stretched out her hand, clasping Katja's warmly. "Antwerp not good enough for you? Or are you back for social reasons?" Katja saw a mischievous twinkle in her eye.

"Just a bit of a training update," Katja said.

"Well, it must be a very foolish person who thinks you need more training." Katja looked around the vaulted space beneath the main museum. It stretched the entire length of the building and was packed with exhibits draped in cloth or wrapped in bubble wrap.

"Wow, you've got a lot more stashed away since I was last here."

Erika nodded. "Yes. But I'm going to have to disappoint you when it comes to your mysterious Count."

"How so?"

"Well, when we spoke, I'd checked the computer, and it showed we had six portraits of his in the museum."

"So, what's the problem?"

"The problem is I can't find them."

Katja looked at her. "That's impossible, you know where everything is, even without a computer you could find a paintbrush in the dark down here."

The old lady smiled. "That's a bit of an exaggeration, but I can normally put my hand on most things."

"So where do you think they are?"

"Well, if the computer says we have them, then they should be here."

Katja racked her brains. "Have you ever had to store paintings off-site? During refurbishments for instance."

Erika shook her head. "No, we have ample storage here, we would have just moved paintings to another storage area."

Katja knew that the museum was built on the foundations of the old Eekhout Abbey and that there were numerous old catacombs and cellars not open to the general public available for storage. And then she remembered something.

"What about the big flood back in the nineties...?"

"Nineteen ninety-five," Erika said.

There was nothing wrong with her memory, that was for sure, Katja thought.

"Yes. Didn't the museum have to take precautions in case of flooding?"

"You're right. Some of the old cellars that used to be beneath the abbey were tanked. They may have stored some of the less popular artworks down there."

"Can we take a look?" Katja asked.

Erika went over to a small wooden key cupboard and fished out an old ornate wrought iron key.

"Follow me."

They headed down a narrow passageway leading from the primary storage area and deeper underground. They arrived outside an ancient three-planked oak door with massive forged iron hinges. Erika wiggled the key into the lock.

"As far as I remember this has been tanked."

The lock gave a dull clunk, and Erika pulled at the handle. The hinges screeched, and the door swung open. Erika flicked a switch on the wall, and a fluorescent light blinked on. Katja looked around. The room was mostly empty. There were rusty metal shelves stacked with a few dozen pictures sealed in thick plastic sheeting.

"It's warm in here," Katja said.

"Yes. All the storage areas are connected to the HVAC, centralized climate control. It's kept at about 18 to 21 centigrade."

Erika looked at the half-empty shelves. "It doesn't look like they stored many paintings down here. So if they are here, we should be able to find them pretty easily. The tourists are only really interested in the usual suspects, so I guess these slipped through the net."

"Yes, the Flemish primitives, Van Eyck, Memling, Brueghel, Bosch…" commented Katja.

Erika looked keenly at her. "That degree you got at Bijloke must come in useful when you're locking up drunks on a Saturday night."

Katja laughed. "I enjoyed my time in Ghent."

"Here we are." Erika lifted a small picture from the top of a pile. Katja made out the portrait of a young woman sitting in front of an arched window overlooking a  canal.

"Let's take them upstairs," Erika said. "We'll need gloves on to study them more closely." Back in the main storage area Erika carefully unwrapped the six paintings and propped them against one of the walls.

"I've not seen these paintings before." Erika pulled down an art guide from a shelf and flicked through the pages. "Here we are. Count Brandt Van Zwart."

There was a self-portrait in the book alongside his biography. It showed a man with a cruel looking face, jet black hair, a small goatee beard, and a neatly trimmed mustache. He wore a long black coat threaded with silver and secured with a silk cord tied in an elaborate knot.

"He has a mean look about him," Erika said. She turned another page. "He did portrait work in the seventeenth century. But other than these six, he doesn't seem to have painted anything else."

Erika looked at them. "To be honest, they're not great. In fact, I find them a bit sinister. I think they were moved down into storage while I was away on holiday. Despite what most people think, I don't actually live down here," she said with a smile. Katja bent down to study them. "So they've never been on public display?"

"Neither have they been authenticated," Erika said.

"May I touch them?" Erika handed Katja a pair of gloves. "Be gentle, they're a little worse for wear."

Katja reached out and touched the face of one of the girls. She moved down the line caressing all the faces until she reached the last one.

Erika looked at her, intrigued. "What is it?"

Katja stood up. "I don't know if it's anything, but all of the paintings apart from this one has been built up from layers of paint."

"That wasn't unusual back then, either through technique, covering up mistakes or reusing canvases. Picasso painted the *Blue Room* over a picture of a bearded man because he couldn't afford a new canvas," Erika said. Katja moved down to the last picture, running her finger across the face in the painting. "Yes, Van Zwart was a master at layering. But this one is different to the others. It's only one coat."

Erika bent down and touched the painting. "I wonder why?" She looked down at the paintings lined up against the walls.

"There are various techniques employed to check the validity of paintings these days. We might be able to look a little deeper at these if you like."

"You mean X-rays?" Katja said.

"Yes, and you're in luck. We received a combined grant with Ghent University last year, and part of the deal was we get to share a portable X-Ray machine."

"Where's the system now?" Katja asked.

"At the moment we have it, but only for a week or so. Then it goes back to Ghent for a research project."

"Great. Would it be possible to look at these pictures today?"

Erika looked at her. "I have a pet radiographer I could call on. Is this part of an ongoing case?"

Katja shook her head. "No, just my obsessive nature."

Erika chuckled. "That's what makes you so good at your job my dear."

# EIGHTEEN

KATJA AND ERIKA watched as Wim Van Den Bergh, a young, lank-haired technician, fiddled with the settings of a portable X-Ray unit. He looked over his shoulder.

"Won't be long. Just tweaking the kilovoltage."

He tapped the keys and settings scrolled past on one of the two open laptops that sat on the workbench in front of him. His slim fingers danced across the keys.

"What's so interesting about these pictures that you want to probe beneath their skin?" Wim asked.

"Well, for a start I have a thing about witches. And secondly, there's a possibility the man who painted these portraits murdered the girls who sat for him," Katja replied.

Wim gave her a look.

"Some sort of medieval serial killer. Cool. So, what's that got to do with witches?"

"One of the girls he painted, Cathelyne Verpoort, was burnt at the stake as a witch."

"So, she avoided being killed by the artist but ended up on the stake. That's harsh."

"Yes, there isn't much historical information about her death, just some mythology passed down through the centuries. These paintings might be the only physical proof that she existed, apart from her name cropping up in various lists of witches burnt in Bruges," Katja said.

Wim tapped some more keys. "So you're going all Patricia Cornwell on the case huh?"

Katja shook her head. She remembered how obsessive the author Patricia Cornwell had become while trying to prove her theory that Jack the Ripper was the artist Walter Sickert. She'd spent ten years researching the subject, bought 32 of Sickert's paintings, and splashed out more than six million dollars, and then wrote two bestselling books on the subject.

"I don't have the time or the millions to spend on it, but a colleague of mine piqued my interest."

"How?" Wim asked.

"He thought it could be the Bruges equivalent to the Jack the Ripper case. Apparently, they found the bodies of five dismembered prostitutes floating in the Waterhalle, so I imagine whoever was responsible would be viewed as a serial killer."

Wim grinned. "Could have been just one helluva' party." He tapped the keyboard. "Okay. We're all set."

The camera hummed into life. The machine scanned one of the pictures propped in position against a wall at the far end of the room. The top layer of the picture faded away, apart from the face and hands, which remained unchanged.

"Whoa!" Wim said. "I was not expecting that."

They all stared at what the X-Ray scan had revealed. The model in the portrait was now completely naked.

"This explains why the paint was in layers," Erika said. "Can we scan the others?" Katja asked.

"Why not?" Wim replied. "Things can't get any weirder."

She helped Wim put the next painting in position. The machine hummed once more, and the results were the same. As they worked their way through the remaining four portraits, they were all naked underneath the top layer. Erika put the un- layered, and final, picture against the wall. The machine hummed, but there was nothing beneath the picture's surface.

"Looks like she was a little prudish," Wim said.

Katja moved closer to the screen. "Is it possible to tighten in on her neck?"

"No problem," Wim said.

He altered some setting and the screen filled with the young girl's face and neck. Beneath her chin, and to one side of her neck, was a sickle-shaped mark.

"What's that?" Erika asked. "Some sort of birthmark?"

"I think this is Cathelyne Verpoort," Katja said.

# NINETEEN

THE WATER WAS a murky brown soup. And even with Dieter's powerful quartz divers lamp, he could barely see more than a few feet in front of him. His umbilical stretched away behind him and up to the surface. The thick tube provided him with coms and back up air, as well as relaying a video feed from his helmet camera to Roland in the van. Experience had taught them it was essential to have back up.

The problem with the canals was illegal dumping. Dieter was always on the alert for old bikes and shopping carts that could snag his equipment. His intercom crackled.

"I can't see shit up here," Roly said.

Dieter keyed his face mic. "Pretty much the same shit down here," he said.

"Yeah, but my shit's in high-def," Roly quipped.

Dieter turned on a small handheld hydrophone, a sensitive underwater microphone, and panned it slowly round. If there weren't any canal boats or tourist boats passing, Dieter would hear the faint sound of the beer being pumped through the pipe, and more importantly, the noise of any leak bubbling out into the canal. He turned up the gain and listened. It was faint, but he could make out the rhythmic pulsing noise from within the beer pipe. He slowly swam toward the sound until he could make out a dim shape in front of him. It was the pipeline…it passed through a concrete collar anchoring it to the canal bed.

He gently moved his flippers so as not to disturb the loose silt beneath him, and drifted towards the concrete block.

As he glided closer, he could make out a thin trail of silver bubbles in the beam from his headlamp.
They were coming from behind the block. There was an old piece of rope wrapped around the concrete.
The sound from his hydrophone changed. Something was coming nearer.

The dull thump of an approaching boat's propellers filled his ears. The pressure from the approaching bow wave began to buffet him. And as Dieter fought to maintain his position, something moved in the gloom. Rising up from behind the pipe. It spun around him. It was a human body. A torso without a head. He screamed inside his facemask.

# TWENTY

TOMAS WAS HAPPY. The tour had gone well, and they were on the return trip to Boottochten Bridge, passing the back of the old Police station. His witchcraft story had proved popular, and he was sure his tips would reflect that. He pointed across the canal.

"On your left is the police station, and next to it the Bourgogne des Flandres brewery. So, it's very easy to get drunk and arrested without having to walk too far."

The tourists laughed.

Tomas looked ahead. Bubbles ruptured the water in front of him. He slowed the engine. Something broke the surface of the water, and he wrenched the tiller to avoid it. But it was too late. The boat smashed into it with a dull thud. And then things got a whole lot worse.

# TWENTY-ONE

WARD PEERED THROUGH the grimy leaded windows.
Outside the streets were busy with tourists. Queues for the
boat tours stretched down the road while ducks and swans
bobbed along the canal. The tour guide's patter echoed
across the water from the passing boats.
He went back to his desk and began looking through the
files on the table. They were mostly petty thefts, assaults,
house burglaries, pickpocketing, and the odd car theft.
None of the cases he'd seen so far would produce a big
enough splash to raise his profile and improve his chances
of promotion, even if he could solve them. He moved to
the next row of files. Outside there was the low throb of an
approaching canal boat and the sound of water slapping
against the ancient stone walls of the station. He studied
another file looking for keywords that might signify
something of enough importance to dig deeper. Parking
violations, stolen cars, and drunken fights were swiftly
dumped on the waste-of-space pile. And then he saw it. A
tourist had reported that his son had been offered drugs in
the market at the skating rink. He skimmed through more
files and found three other reports, all logged during the
Christmas season. There was no real evidence, other than
the dealer had long blond hair. Ward smiled. This ticked
all the boxes: drugs, children at risk, and more than one
complaint. He stacked the four files in a separate pile and
rubbed his eyes.

The pulsing fluorescent lights and the deep throb of the approaching boat's engine were starting to give him a headache.

There was a dull thud, a woman screamed, and the prow of a boat smashed through the window. Bricks exploded into the room, and a wall of freezing water slammed the steel table into him, pinning him against the wall behind. The engine roared as the driver threw it into reverse. More water swept over him, and his head was soon beneath the surface. He was almost out of air. His vision dimmed, and he heard the blood pounding in his ears. Sodden sheets of paper clung to his face. And then it all went dark.

# TWENTY-TWO

HOOG WAS SWEATING in the dank chill of the underground space that passed for his drum room. The catacombs beneath the station were a perfect fit in terms of acoustics and soundproofing. When the firing range had been set up, the whole area had been soundproofed, and he'd manage to scrounge some extra panels to fit out the small space beyond the range. He'd had the percussion bug for a couple of years now, and like most of his hobbies, it had become an obsession. He'd watched footage of Cozy Powell on "Dance with the Devil", and in his opinion, the man had been a rock god. He always wound down a practice session with the classic Phil Collins drum solo on "In the Air Tonight". As he built to the climax, the ground beneath his feet shuddered. For a moment he thought he'd imagined it or that it was some acoustic quirk. He stopped drumming, stilled the cymbal, and listened. And then he heard something that sent shivers up his spine. The sound of rushing water.

He dropped his sticks and ran towards the noise. As he raced through the catacombs towards the exit, he heard the roar of an engine. It was impossibly loud. Like it was in the room. A wave of freezing water washed against his shins. The overhead fluorescents flickered and winked out. He fumbled for his phone and found the flashlight. The roar of the engine was deafening now, and the back of his throat burned from diesel fumes. He waded through the gun range and reached the last room below the station.

It was lower than the other rooms, and as he stepped down into it, the water reached up his chest. He shouted out.

"Ward!" He panned his phone light around scanning the room. It was completely flooded. Hoog knew Ward had been working there earlier but guessed he had left. Dark brown water still swirled through the smashed window, and he heard raised voices from outside. Hoog imagined one of the tour boats had got out of control and rammed into the station. He saw some bubbles breaking the surface in front of him. He put his phone on a ledge behind him and ducked below the water. Visibility was almost non-existent. Sheets of paper floated past him, sticking to his face. He ripped them clear and felt around with his hands. He saw a dark shape in front of him. The steel table upended and leaning against the wall. He was about to move on when he saw something glowing beneath the water.

He moved towards it. Straining to see what it was; a luminous watch dial. He ducked under the water and reached for it. Felt cold flesh and grasped a wrist. He shoved the heavy table away and grabbed the body that floated free and pushed up to the surface. He dragged Ward towards the stairs leading out of the catacomb. Hoog yelled up the stairs.

"Need some help here!"

He heard feet running down the stairs towards him and shouting f room above. He looked down at the water flowing into the room and saw something floating just below the surface. As it drifted nearer, he saw what it was. A human torso.

# TWENTY-THREE

WIM HAD HEADED back to Ghent University, and Erika and Katja had begun looking through the bibliographical archives. Erika had collected a pile of books and was using the museum computer to investigate things further.

"She's certainly an elusive figure. Apart from the mythology that Jochum and the tour guides are continuing to extol, there's very little about Cathelyne Verpoort to be found. Even Mr. Google hasn't come up with anything that links her to our mysterious Brandt Van Zwart."

Katja rubbed her eyes. She'd been straining them trying to read some of the old manuscripts, and the fine print had given her a headache.

"Maybe we're looking in the wrong place, or looking for the wrong person."

"What do you mean?" Erika took her glasses off and polished them vigorously on the sleeve of her sweater.

"Again, It's one of my hunches. But when I was looking through the lists of witches burnt in Bruges, Cathelyne Verpoort came up in a number of lists, and she was always mentioned along with Mayken Luucx."

Erika looked at her keenly. "What's the connection?"

"I'm sure I saw something about another name," Katja said. "You think Cathelyne was known by another name?" Erika said.

"Maybe." Katja tapped some keys. "I'll try a search for Cathelyne Verpoort and Mayken Luucx and see what comes up." She tapped search.

Erika looked over as the search engine spat out a list of sites. "Royal Academy of arts and fine arts Belgium…try that." Katja tapped the link. "There." Erika pointed at the screen. Katja read it out. "Besems Calla, Zie Verpoort, Cathelyne." Katja hit another link. "Humanistica Lovaniensia Journal of Neo Latin studies. It lists the questions the aldermen asked the witches under torture, and she was one of them."Erika read the words on the screen. "My God, you forget the brutality of the times."

"Yes. I read somewhere that during the European wars of religion almost 50,000 witches were burnt at the stake, eighty percent of them were women and usually over the age of forty."

"As I'm sure you know, it was persecution fueled by many things, but mainly to serve the agendas of men," Erika said.

"Yes, there was no hashtag *'me too'* back then. Women had no rights whatsoever. Can we do a search using her alternative name and see if anything comes up in any of the bibliographical archive databases?"

Erika nodded. She was already accessing the database. "Hold on. Let's see what we have here," Erika said. The winking search icon blinked as the machine completed its search.

"It only comes up in one book," Erika said. "And according to the database, it's upstairs." Erika had managed to track down the ancient book and had scanned the relevant texts, translating as much as she could. Katja could see she was very excited with the results.

"Put these on," she said, handing her a pair of protective gloves. Katja slipped them on, and Erika held up a small, leather- bound book, mottled with age. Katja could just make out a faded name on the cover. *IGNIS*

"From the Latin meaning fire or an inferno," Erika said. Katja opened the book, straining to read the tiny, faded lettering inside. Erika produced some pages of text. "I took the liberty of copying the relevant pieces for you."

Katja scanned the words. "Did you translate this?"

"No, that honor falls to Google."

Katja studied the text. "Is this some kind of mystical grimoire like *The Key of Solomon* or *The Sworn Book of Honorius*?"

"Not exactly. Have you heard of Cornelius Agrippa?" Katja shook her head and kept reading.

"He was an influential occult philosopher in the sixteenth century. He wrote three books on the occult sciences, and a fourth book appeared after his death. The fourth book was about spirit conjuration and damaged his reputation during the time of the witch trials that were sweeping Europe."

"So, if he didn't write it, who did?" Katja said.

Erika held up the leather-bound volume of IGNIS. "Some people say it was the same author as this." She placed the book back on the table. "There's no record of anybody by that name. So, it might be a collective work with no single person taking the credit...this is the only surviving copy. It was banned throughout Europe, and anybody found in possession of it was deemed to be a witch and burned at the stake. Which is pretty ironic, once you know the substance of the work."

"Why don't I take you to lunch, and you can fill in the blanks," Katja said.

"What a good idea, I took the liberty of booking a table at The Olive Tree."

It was evident that Erika was a regular at the Olive Tree from the way the Greek waiters fussed over her, and she was soon seated at a corner table by the window with a steaming plate of moussaka and a bottle of the house red.

"Mmmm that looks delicious," Katja said, "If I hadn't eaten already I would join you. But as I'm off duty I'll have some wine at least."

Erika took a sip of her wine. "I'm glad Bruges is still up to your standards. I was worried that Antwerp might steal you away for good."

"It has its good points, but being back here reminds me of what I liked about Bruges in the first place."

Erika broke off a piece of garlic bread, nibbled a bit and put it down before speaking softly. "How is Jochum these days? I haven't seen him for a while. He's always off doing some new dance class, at the gun range, or banging on his drum kit."

Katja put down her glass and studied the old lady. There was nothing that got past her. When she was seeing Hoog, they'd often visited the Groeninge, and Erika had been a bottomless pit of information on the numerous works of art on display. When she and Hoog had gone their separate ways, Katja had often thought that Erika had been more upset than her.

"Well, he's still the Hoog we all know and love."

"Charming, abrasive, funny and always right…in his opinion anyway," chimed Erika.

"Pretty much. Anyway, we're not sitting in this fine restaurant to talk about Jochum, are we?"

"I suppose not." Erika went on, "the book lays out an alternative view of the witch trials and their consequences, including the formation of an order calling itself IGNIS."

"And what's the connection between Cathelyne Verpoort or Besems Calla with the contents of the book?"

73

"Well according to the book, Besems Calla, who we know to be Cathelyne Verpoort was the first member of IGNIS," Erika said.

"How could she be. She was burnt at the stake as a witch. It's one of the few things we know for sure," Katja said. She could feel her hopes of bringing some clarity to the Waterhalle murders slipping away as the fog of myth and conjecture rolled towards her.

Erika smiled. "Not according to the book."

"Go on, you have my full attention."

Erika took a sip of wine. Before speaking.

"According to the book, IGNIS was an order formed by the belief that witches burnt at the stake were freed from their mortal shackles to possess their persecutors, and by doing so allow the order to establish itself throughout Europe."

"Could this have been a kind of religion formed by the author of IGNIS, rather like L.Ron Hubbard and Scientology?" Katja said.

"Well as you know, there's not a lot out there about IGNIS and nothing to say this isn't a work of fiction. So I can't answer that." Katja took a sip of wine. "So, if Cathelyne was the first to possess her own persecutor…who exactly did she possess? There were numerous people involved in her arrest and torture; jailors, elders, the men that set the fire."

Erika took another forkful of the moussaka before replying. "I think you have enough pieces of the jigsaw to make a logical guess at that. After all, you've recently uncovered new information that suggests Cathelyne wasn't burnt at the stake just because she was in the wrong place at the wrong time or because she had a birthmark."

Katja thought about this. Erika was right. Out of all the people involved in Cathelyne's torture and death, there was one person who had the motive and the power to ensure her tragic death.

"The Count!" Katja said.

"Exactly. It could have been revenge for Cathelyne's refusal to pose naked, or maybe Brandt Van Zwart really was a serial killer, and felt cheated because she was the one that got away."

"That makes as much sense as anything. But there's still no real explanation as to why Cathelyne became the founder member of IGNIS, or where she got her supposed powers from. After all, she was just a prostitute that cheated death one way only to end up being burnt at the stake. There's something fundamental missing from the equation."

Erika put her napkin down. "Yes, I agree. But witches and their various powers are not one of my specialty subjects. I think it's time you met with an expert. I know someone who lives and breathes witches."

"Who's that?" Katja asked.

"Aart De Vries, he wrote his doctoral thesis on witches and was one of the curators of the witch exhibition we had at the Sint-Janshospitaal Museum a few years back. He's a strange beast, but he knows more about witches and their cults than anybody I know. He has a small office space in the attic at the museum. He's there most days. I'll tell him to expect you."

She paused for a moment, glanced at the menu, then added, "Dessert? They do a lovely honey coated ice cream."

# TWENTY-FOUR

WARD WAS TRYING to sleep, but someone kept shouting. The voice sounded muffled like it was underwater. Someone was punching him in the chest. Thump, thump, thump.

He was freezing cold. He was going to be sick. He felt it rising up into his throat as his eyes opened wide. Hoog was looking down at him.

He vomited to one side.

"Better out than in," Hoog said with a grin.

Ward looked around. He was lying on a table. The catacomb he'd been working in was still under a foot of water, and there was a pile of bricks heaped on the floor beneath the smashed window. Two paramedics were working on him, checking his heart, pulse, and eye reactions.

"We'll get him to the hospital and give him a good check over, but I think he'll be fine." The younger of the two paramedics said.

Ward cleared his throat. Gestured to the flooded room.

"What the hell happened?"

Hoog gripped his shoulder. "One of the canal boats lost control and slammed into the window. If the canal level hadn't been so high, we wouldn't have taken in so much water. The pumps have cleared most of it already. But it's going to be pretty draughty for a week or so."

The paramedics carefully lifted him onto the nearby stretcher and tightened some restraining straps. "How did you find me?"

Hoog flicked a look behind him. "I was practicing my drums when I heard a god-awful crash and the sound of water. The filing room is lower than the other rooms in the catacombs, so I was able to wade down to where you were and drag you out. You were pinned under the table. You'd blacked out. It was touch and go."

The older medic nodded at Ward "Let's get you to the ambulance." The paramedics carried him toward the stairs.

Ward shot a look at Hoog. "I owe you a serious amount of free beer."

Hoog smiled. "For sure."

# TWENTY-FIVE

THE SINT -JANSHOSPITAAL Museum was a vast open space with polished wooden floors and a dramatic arched ceiling ribbed with oak beams like the upturned skeleton of some enormous ship. With its wrought iron stairways and dominant Memling triptych, it was an impressive sight. Behind the triptych, two arched stone windows with leaded glass allowed natural light to flood into the room. Katja knocked on the door of an office off from the main gallery. "Come in," a voice said from behind the door.

She pushed open the door and found herself in a small, cluttered space, dominated by Pieter Brueghel and Hieronymus Bosch prints on the walls. She was greeted by a short, cherubic- faced individual who strode toward her with his arm outstretched.

"Katja Blondell?"

Katja nodded and shook his hand. "Thank you for seeing me." Katja looked around at the many prints and etchings crowding the walls, including an engraving of *St James at the sorcerer's den,* by Brueghel, behind Aart's desk.

Aart De Vries sat down and gestured to a seat opposite. "Erika brought me up to speed about your interest in Cathelyne Verpoort and the Waterhalle murders."

Katja settled herself into the chair. "Erika said you knew more about witches than anybody."

De Vries gave a wry smile. "High praise indeed. The Waterhalle murders is a popular story, and you wouldn't be the first to try and pin the murders on Count Brandt Van Zwart," De Vries said. "But it seems you have made an interesting discovery when it comes to our friend, the count." He tapped some printouts of the nude portraits Erika had emailed him. "If we are to believe that the five bodies found in the Waterhalle were Cathelyne's friends and that she alone had refused to pose naked, it would certainly give him the motive to set her up."

"Not that a rich psychopath needed one back then," Katja said.

De Vries nodded. "True indeed, they weren't the most enlightened of times. She was at the scene of the crime, was a woman, a prostitute and had a birthmark. She ticked all the boxes."

"And someone eviscerated her friend's bodies and dumped them in the Waterhalle on the first night she returned, having not been back there for a while. That's a big coincidence."

"I agree." De Vries rubbed his chin thoughtfully. "So, let's look at the facts we know already."

De Vries shuffled some notes around on his desk, more comfortable with old school note taking, than flicking at a handheld screen.

"It's interesting to note what happened during, and after, Cathelyne was burnt at the stake. In the manuscripts that survived, I found a reference to something called *'Invisibillis Ignis'* Latin, for invisible fire."

"I haven't heard of that," Katja said, leaning forwards.

"No, it's not widely known. But basically, the records show that when the fire was lit, and Cathelyne began to burn, those responsible for her torture and abuse showed all the signs of being burnt alive themselves."

"So they suffered all the symptoms of fire without visible flames?" De Vries nodded. "Like the ethanol fuel used in racing cars, which burns with a pale blue flame and is practically invisible."

"That sounds more like witchcraft than anything else," Katja said.

79

"Yes, but then the Count appears to have had some sort of epiphany or a personality change." "How so?"

"He went from being a cruel, and possibly murderous psychopath, to someone who traveled Europe trying to save women accused of witchcraft."

"That is a pretty big shift of view on his part," Katja said, mulling over the new facts.

"It gets better. Because from that day forth he was accompanied on his travels by a Negress slave. But I'm getting ahead of myself. You wanted to know how Cathelyne went from dodging the attention of a psychopath to becoming the founding member of the order of IGNIS."

"Yes, my feeling is there's somebody missing from the picture." De Vries nodded. "You're right. But before we get into that, I think it would be useful to give the period some context."

"Go on," Katja said, settling into her chair.

De Vries moved the papers on his desk into a neat pile as he talked. "During the sixteenth and seventeenth centuries, crops were destroyed, farmlands flooded, and icebreakers were needed just to make the canals navigable. Along with the violent storms sweeping across Europe, this led to massive famine. Millions of people were starving to death, and they were desperate to find a reason for this terrifying event. Witches were the ideal scapegoat." He gestured to the etching behind him. "Brueghel based these images on manuscripts written by misogynistic men in positions of power." "People like Count Brandt Van Zwart," Katja said. "Yes." He steepled his fingers and looked at Katja with a half-smile. "But what we're looking for is another player, an enabler. Maybe even an über witch."

"If there is such a thing," Katja said. De Vries stretched his arms in the air. "Why don't we take a turn round the museum, and I'll tell you what I know, and what I think I know."

The museum was quiet, and they were able to move easily past the pictures and exhibits. They halted beside Hans Memling's *St. Ursula Shrine*, a chest in the shape of a gothic chapel, with paintings on both façades and tondi on each side. It's gilt decoration and ornate design was a triumph of artistry. De Vries stared at the exhibit before turning to Katja. "The concept of an über witch has been around for centuries. Part of it is mankind's need to believe in a higher power, whether it be good or evil. During the height of the witch trials, as thousands of innocent women were burned to death at the stake, there grew a belief that those who perished in flames were reborn…"

Katja nodded. "The order of IGNIS. A sort of witch-based belief in the resurrection,"

"Yes. Whether this was real, or a source of comfort to those facing death at the stake, we don't know. But the belief in IGNIS began to spread. From the reaction caused by the publication of the book, it was obvious that the authorities didn't want that kind of dogma circulating amongst the masses."

"Of course, the threat of being burnt at the state would have been diluted if it was believed that there was an upside to the ordeal," Katja said.

"Precisely," De Vries said. "Which explains why only one copy of IGNIS survives, and so little information exists about Cathelyne Verpoort in ancient manuscripts."

Katja nodded. "Go on."

"As you know, part of the IGNIS mantra was the conviction that as supposed witches died at the stake, their souls would be channeled into the body of one of their persecutors."

"But who did the channeling?" Katja asked.

"I'm getting to that. In 1630 Frederick Olfert, a sorcerer living in Bruges, was accused of witchcraft and hanged. His death was witnessed by a young Maasai slave, Marja Nalangu. As he died, Olfert's soul was believed to have possessed Marja, along with his powers. Can you guess where this is going?"

Katja nodded. "Marja Nalangu. The African slave girl that went on to accompany Count Brandt Van Zwart, you're saying she's the über witch," Katja said.

"Though she didn't realize the full extent of the powers the sorcerer had gifted her until some years later." De Vries said.

Katja nodded. "When she saw Cathelyne burnt at the stake in 1634. That's when she realized she was able to channel Cathelyne's soul into one of her persecutors, which at that point seems to have been Count Brandt Van Zwart." They headed back through the museum. "That would also explain Zwart's sudden change of heart," Katja said.

"Because by then he was possessed by the soul of Cathelyne Verpoort and in the thrall of über witch Marja Nalangu."

Katja shook her head. "That takes gender fluidity to a whole new level." De Vries smiled. "Things were a lot simpler when I was young."

"Maybe you just weren't paying attention." "I was a bit of a swat," De Vries said.

"So what happened after that? Marja couldn't have been present at every witch burning throughout Europe," Katja asked.

"That's true, but if she was able to channel a certain amount of victim's souls into men of power, maybe she also gifted them with the same channeling abilities."

"So it became a self-propagating situation," Katja said.

"Yes. Marja channeled the victim's souls and her abilities into the men of power, and they repeated the process for the next victim."

"That's a bit of a stretch for me to take on board," Katja said.

"As I said, that is more of what I think was happening rather than something that can be proven,"

De Vries agreed. "I understand that. And it's not like we're going to be bringing anybody to justice for any of the atrocities that happened back then," Katja said.

"No. But it would be interesting to know how Marja's relationship with the Count evolved during their travels through Europe."

They arrived back at De Vries office and went in. "Can I make you a tea or a coffee?"

"A coffee would be good." He handed her a mug and pointed at a small tray beside the machine.

"There's sugar and milk there."

"Thank you." Katja spooned in a couple of sugars and took a sip. Her head was spinning with all the information, but she still had questions. "What other powers were Marja thought to have possessed?"

"Well, for all intents and purposes, she was immortal." "But?" Katja sensed there was more to that statement.

"Well, even though she was immortal she could still be killed. But if that happened, her soul, along with her memories, would possess her killer."

"That's an interesting form of immortality," Katja said.

"Yes, Marja was also a kind of spiritual curator able to store souls, and memories, and channel them into whoever she so wished."

Katja thought about this for a moment, "Like a Russian doll of souls."

De Vries smiled at the comparison, "That's a fairly accurate analogy."

"So she would live forever while everyone she knew grew old and died."

"That's the downside of immortality," said De Vries.

Katja paused for a moment, then, "How powerful was she? Could she shape shift, fly through the air, cast spells?"

De Vries shook his head,

"Nothing to compete with Harry Potter, as far as I'm aware. Though she did have one more trick up her sleeve. But it was an unusual gift because of the sacrifice needed to achieve it."

Katja looked at him. "What sort of sacrifice?" she asked, a feeling of dread creeping over her. De Vries looked grim before delivering the answer, "Self- immolation."

"My God, when would she want to do that?" Katja asked. "If she needed to transmigrate."

"That's a new one on me."

"It's when the soul passes into a different body after death," explained De Vries.

"I wouldn't put myself through that to become someone else." She paused, "Accept perhaps Héloïse Adelaide Letissier."

It was De Vries's turn to look blank. "French pop singer, Christine and the Queens...Chris? Never mind, but none the less, I'm not a big fan of self- immolation, or any immolation to be fair."

"I can understand that. But according to folklore, you would be looking down at your corporeal body while this was going on. So, you wouldn't actually feel any pain."

Katja thought about this. "I'd have to be pretty sure about that before I lit the blue touch paper."

De Vries laughed. "Lucky you're not an über witch then." Katja paused for a moment as all of the conflicting facts and myths whirled around her head

"I don't think I have enough evidence to convince my colleague that witches actually exist, never mind getting him on board with transmigration. But you've certainly given me enough to think about, that's for sure."

De Vries tidied up the pictures and papers strewn across his desk. "I imagine you're talking about Hoog?"

Katja nodded. "Yes, I dragged him here about three times when the exhibition was running. We were a little closer then, and he indulged my interest in all things witch."

There was a low-pitched buzz from her pocket, and she fished out her phone. Looked at the screen and saw Hoog's ID.

"Speak of the devil."

# TWENTY-SIX

THE POLICE STATION was in controlled chaos. Hoses were being carried in through reception, and the sound of distant pumps throbbed from below. Hoog had called Katja and brought her up to speed with the canal boat accident, Ward 's condition, and the discovery of a human torso as she'd walked back from the museum. He met her at the front desk.

"Will Ward be okay?" she asked.

"Yes, he'll have a bit of a sore chest from my clumsy CPR, and some fluid on his lungs for a few days, but they'll check him over before they release him from the hospital."

"Thank God, he must have been terrified. You don't expect to have a boat smash through your office window as a rule."

"For sure. Lucky I'm an obsessive drummer, or he could have drowned."

"Yes, I won't mock you anymore on that score," Katja said.

"We can walk over to the scene," Hoog said.

"Did the people on the boat see anything?"

"No, not really. The tour guide told them it was a dead dog."

"Smart," Katja said.

"He was protecting his tips and his business," Hoog said.

"One of the divers working for the brewery was investigating a leak in the beer pipe when the torso broke loose in front of him. He nearly had a heart attack. We've had a word. Told him to keep it to himself in case it prejudices the investigation. The last thing we want is the press getting hold of it."

"Do we have a cause of death yet?" Katja asked.

"Coroner's at the scene but I imagine not having a head would be a contributory factor," Hoog replied with a grin. They turned right into Wollestraat, headed across the bridge and right again before ending up walking alongside the Dijver canal. They approached a metal sculpture dedicated to the former mayor, Frank Van Acker. Known as the *Bouquet of Flowers*, it was a highly stylized gothic collection of twisted metal flowers spilling out of a container. Katja remembered Hoog had joked about ripping one of the flowers from the display and handing it to her as a token of his love. She looked at him as they passed it and wondered if he remembered. His face was turned away, whether it was deliberate or not she couldn't tell. She saw a crime scene tent ahead, cordoned off with crime scene tape that crackled in the light wind. Hoog nodded to an officer standing outside the tent. He pulled back the canvas flap, and they both went inside. The torso lay on a plastic sheet. Kruger, the coroner, a silver-haired man with steel-framed glasses and an intense look, was fussing around the corpse.

"How's it going?" Katja asked. Kruger looked up.

"Hi Katja, welcome back. Antwerp too exciting for you?" Katja smiled at him. "Compared to this I'd say it's neck and neck." Kruger bent down to study the torso. "The amputations happened post mortem…cause of death would appear to be blood loss, though I'll know more when I get it back to the lab."

"Do you have a rough time of death?" Hoog asked.

"As it was immersed in cold water, it's difficult to give an exact time of death."

Kruger looked up. "There're a couple of things which may be of interest to you. The torso was secured to the pipe with a piece of rope and some kind of slipknot. I think it was designed to release the torso when the water pressure exceeded a certain level."

"Like a bow wave?" Hoog asked. Kruger nodded. "Yes."

"So the body had to have been placed after the last boat of the day, and before the first boat in the morning," Hoog said.

"Yes, and because we're at the end of the season there aren't as many boats doing the tours."

Hoog flipped through a small notebook. "Tomas, the tour guide said it was his first tour of the day, and that was at ten o'clock. As far as he was aware, no one else had been out before him."

"So the body was probably put there overnight," Kruger said.

"I imagine there will be CCTV from some of the buildings overlooking the canal, as well as our own."

Kruger pointed to some wounds in the side of the leg stumps.

"These wounds were made anti-mortem, and if you asked me to guess, I'd say it's where the blood was drained from. It could have been a gradual process."

Hoog nodded. Something was gnawing away at the back of his mind. Something about torsos.

"I'll let you know if the tox report or DNA analysis comes up with anything." "Thanks, Kruger, appreciate it," Hoog said, straightening up from beside the corpse.

They walked along the canal side opposite the police station. The damaged window had been boarded up, and the tourist boat had headed down to a nearby dry dock for repairs. Repairing the ancient brickwork and windows of the station was going to take some time and specialists. The heritage people wouldn't be rushed. They crossed over the bridge into Wollestraat and headed back toward the station.

"I've seen something like this before, I know I have," Hoog said.

Katja looked at him. She could see from his face he wasn't going to rest until he had found the connection.

"Well, when we get back to the station we can do a search through all of the case databases. I know what you mean though. Problem is, I watch a lot of procedural detective series. Netflix, Amazon Prime, Sky Atlantic, not to mention all the Nordic Noir stuff. It gets to a point where you're not sure if the case you remember is from real life or some boxed set you fell asleep in front of."

"I'm the same. *The Bridge* was one of my favorites, I loved *Beck*, *The Killing*, *Wallander*, of course... *Fortitude* lost the plot after the first series, *Trapped* was good, but *Jordskott* hurt my head." Hoog said. Katja turned to look at him. She'd forgotten how much they had in common. "I agree. Once you start making a tree one of the main characters, you're on a slippery slope."

They turned into Kartuizerinnenstraat and walked down to the station. Armed with cups of strong coffee and fresh waffles they scanned through the previous night's CCTV footage from the station and some of the hotels and businesses that overlooked the canal. "The boats only run on Saturday and Sunday between the 4$^{th}$ of November up until the 16$^{th}$ of December," Katja said, reading from her laptop. "So whoever set this up did their research," Hoog said. "Or more likely, just waited until the time was right. But they hadn't counted on the dive team checking for leaks from the beer pipeline." It had been a tranquil night, and as she moved through the footage, it looked like a still photograph of the canal until the odd passing tourist broke the illusion. The surface of the water suddenly shimmered. Katja paused and inched back.

"Here we go." She checked the time code. It was displaying after midnight. The surface of the canal rippled. The ripple formed a line heading towards the canal bank on the opposite side to the police station. Katja tightened in on the image and paused it. Hoog stared at the screen. "Something, or somebody, under the water?" "Could be." She started the playback again. The line of ripples faded away and the area beneath the canal side opposite the station became the center of motion as the water blurred. "I'd say that's when it was placed," Katja said.

"Can we reverse the trail and track where it came from?" "Let's see." Katja flicked between various CCTV feeds from around the area. She paused the view, and the picture showed the canal disappearing under a bridge into blackness.

"Okay. We can see the water surface pattern heading down the Djiver canal up to Boottochten Bridge then it goes under it and doesn't come out." Katja opened Google earth and studied the terrain. "Arentshuis, It's an art museum,"

Hoog nodded. "Might be worth checking the area out. But I want to scratch this itch I have about the torso first." Katja started a search. It didn't take long for the stories to pop up. They soon narrowed their search down to a story in the Louisiana Times.

Chandler Travis, a retired detective from London, and Duke Lanoix, a local Sheriff, had, with the help of some anthropology students, uncovered a link between some torsos turning up in a Louisiana swamp and a Jack the Ripper conspiracy in nineteenth-century London.

Katja scrolled down the screen. "I remember this now. They got a lot of flak for debunking the Ripper conspiracy..."

"Too many people earning a living pedaling that hokum to let it die," Hoog said. "The autopsy report on the corpses found in the swamp all showed the same ante-mortem puncture wounds in the side of the thighs," she scanned the report. "Also, a member of an environmental group who was kidnapped and used as a human blood pump had the same wounds." Hoog looked over at the screen. "Governor Roman Blackburn, the man behind a carbon credit scam up at the plant, and the weird experiments in the swamp, wound up dead. So, he's got a watertight alibi." Katja smiled at Hoog's strange sense of humor. "It's always good to look at the positive side of things."

Hoog read down the page, "Seems Blackburn had a couple of hounds. A rare breed, Dogo Argentino." He punched up a picture of the dogs. "Pretty distinctive wouldn't you say?"

"I'd say. So, do you think there's a connection between that case and ours?"

Hoog went on. "Looks like it. The wounds, amputation of the limbs and head, and the method of disposal in water. The only difference in our case is whoever placed our torso wanted it to be found, whereas the ones in the swamp were used for experiments and then dumped for the alligators to snack on."

"They eventually found ten torsos, or what remained of them. His partner, Marsha Brochell was never found. From what I've read it seems highly likely that she was heavily involved in everything including the experiments that went on out there in the swamps. And if she's still on the loose..." She left it hanging. "You think our torso could be her handiwork? Damn! If the press gets hold of this, the tourist industry will go into
meltdown," Hoog said.

"Until a century has passed, then they'll sell it as part of the authentic tour."

"For sure. A tragedy in one century becomes a tourist attraction in the next." Hoog thought for a moment. Tapped the picture of the Dogos on the screen. "If Marsha is connected to our torso, I'm betting those dogs won't be too far away."
Katja looked at him. "What makes you think that?"

"If Marsha had feelings for Blackburn, it's very likely she'd have a soft spot for his dogs. They might be the only thing left that reminds her of him. But I'm jumping ahead here. We don't have any proof that she's involved. Copycat killer and economic terrorism are still on the table." Katja nodded reluctantly. "That's true. What else do we know about Marsha?" Hoog flicked through the reports on screen. "Officially she was a corporate astrologist."

"Seems she was heavily into voodoo and all kinds of weird shit." Katja was digging into the case records, and it wasn't pleasant reading. "Kidnapping, unauthorized experimentation, murder..." Hoog smiled and looked over at her. "Don't be so judgmental, if she were a witch you'd be all over her."

"Touché. I'll check CCTV and registrations through the ports over the last few months and see if anything turns up. If she traveled with those dogs there'd be records somewhere, you can't just pop them in a handbag and smuggle them through."

"That's for sure. But it seems to me that we could use the similarities between our case and the Louisiana one to our advantage."

"How?" Katja asked, sensing that Hoog was about to suggest some cunning scheme to outwit the bureaucracy that hogtied police investigations with their budgetary constraints.

"I'll speak to the chief and suggest we get these guys over there to help us. If we team up with them, it'll increase our chances of solving the case."

Katja thought about this. She didn't think it made much sense, but selfishly nothing would please her more than having some investigators that were as interested in history as she was.

"Good idea." She said. Hoog looked at her. "Really?"

"Why not? It can't hurt to have a different viewpoint on a case. And my guess is they'll spot similarities we might miss."

"Okay. We might have to get an interpreter in," Hoog said with a smile. "Right," Katja said. "For the American and English accents. You should do stand-up...oh but wait. You're not funny." She tapped the screen, which displayed a picture of Duke, Chandler, and an attractive blond girl on the front page of the Louisiana newspaper.

"She looks cute." Hoog shot Katja a look. Was she hinting that he had an alternative motive for wanting the three of them on their team? Or just playing with him?

"If you like that sort of obvious beauty," he said. Katja smiled. "Show me a man that doesn't?"

Hoog grinned. "Okay, I'm going to see the chief. Compared to the potential loss of tourist income, I imagine he'll get authorization for flights and accommodation."

"That makes sense," Katja said as she stood up and stretched. "I need to get some of this damp out of my bones and eat something other than biscuits. What say we meet up in the tearoom in half an hour?"

"Sounds good. I'll see you there."

She watched Hoog as he disappeared up the stone stairs before closing down the laptop. The years she'd spent in Antwerp seemed to be fading away with each hour she spent with Hoog. She was starting to feel like she'd never been away, and more worryingly that they had never been apart.

# TWENTY-SEVEN

HOOG AND KATJA sat in T Eekhoetje, a small tearoom in Eekhoutstraat just around the corner from Market Square and the Belfort. Hoog tucked into a couple of goat cheese croquettes, along with a mug of strong coffee. He looked up as a dark-haired server floated past, her hips seemingly detached from the rest of her body. Like an Irish dancer, it was all going on below the waist.

Katja noticed Hoog's look. "See something you like?" She said and inwardly cursed herself. How could she be so juvenile? It worried her that Hoog still brought out feelings of jealousy in her...they were over. Had been for years. *Keep telling yourself that girl.* She quickly covered, "The carrot cake is tasty."

Hoog mentally changed gears. He was not sure if he was being played. "Sounds good," he said, forking another croquette into his mouth. "I love this place."

"More than the Bagelsalon?"

Hoog shrugged, his mouth full. He swallowed. "It's a close- run thing." Hoog smiled to himself.

"What?" Katja looked at him.

"I just remembered the first time you brought me here," Hoog said. "You kicked me under the table when I stared at one of the waitresses." Katja shook her head. "Old mammaries never die."

Hoog nearly choked on his coffee. "Where do you get these sayings from?" "Wherever I can find them," Katja said with a smile.

Hoog looked over to where the server was chatting with her colleague. "Can't blame the management for hiring tip bait. There're a lot of tearooms competing for the same tourist euros. I only came here because it's nearer the station."

Katya dug into another slice of her farmer's omelet before looking back at him. Hoog had spoken to the chief who'd been given approval from the commissioner and the mayor to bring in more help. Reading between the lines, it seemed that money was not an issue and that they needed the case cleared up, and fast.

She'd listened to Hoog extolling one of his more elaborate theories of criminology while they'd waited for their food. The subject of his opinion had been described by Carl Jung as synchronicity, a situation where highly improbable events combined in a way that couldn't be explained by cause and effect. Hoog had gone on about quantum physics, and how everything in the universe was connected as an indivisible whole. Something that Einstein referred to as *spooky action at a distance.*

Katja had wiped her mouth with a napkin and looked at him.

"So, you're saying that sometimes what seems like too many coincidences could be explained by Bell's theorem?"

"I'm not saying this is something absolute, just that there are many instances of it happening in our day to day lives at a low level."

"You mean like when I go to call my mother, and my phone rings, and it's her?" Katja asked.

"Exactly, or you're thinking you haven't seen someone for a while, and you bump into them in the street." He took another slug of coffee and continued, "But when the number of coincidences becomes significantly larger, then you need to pay attention."

"How many are we talking about?"

Hoog forked the last croquette into his mouth and put the fork down. "Well, the number seven seems to be popular."

"And that's part of the Hoog modus operandi for crime solving is it?"

Hoog chuckled as the server filled his mug with fresh coffee. "In some cases," he took a sip of coffee, "others need different techniques. I'm just saying that some situations more clearly demonstrate synchronicity than others."

Katja put her fork down. "Well the torso was in the canal right opposite the police station, so that's one coincidence."

"Yes." Hoog agreed.

"The fact that it's a torso, and has the same wounds as the torsos in the Louisiana case is another, two for the scorecard."

"Yes. There's also the possibility that the torso was secured so that it would surface when a boat approached. Creating maximum exposure and subsequent fear and financial damage."

Katja continued, "That makes sense. The fact that the boat tried to avoid it and ended up smashing into our basement, and delivering the torso to us, was a lucky break."

The server came over and began to clear their plates away.

She caught Hoog's eye. "Anything else?" she asked.

Hoog looked over at the cake display next to the register.

"I may be able to force a slice of carrot cake down."

The server turned to Katja. "Anything for you?"

Katja tapped her stomach and smiled. "I don't think so."

The server grinned and hurried away.

Hoog snorted. "You're not worried about your weight?

You're as thin as a rake." Katja gave him a look. "Maybe, but there are some pretty large rakes around these days."

Hoog shook his head. "I don't eat out much so I have some space left for cakes." Katja looked at him. He was right. In the two years she'd been in Antwerp, he seemed to have just become even more wiry and muscular. He'd always had a fast metabolism, and that combined with his mania for dancing meant he could probably get away with the odd slice of cake. "So, what other connections has our case with theirs?"

Hoog waited until the server had placed his carrot cake in front of him before replying. "I can't think of anything at the moment. But I'm sure once they join the investigation, they'll spot additional links."

"How soon before they get over here?"

Hoog checked his watch. "I was waiting for all the time zones to align. That way we can get everybody's travel arrangements in sync. I'll start with the English guy and take it from there." He reached into his pocket and pulled out his phone.

# TWENTY-EIGHT

THEY WERE IN the middle of their cable-car journey when Chandler's phone rang. The caller was Jochum Van De Hoog, a detective from Bruges in Belgium. They were alone in the car, so he'd shrugged at Roxie and listened to what Hoog had to say.

They disembarked from the pod and made their way to the Skylon restaurant for brunch. It had a great view looking out over the river and served tasty food. He felt sure that Roxie had heard enough of the call to understand the situation. But he would let her make the decision.

They were soon seated and tucking into heaped plates of crispy bacon, black sausage, and fried bread.

"Mmm, delicious," Roxie said between mouthfuls.

"Yes, and the view comes for free," Chandler said, as he crunched through a piece of bacon.

Roxie took a swig of coffee. "So, do you want to tell me what's going on? You looked pretty excited by the call."

Chandler put his fork down, wiped his mouth with a napkin, and leaned forward. He held one of Roxie's hands. "Well, I'm sure you heard enough to work some of it out." "I heard you say that if Duke were interested, you'd set up the travel arrangements, and something about Bruges?"

"Yes." Chandler looked around and checked there weren't too many people within earshot. "The Bruges police had a headless torso turn up in one of their canals."

"I'm guessing there's something special about it?"

"Yes, it has the same ante-mortem puncture wounds as the ones in our case. Detective Hoog, the Belgian detective, did a search on the database and our case came up. There were enough similarities for him to get his chief to recommend we join their investigation along with Duke. Funded by the city of course. They want to get the case solved as quickly as possible to prevent any damage to their tourist industry." He looked at Roxie. "I could say no."

Roxie shook her head. "We both know that's not going to happen. Besides, an all-expenses paid trip to a beautiful medieval city accompanied by me, and you get another chance to hook up with your old buddy and talk jazz and criminology. What's not to like?"

"Well if you insist," Chandler said.

Roxie laughed. "I've seen the film *In Bruges*. I can't wait to get there. How long will it take?"

Chandler looked at his watch. "If Duke agrees, he could get an overnight flight to Brussels and meet us at the train station around lunchtime tomorrow. We can then catch the local train to Bruges together."

"Sounds good." Roxie already had her phone out, and her fingers were flicking across the screen. "We could catch the Eurostar just before nine tomorrow from St. Pancras and be at Brussels Midi by midday. That should fit in with Duke's flight. He'll have the morning to catch up on his sleep before we arrive."

"That could work. So, we have the rest of the day and the evening if you want to do anything special?"

Roxie looked through the restaurant windows at the majestic view of the river and thought for a moment. "Well, we could go and look at Madame Tussauds, along with all the other tourists…or go back to your flat and fool around." Chandler grinned, "I don't see any point in overthinking that decision, do you?" He waved at a passing server and made the universal sign of writing a check.

Roxie finished her coffee and started tapping on her phone. "Premier Plus?"

"Why not." Chandler said.

Roxie tapped the screen. "Done!"

# TWENTY-NINE

CHANDLER SIPPED ON a coffee and a slice of cake at a café at St. Pancras International. Roxie's eyes had resembled two saucers when she saw the many floors of shops within the station complex. If there was one thing she liked as much as London's history, it was shopping. Her wardrobe wasn't geared up for the winter climate in Bruges, so she'd made a beeline for the various clothing stores on the upper and lower floors. She appeared half an hour later and sat down next to him in a flurry of carrier bags and guidebooks.

"They don't have much on offer in the winter clothing line," she said.

"Coffee?" Chandler asked.

"Oh yes," said Roxie.

Chandler waved at a server, and their order was soon in hand. He looked at Roxie. "You do know that Bruges has the most amazing shops for women, and they're not short of winter clothing either. We can buy everything you need there and get a larger case to bring it back in."

The server placed a skinny latte in front of Roxie and an almond croissant.

"Thank you," Roxie said, before kissing Chandler on the cheek. "Perfect!"

"Yes, trust me. Bruges is a hedonists paradise. I believe they have hundreds of beers. I'm not a fan myself, but still..." He looked at his watch and the large clock at the back of the station, "The train leaves at 12:58, so we can board anytime we want."

Roxie sipped her coffee. "Great. This is so much better than flying."

Chandler nodded. He remembered the endless queues and cramped legroom when he'd flown over to Louisiana and the same thing when he and Roxie had made the return journey back through Heathrow. With the complicated situation brewing on the Brexit front, traveling around wasn't going to get any easier.

Chandler stowed their bags in the overhead racks and settled into the comfortable seats in the Eurostar carriage. The train pulled out of the station, and they were soon speeding through the English countryside.

After what felt like minutes, they were arriving at Brussels-Midi station. They grabbed their bags, stepped off the train and headed down the platform.

"Where are we meeting him?" Roxie asked.

Chandler looked at his phone. "Somewhere called Sam's café?" He looked around. "There's a café over  there."

He saw a glass-fronted area with a coffee cup sporting wings embossed on it. He was too far away to make out what it said.

"Did he give you any other clues?" Roxie asked.

Chandler looked down at his phone.

"He said to look out for the zebra."

Roxie smiled. That sounded like the sort of mysterious clue Duke would give out. "Well, there's something down there with a coffee cup on the side, so if it's not Sam's, we can ask them where it is…"

They walked toward the shop, and Chandler soon made out the name 'Sam's café, on the door. Beyond it were some small circular tables on chrome stands. He also spotted what looked like a horse wearing a zebra suit sitting at one of the tables.

"There's the zebra," Chandler said. "How cute," Roxie said.

"There he is." He'd spotted Duke immediately. Tired but happy, he dominated a small table in the corner of the room and was seated in front of a plate piled high with pastries. He waved them over, standing up to shake hands with Chandler and giving a hug and a kiss to Roxie.

"Great seeing you guys again."

Roxie and Chandler pulled out two chairs and sat down.

"Likewise," Chandler said, as he moved his luggage to one side of the table. "The next train to Knokke isn't for forty-five minutes, so we have some time. And looking at those pastries, it looks like we're going to need it."

Duke grinned and took a sip of his coffee. "Thought I'd sample the famous Belgian pastries and then I couldn't make up my mind which one to choose. Help yourselves."

Roxie wasted no time before pouncing on a Pain Au Chocolate and biting into it. "Mmmm, that is yummy, how was your flight?" Duke swallowed a piece of waffle before replying. "Pretty good. They put me in business, so I had more room for my gut." He slapped his belly with a hand. "I've put on a few pounds since I stopped running around the swamps with you guys. But these pastries are calorie free right?" Roxie forked a waffle piled high with strawberries and cream. "No doubt about it." "How was London?" Duke asked Roxie. "Really old. I loved it. Chandler gave me the full tourist treatment."

Chandler squeezed her shoulder. "No more than she deserves."

"Sounds like you've been having a great time. I don't suppose you've been missing the swamps."

"Well…" Roxie shrugged, "What can I say, I'm still digging London."

"If you think London's old just wait till you get to Bruges, you'll be ecstatic. It's one great big fairy tale. Horses, bells, and as much beer and chocolate as you can stand."

Roxie stared at the pastries, trying to choose. "They have these in Bruges, right?"

"They have everything you can think of made out of chocolate," replied Chandler.

Roxie fixed him with a raised eyebrow. "Everything?"

"Everything."

\*\*\*

The train was a sleek silver double-decker, and they were soon settled on the top deck. It was relatively quiet, and there were few passengers. The journey to Bruges took about forty-five minutes, and apart from the ticket collector checking their paperwork, they were left to themselves. Duke took the opportunity to catch up on his sleep, leaving Chandler and Roxie looking out of the windows at the countryside speeding past. Roxie stretched out her legs beneath the table. "I can't wait to check out Bruges."

"You'll have plenty of time for that once you've cracked the case," Chandler said with a smile.

"Very funny. Do you really think there's a link to our case? Or just some wacko looking to make a name for himself."

Chandler straightened up in his seat. "All I know is, the Belgians are more than happy to spring for our trip and accommodation. They want to get the situation under control as fast as possible. Which means you get to visit lots of old buildings, and it doesn't cost me a penny." Roxie smiled. "That would appeal to your parsimonious nature."

"Parsimonious? Nice choice of word," Chandler said.

"I had to look it up, and I was saving it for a special occasion. You'd better not have cut corners on the accommodation front."

"No, I managed to get us booked into the Bonifacius. It's a guesthouse made from two sixteenth-century carriage houses…and…" he paused dramatically. "It was used as the green room when they shot *In Bruges* and…it overlooks a canal."

Roxie hugged him. "Perfect."

The train slowed as it approached Gent-Sint-Pieters station.

Roxie looked out. "Wow! They love their bikes here."

"Yes, it's a big university town," Chandler said. Duke sat up, rubbing the sleep out of his eyes. "We there yet?"

Roxie looked at the illuminated digital station guide at the end of the coach. "Nearly. Next stop is Bruges."

They trailed behind the passengers headed along the concourse that exited from the station. Hoog and Katja were waiting by the exit. Chandler recognized them as police immediately. There was something about being in the police; you could always spot fellow police officers. The Belgian's already knew what they looked like from the newspaper pictures and waved a cheery greeting.

Hoog stretched a hand out to Chandler.

"Jochum Van De Hoog."

"Pleased to meet you," Chandler said.

Hoog held a hand out to Duke. "You must be Duke."

Duke gave him a broad smile and pumped his hand. "What gave me away?"

Katja reached out to Roxie. "Katja Blondell, you must be Roxie."

"Pleased to meet you, Katja."

"We have a car outside," Hoog said.

They cut across the ring road that circled the town and wound their way through the cobbled streets weaving alongside the canal past signs to the Groeninge Museum and Sint Jan's Hospital. Roxie stared wide-eyed as they passed tourists taking the horse- drawn carriages around the city.

Chandler looked at her. "Do you like it?"

"Like it? Like it? Let me out, now!"

Katja smiled at Roxie's enthusiasm. "Easy, they aren't going anywhere, trust me. We'll drop you at your hotel, and you can freshen up, grab a bite to eat and meet us down at the station, it's only a short stroll beside the canal from your hotel."

Moments later they arrived outside their hotel and Hoog unloaded their luggage.

"See you all later," Hoog said, as they pulled away.

They headed into reception and signed in before climbing the stairs to the floor where they were staying. Duke headed up the stairs hunching over to avoid banging his head on the low beams, his bulk filling the narrow stairway of the ancient building.

They reached the top floor, and Duke said as he turned to Chandler and Roxie, "I'm gonna crash for a couple of hours, so I'll see you at the police station."

"Don't you want to eat?" Roxie asked.

"I'm good. I ate my own bodyweight in pastries."

"He's right," Chandler said. "Okay, have a good sleep, and we'll see you later."

Chandler watched as the big man headed off to his room.

"You're not tired are you, Old man?" Roxie asked, with a Mischievous grin.

"No, I'm fine."

"Good. Because this could be our last chance to roam the streets before this case sucks the life out of you."

Chandler put a smile on his face and hoped he was convincing.

"That sounds great. We'll hit the markets and maybe get a bite to eat alfresco."

Roxie smiled and gave him a hug. "I don't mind where we eat, either Al Fresco's or some other place we see on the way."

"There are plenty of other places. We don't have to eat..."    "At Al Fresco's?" Roxie said with a smile.

"Exactly."

"You know what I love about you?"

"Er, no," Chandler said.

"I like the way that even when I pretend I don't know what alfresco means you go along with it."

She picked up her bag, slipped a key into the door and headed into the room.

"C'mon, we should just have time to freshen up before we go out." Chandler looked at her. "When you say freshen up..." But Roxie was already stripping off her clothes and heading for the bathroom. "Last one in the shower buys the waffles." Chandler dropped his bag and ran after her.

# THIRTY

HOOG, CHANDLER, AND Duke sat down one side of a long table, opposite Roxie and Katja. They were seated in one of the catacomb rooms beneath the station. It was still damp from the flood, and the gentle burble of a pump could be heard along with the whine of de-humidifiers in an adjoining room. The table in front of them was piled high with paperwork, print outs, and photocopies. A temporary corkboard had been fitted to one wall and was populated with printouts of the Count's portraits along with his details and pictures from the art book. There were blow-ups of a still from the diver's video showing the knot securing the torso to the concrete collar. An old illustration of the Waterhalle sat in the center of the other printouts. Colored string and pins linked information of interest. Roxie couldn't take her eyes off the board. Her interest in all things historical undimmed by her time in London.

Hoog gestured around the space. "Sorry about the damp. As you English would say, somebody barged in."

Katja sighed. "Please excuse my colleague's sense of humor and his borderline racism, but the flooding is part of the reason you're here." She laid some photos down.

"The driver of a tour boat took evasive action to avoid hitting this," she tapped a morgue picture of the torso.

"He then, as my colleague put it, barged into our window. Even though technically it wasn't a Dutch barge." Chandler looked at the photos on the board, memories flooding back. The thick heat of Spirit's Swamp out in Louisiana and the terrifying discoveries they'd made out at the Rafetti place. Since he'd arrived in Bruges, he'd felt a strange connection to the City. As if he'd been there before. Maybe he'd been reading too many guide books, and it was a false memory. The last time he'd felt that way had been when Governor Roman Blackburn had been killed out in the swamp. He remembered the confusion he'd felt when Roxie's investigations had discovered, he was a chimera, a biological freak, sharing DNA with Mary Kelly, a victim of Jack the Ripper, along with being genetically linked to the Blackburn dynasty. He tried to focus on what was being said in the room. Duke leaned forward. "What are we thinking here? Copycat killer with an ego to feed, economic terrorist, or something else?" "Could be any of them or none?" Hoog said. "But we need to make sure that none of the details leak to the press at this early stage. Along with the export of our local beer, the Bruges tourist industry brings in over 1.5 billion euros a year. And that's something we don't want to damage."

"That's a lot of beer and chocolate," Roxie said.

"Exactly. So, whoever's behind this, we need to catch them. And quickly," Hoog said.

Roxie pointed to the corkboard. "Does that have any connection to your case?"

Hoog smiled and indicated Katja. "It's a personal project of Katja's, a cold case from the 17<sup>th</sup> century..."

"1634 to be accurate," Katja said. "The eviscerated bodies of five dead prostitutes were discovered in the Waterhalle one night, and another prostitute, Cathelyne Verpoort, was found guilty of their murders and burnt at the stake as a witch."

"That is so cool," Roxie said.

"Not for her, obviously," Katja said. "The main suspect was an artist called Count Brandt Van Zwart, who the five victims had previously sat for."

Roxie stood up and went over to the corkboard. Her eyes were bright with fascination as she looked at the nude portraits and the clothed picture of Cathelyne.

She tapped Cathelyne's portrait.

"I'm guessing this is Cathelyne?"

"Yes," Katja said, "we used an X-ray machine to see through the layers of paint, Cathelyne's was the only portrait that he painted fully dressed."

"You think the Count set her up as revenge for her refusal to pose naked?" Roxie asked.

"Yes."

Roxie peered at the picture of the Count, her brow furrowed and she looked towards Duke. "Does he remind you of anybody?"

Duke looked at the picture. "I wasn't going to throw any more coincidences into the mix, I think that's Hoog's area of expertise."

Hoog smiled. "I was wondering when you were going to bring that up. He is how you would say, the elephant in the catacomb. Not only does he look like the killer in your last case. But Governor Blackburn's name, Brandt for Burn and Zwart for black, is also a coincidence. Yes?" Roxie went and sat down. "I'm sorry, you must think I'm a typical mouthy Yank muscling in on your case," she said. "Not at all. Happy to have you on board," Katja said. "I thought he looked familiar when I saw his picture in the Louisiana Newspaper, but as you've probably guessed, I'm face blind. Luckily, we have software that helps with that nowadays. But if I don't recognize you out in the street don't hold it against me."

Hoog shook his head. "She's joking. I had a feeling you two would bond over the historical side of things, but at the moment, given that our case has nothing to do with the 17$^{th}$ century, we should focus on identifying the victim and tracking down the killer."

Roxie held up a finger. "I agree, but given that our previous case turned out to have a historical connection, which led us to the contemporary conspiracy and murder suspect, I don't think we should dismiss the possibility that this might be a similar situation. After all, a crime is often the end result of a very long sequence of previous events."

She looked at Hoog. Hoog threw up his hands in a conciliatory gesture. "Okay, I'm the last person to ignore the laws of synchronicity."

Roxie looked at Katja. "We should get into this later." "For sure," Katja said.

Roxie turned to Chandler. "Do you remember the night you went to the Rafetti house?"

"Which part of that particular nightmare do you want me to relive?" Chandler asked.

"Nothing upsetting, I promise," Roxie said. "Do you remember the old pictures in the hallway? There were a couple of lacework pictures of the Belfort. And we also found some souvenir mugs from Bruges."

"Yes, I remember. So, you think Blackburn or Marsha could have had some sort of connection to Bruges?" "It's possible. I'm ruling out the Rafetti sisters as I don't see them as your average tourists," Roxie said.

Duke scratched his chin. "That's for damn sure."

Hoog looked around the table. "Okay, I'm going to check in on Ward at the hospital, so we'll catch up later, but right now it seems we have more hunches than the hunchback of Notre Dame. But what we don't have is any evidence that would help us to locate the criminals responsible for our headless friend's death."

109

# THIRTY-ONE

MARSHA HAD WATCHED the activity around the scene of crime tent beside the canal and had witnessed Hoog and Katja entering the tent. The diver had done an excellent job placing the torso, and it had reacted perfectly to the approach of the tour boat. Its collision with the station had been an unexpected bonus for the police as it had helped divert attention from the macabre discovery and prevented immediate damage to the tourist trade. She imagined they would keep things under wraps until they knew what they were dealing with. It made no difference to her. The discovery of the torso had already started a chain of events that would ensure the successful outcome of her plan. All she had to do now was wait. Marsha made her way down the canal path towards the tree-lined Groenerei and let herself back into the house. She walked through the hall and into the kitchen. The dogs ran towards her and licked her hands, a welcome home and a subtle hint that they were hungry. She filled two bowls with fresh meat and placed them on the floor before heading downstairs to the cellar. She 'd arranged candles around the area, which stretched the length of the house. The golden light, and the echoing sounds from the canal outside imbued the cellar with the atmosphere of an ancient cathedral. She didn't want the harsh glare of 21$^{st}$ century lighting to dazzle him when he returned. He was already going to be disorientated and confused until she had finished the process.

She looked over at the glistening shape that lay in the oblong ceramic trough on the heavy wooden table at the far end of the room. The hum of the electric pump that controlled and filtered the blood supply filled the quiet space. It wouldn't be long before the procedure was complete. As she waited, she mused on the journey that had brought her to where she now stood.

As Marja Nalangu, a young Maasai slave girl, working in Bruges in 1630, she had watched in horror as Frederick Olfert, a sorcerer, was taken to the Groot Market and hanged. As his life ebbed away, his eyes fixed upon her, and she found herself possessed by an overwhelming presence.

Under cover of darkness, she had cut him down from the gallows and used a wheelbarrow to carry his body away before burying him in a rough patch of ground behind the house where she worked. It would be years before she realized the extent of the powers he had bestowed upon on her. When she realized she could foresee the future, she soon learned it was changeable, and that her view was only one of the many that were possible. Though she was able to influence the future to some extent, that influence required her to manipulate both the past, and the impending future to produce the desired outcome. Both her and Roman's futures were at a crossroads. The events she had planned would ensure that Roman's present transition would be the last one he would have to suffer through. The immortality the sorcerer had bestowed upon her had come at a price. Watching her mortal companions die throughout the centuries had riven her with loneliness. With Count Brandt Van Zwart already absorbed into IGNIS, she had taken him as her lover and companion. As he grew older, she had no choice but to use the sons she bore him as a way of extending his bloodline, channeling the count's original soul and memories into their corporeal beings. But despite her many attempts to make them immortal, she had met with failure. She could only watch helplessly, as one by one they grew old and died, leaving her bereft, and alone.

From her vision into the future, she knew there were ways to extend life using blood, but she couldn't duplicate the process to achieve success. In desperation, she'd worked at Sint-Janshospitaal as a nurse and attempted to transfer blood into her companions using younger men as the source. But it made little difference, and in some cases, had hastened their deaths. One by one she buried them behind the house where Frederick lay. Finding a way to extend life would enable her to channel the count 's soul and memories into a companion who would always be by her side.

She remained in Bruges over the centuries as its fortunes waxed and waned, and warring factions tore it apart. By the eighteenth century, the persecution of witches was over. And her last companion was dead. Now, with only his soul and memories curated within her, there was no reason to remain in Bruges. She needed to continue her quest elsewhere and to do that she needed to adopt a different identity. She needed to become someone that could add to her powers, someone that would help her find a companion with whom she could share eternity.

She had traveled to America and the city of New Orleans and sought out Marsha Brochell. Marsha's great grandmother was Leatrice Brochell, one of the first vodoun queens to practice in New Orleans. By becoming her, Marja's powers would increase enormously. She followed Marsha through the streets of New Orleans and watched as she walked down the crowded length of Bourbon Street before entering the old Absinth House. Marsha ordered a drink, charming everyone she met with her easy laugh and sparkling eyes. The teenage Marsha Brochell had the same tawny skin and poised beauty Marja had received through her Maasai roots. Marja knew then that she would feel right at home when she entered into what was to become her new body. But first she needed to engineer her transition into Marsha without raising suspicion. The last thing she needed was a confrontation with a vodoun queen.

She knew Marsha made a habit of going down to the sugarcane fields to watch the burning. The crop would be set on fire, burning the dry leaves and flushing out any venomous snakes without harming the stalks and roots. Marsha liked the excitement as the men chased the snakes away from the field. Marja waited patiently as the workers set the fires. Within minutes, orange flames were leaping high into the sky, and black smoke swirled above the burning crop. Marja looked over at Marsha…and walked into the fire. Marsha began to scream, but then stopped. As Marja's soul entered her.

A young boy ran up to her. "What is it?"

Marsha smiled. "I thought I saw someone in the flames."

The boy grinned. "Nothing in them flames 'cept angel spirits."

"Maybe," Marsha said.

A man called, and the boy turned to go.

"See you later," he shouted, before running off.

Marsha watched him go as Marja's memories gradually filled her mind. Since then, she'd helped numerous influential men profit from her foresight. Like sugar plantation owner John Palmer Sturridge and stockbroker Jessie Livermore, all made millions from their association with her. And she, in turn, used them to further her influence. And then she'd met Francis Tumblety, one of the prime Jack the Ripper suspects who had fled to America and adopted the pseudonym Francis Blackburn. Together they began a series of experiments out in the Louisiana swamps in their shared quest to find the secret of immortality. Despite early promise, it was left to Tumblety's heirs to continue the experiments with the help of the Rafetti sisters. And then finally, with Governor Roman Blackburn, Marsha was near to giving him the immortality she'd craved for her companions for so long. But then a Victorian coach had been discovered in Spirit's Swamp containing the bodies of five women from nineteenth century London, and ex-Detective

Chandler Travis, and Louisiana Sheriff Duke Lanoix had arrived on the scene.

Their investigation linked the Blackburn's to a massive conspiracy stretching back over a century and exposed their complicity in an oil field disaster and the ensuing cover-up. Marsha had tried desperately to save Roman from the future she had foreseen, but Roman had ignored her advice and lost his life during a deadly confrontation out in the swamp.

Marsha was able to save the results of their biological experiments, and along with his precious Dogos Argentinos, had made her escape to Bruges.

She shook her head clear of the memories and looked around the dank basement. Roman Blackburn's rebirth and his reappearance as Brandt Van Zwart would complete a journey of over five hundred years. The combination of her powers and the scientific advances they had made would soon give him the immortality she already possessed. As the curator of his soul and corporeal memories, she would decant them both into his reformed human shell when the time was right. Once he was on his feet, she would be able to  carry out the final part of her  quest.

Since the formation of the IGNIS order in the 17<sup>th</sup> century, its members had spread throughout Europe by possessing their persecutors. But there was a flaw within the order. Unlike Marsha, other members of IGNIS were discovering their longevity had its limits. Immortality in their case had been measured in centuries. Now Marsha was back in Bruges, to align the power of IGNIS with her own, and empower the members of the order with an unlimited lifespan.

She looked across the room towards the trough.
The speed of his transformation was astonishing.
A process that had previously taken twenty years had become a transition of less than a month. And now the final stages were nearing completion in front of her eyes. As she stared into the gloom, something stirred. There was a sucking noise, and a hand slithered over the lip of the trough.

# THIRTY-TWO

ROXIE AND KATJA sat in the catacomb room working through their notes. Roxie studied the printouts of the Brandt Van Zwart pictures, a piece of knotted rope in a plastic evidence bag from the canal, and some pictures of the headless torso in the morgue.

Katja picked up the bag containing the rope. "Kruger, our coroner, thought that the knot used on the torso was one that self-released when subjected to a reasonable amount of force. He got back to me to confirm that. Apparently, it's called a Tumble Hitch. It's similar to a slipped Buntline."

"So, the pressure of the bow wave from the approaching tour boat, moved the torso, which yanked on the knot, releasing it," Roxie said.

Katja nodded. "Yes. Whoever planted the torso wanted it to be witnessed by as many people as possible. Luckily, things didn't go to plan."

Roxie studied Brandt Van Zwart's bio entry in the art book from the Groeninge Museum. She looked down at the still of the knot from the diver's video feed. "Do you have a digital copy of the artist's bio page?" Roxie asked.

"Yes, I took a picture on my phone and uploaded it. Just a sec." Katja flipped open her laptop and scanned through her emails. "Here we are." She downloaded a link and the screen filled with the page from the art book.

"Can you zoom in on the Count?"

"Any particular area? Katja asked.

Roxie looked at the screen. "The knot on the cord around his waist."

Katja zoomed in on the knot. Roxie lifted up the still from the diver's video feed and held it alongside the laptop screen.The similarities were obvious. "They're the same knot," Katja said.

Roxie nodded. "It could be a coincidence, or it could be a mistake."

"A mistake by who?" Katja said.

"By the people responsible for our headless friend's murder," Roxie paused, her mind spinning with the possibilities, and then continued. "I think a couple of things happened that no one could have planned for. Firstly, the driver of the boat took evasive action, and the torso ended up inside the police station, and not on public display. Secondly, a diver was working in the canal and filmed the knot and the torso in position before it broke free."

Katja nodded. "So, if the engineers hadn't been there that day we wouldn't know that a specific knot was used to release the torso."

"Exactly. So, we wouldn't be comparing it to a knot used in the seventeenth-century, worn by a suspected serial killer."

"Count Brandt Van Zwart." Katja looked at the pictures on the corkboard and the laptop screen. Things were starting to come together. "Yes. And if you go with your witch guy..." Roxie said. "De Vries?"

"Yes, you said he thought that the Count was the first member of the order of IGNIS, and had Cathelyne's soul channeled into him by the über witch...."

"The slave girl Marja Nalangu," Katja said.

"Yes, who in turn had gained her powers from the sorcerer guy...,"

"Frederick Olfert," Katya prompted.

116

"Right, so if we accept that Brand Van Zwart was a member of IGNIS, then the person or persons that set up the discovery of the torso using that knot could have links with the IGNIS order back in the seventeenth century," Roxie said.

"I think we'll need more than a knot to convince anybody of that link. But it's a start."

"I agree, and from what I've seen of Hoog I think you're a long way from convincing him," Roxie said.

"You're probably right. Jochum believes that no single criminal action exists in isolation and that there are always links and coincidence's stretching back a long time before the actual crime."

"Like a paper trail or a digital footprint," Roxie said. But even as she said that her mind was wondering why Hoog had become Jochum all of a sudden. It was something she would ask Katja about later. No point in cluttering up two separate investigations six hundred years apart with personal issues. She saw Katja looking at her oddly as if she'd realized her mistake. Roxie thought back to all the signs she'd noted and dismissed while she'd been with Hoog and Katja. The odd glance, the space between them and the way they talked around each other. But now she was convinced, they either were or had been an item. She felt sure that Katja would spill the beans at some point, but for now, she needed to concentrate. Katja was filling her in about the importance of the time before the crime.

"…and normally you work back through the case until you reach a point where the criminals weren't so careful because they hadn't worked out all the details of their plans and therefore hadn't covered their tracks." Katja looked at her for a response.

Roxie studied the pictures. "So, if we took that to its ultimate conclusion then whoever put the torso in the canal started planning this back in the seventeenth century." Katja held up her hands. "I know, that's a bit of a stretch even for a conspiracy nut like myself."

"Yes." Roxie leaned forward. "Tell me more about IGNIS."

Katja nodded. "IGNIS was a secret order established in Europe, principally Bruges and Venice during the seventeenth century."

"Like the Illuminati?"

"But a lot weirder," Katja said.

"Because of their belief in soul channeling?" Katja nodded.

"Why do you think that was the core belief of IGNIS?" Roxie asked.

Katja paused. "Well, De Vries, thought it could have been to provide some sort of spiritual comfort to the victims of the witch trials. The belief that their suffering was going to be rewarded in the afterlife."

Roxie frowned. "An afterlife for witches, with a life of power and wealth thrown in. It sounds pretty far-fetched...but hey, why should a belief in the afterlife be acceptable in some religions and not in theirs?"

Katja shrugged. "Exactly, possessions and conjurations have been pretty well documented, and how do we discount the existence of witches while believing in the devil?"

"What else did De Vries say?" Roxie asked.

Katja went on, and Roxie listened while she filled her in on the history framing the witch-hunts that swept Europe when over a hundred thousand people were burnt at the stake. She listened spellbound as Katja explained the mythical powers that the über witch was supposed to have received from the sorcerer, including transmigration from one body to another through the horrific action of self-immolation.

When Katja had finished, Roxie sat for a moment, listening to the gentle slap of water outside the window, and the muted babble of tourists from the nearby bridge. It took a while to even begin to imagine how appalling the world had been all those centuries ago. She tore herself free from the images that swirled around inside her head and turned to Katja.

"I read that most, if not all, of the witches burned at the stake were innocent. Betrayed by people with a grudge or men wanting to get rid of their wives so they could take up with their mistresses.

"This was way before hashtag 'MeToo,' that's for sure," Katja said.

"You'd think that level of brutality and injustice would spark a major kickback at some point. But then again, we're still stoning women today. Some things never change."

"It sounds like you're rooting for the witches," Katja said.

Roxie shrugged. "Maybe I am, after all, before the world went completely mad they were regarded as a force for good, in touch with the power of nature, and not just some old crones cackling around a cauldron."

"Well, at the moment there's no real evidence of the existence of our über witch, apart from folklore and speculation," Katja said.

"Well unless you can find some old family photo albums with the Count and Marja snuggling up together I doubt we'll ever find that level of proof."

"Katja gave her a smile. "I'm seeing someone that might be able to do a little better than a photo album. Duke and Chandler will be there and Hoog too, if he makes it back in time from the hospital. He's just checking on Ward. Do you want to come along? I have some things I need to talk to you about on the way."

Roxie smiled. "I'm all ears."

# THIRTY-THREE

CHANDLER AND DUKE made their way down Nieuwstraat towards the Art Museum on Dijver. They'd reviewed the CCTV footage that Katja and Hoog had compiled from the various buildings that overlooked the canal and checked the images from the police station cameras.

The museum was situated over the Dijver canal between the Boottochten Bridge, where the boat tours left from, and Bonifacius Bridge, which was visible from their hotel.

The disturbance beneath the water on the CCTV footage had indicated that a diver had positioned the torso after midnight, and made his way back along the canal. The trail stopped where the canal disappeared under the museum. They walked around the outside of the building and came to the Arents courtyard, a quiet area with neatly trimmed shrubbery and hedges populated with Rik Poot sculptures of expressionist figures on bronze horses representing the four horsemen of the apocalypse.

Chandler peered at his tourist guide. He pointed to a nearby spire that towered over them. "That's the Church of Our Lady, and the sculptures are the four horsemen of the apocalypse. Apparently."

Duke shook his head. "Does it mention anything about an escape route for a man wearing a wetsuit and an oxygen tank?"

Chandler smiled. He loved Duke's sense of humor. He went over to a large stone pillar, one of two that dominated the courtyard.

"These are supporting pillars from the original Waterhalle that was demolished in 1787."

"I guess that's a piece of trivia that will go down well with Roxie and Katja, but we still need to check stuff out in the twenty-first century," Duke said.

He followed Chandler to the wall surrounding the courtyard that overlooked the canal. Behind them, a horse-drawn carriage trotted slowly between the pillars while the guide explained the history to an old couple seated behind. Chandler took a snap of the sight. "Roxie is going to love this." Duke peered over the wall. A tour boat thrummed past and headed under the bridge, the voice of the guide echoing off the curved stone roof as it disappeared from view.

Chandler walked along until he reached the outside wall of the museum and leaned over. "Have you got the CCTV footage on your phone?"

"Yes, just a minute." Duke swiped at his smartphone. "What do you want to look at?"

"If you look across to the other side of the canal, about two feet up from the water line, what do you see?"

Duke squinted against the sun bouncing off the surface of the water. Then he saw it. Partially hidden by foliage, a dark void in the opposite wall. "Damn. I got you. It's some kind of drainage outlet."

Duke saw a square entrance just over a meter wide and a meter high in the wall, partially hidden by some leafy tree branches dangling in front of it.

Chandler nodded. "Okay. Now run the footage and see if it appears anywhere." Duke tapped the screen and cupped the phone in his hand to cut down the reflections on the screen. Chandler looked over his shoulder as it played out. They reached the end of the footage. "Nothing. It's in a blind spot. He just had to stay underwater until he was beneath it, and then drag himself up and wriggle through. Let's check the other side," Chandler said.

It didn't take them long. In the other smaller tree-lined courtyard, they found a square, cast iron manhole cover that gave access to the drainage outlet in the wall of the canal below. Chandler pointed to some shiny fresh gouge marks at the edge of the metal lip.

"These have been made recently."

Duke nodded. "Let's check the nearest place to park a car. I don't imagine he would get too far in a wet suit without drawing attention, no matter what time of night it was."

They walked out of the courtyard, turned left onto Dijver and over into Gruuthusestraat. They came to a wire metal fence and a locked gate that led into a large and impressive looking building outside of which there was what looked like a building site. Four or five vans were parked up along with a couple of private cars. Chandler looked at his guidebook, and then at a sign on the gate.

"Heren Van Gruuthuse, Lords of Bruges, it's a museum and it's closed until May."

"Looks like they're having some kind of major renovation."

"That's good. They'll have security and CCTV. If our diver parked here they'll be footage."

Chandler looked at his watch. "We'd better get a move on, we're meeting the rest of them at Ghent University in a couple of hours. Katja will pick us up at the station."

Duke nodded, and they headed down the street and flagged a taxi down to take them to the station.

# THIRTY-FOUR

HOOG WAITED UNTIL the doctor had finished checking on Ward before sitting down on the small hard chair next to the bed. "How are you feeling?"

Ward rubbed his head and gave a rueful grin. "A little sore."

"That's not surprising. You took quite a whack from that table."

"Yes. Thing is, I'd just found something in the pile of cold cases the chief gave me."

"Well, I hope you remember the details 'cos those files are papier-mâché now," Hoog said.

"I'm sure. But I think they were scanned at some point anyway."

Hoog shrugged. "You'd think. But there's a reason the Chief gave you those files."

"To keep me busy?" Ward grinned.

"Yes, though to be fair, if you did turn something up in them it couldn't harm your fast track chances."

Ward moved higher up against the pillows. "Well, just before I was so rudely interrupted, I'd found some files with a pattern."

"Go on," Hoog said.

"There were three reports of a man selling drugs on the ice rink. They weren't followed up, but the description was consistent with the same man in all three reports."

"I'm not surprised the reports weren't prioritized, Christmas isn't the most relaxed of events on the tourist calendar. By the time we've sorted the parking violations, bag snatchers and pick- pockets we'd hardly have time to draw breath."

"I know. But if the press found out that we'd let some ice- jockey get away with selling drugs to children, it wouldn't look good for us. And with what we already have on our plates…" Ward trailed off.

"Yeah. The torso case is already soaking up a lot of time."

"How are you getting on with the visitors?" Ward asked.

"Roxie and Katja are getting on like a house on fire," Hoog said.

Ward grinned and held up an iPad. The front page of the Louisiana newspaper on screen. "That Roxie is pretty smart from what I've read, and easy on the eye too. Though I wouldn't say that in front of Mari, obviously."

"Or Chandler, if you want my advice," Hoog said. "Advice taken."

Hoog looked at him. "So, how would you handle the rink pusher, if we had any resources, which we don't, and if you were heading up the case, which you aren't?"

"Well, it wouldn't take much to set up a CCTV system around the rink. Apparently, the guy's a good skater and has long blond hair, so he should be easy enough to spot. Then it's just a matter of catching him in the act. It wouldn't take more than two or three officers to cover the operation in an evening. I would monitor the CCTV back at the station, and we'll need some undercover officers on the rink for the arrest." Ward looked at Hoog. "I thought maybe you and Katja?"

Hoog thought about this. "It might be doable."

"So you'll speak to the chief?" Ward asked, animatedly.

"One thing at a time. Let's make sure you're fit and well first. No point in someone else getting all the glory."

"Guess not. Thanks for dropping by, I know you've got your hands full," Ward said.

Hoog stood up. "Not a problem, we'll have that beer once we've wrapped up our caseload."

"Do you think it's going to happen again? The torso thing?"

Hoog shrugged. "I hope not, but if it does, then I guess we'll have twice as many clues."

"Well, I hope it doesn't come to that," Ward said.

"Me too."

Hoog waved goodbye and headed out into the hospital corridor.

# THIRTY-FIVE

GHENT UNIVERSITY WAS a public research facility containing one of the biggest hospitals in Belgium and was the largest beneficiary of funding from the Research Foundation- Flanders. As such, it possessed some of the most advanced technical facilities available and could provide more than enough computing power for their needs.

They all sat around a table in one of the university's laboratories where Wim worked. Duke clutched his ever-present mug of coffee, while Roxie and Katja shared an almond croissant, and Chandler made do with a cup of tea. Hoog arrived as Wim was setting up the equipment.

"How's Ward?" Katja asked.

Hoog pulled up a chair and sat next to her. "He's on the mend, they just need to keep him in for observation. He was pretty excited about a cold case he'd found before the catacombs got flooded. I'll tell you about it later."

Hoog looked at the pile of pastries.

Wim waved a hand at them. "Help yourself, I'll only have to eat them if you don't."

Hoog scooped one up, and Duke dived in as well. "Thanks, Wim. So, what's this all about?" Duke asked.

Wim took a sip of his coffee and ran a hand through his disheveled hair. "Erika told me about IGNIS and the über witch you believe may have been responsible for starting it. I couldn't help thinking there must be some evidence of her existence somewhere."

"It's a shame they didn't have CCTV back then, finding her would have been a cinch," Hoog said, taking a bite out of an almond croissant. Wim nodded. "Sadly, they didn't. But then I got to thinking. There was a series of documentaries, originally shown on your BBC, and then on PBS, called *Italy's Invisible Cities*. It used high definition 3D scanning techniques to produce a virtual tour beneath Naples, Florence, and Venice."

"I saw that, it was incredible. They were able to do a virtual reality walkthrough in the tunnels and caves beneath the city," Chandler said.

"Yes," Wim said. "They used a combination of ultra-high definition 3D scanning, ground penetrating radar and underwater lidar."

"Lidar?" Katja asked.

"I'll take this," Roxie said. "It's the same technology that's used in speed guns. A bit like sonar, but using light in the form of a pulsed laser."

"That's pretty much it," Wim said. "They take all the technology and combine it to produce an amazing 3D virtual walkthrough of the city. They stitched together millions of data points, mapping the entire city above and beneath. Have a look at this."

Wim tapped the screen of his computer tablet, and a video clip began running on a screen on the wall. The camera swooped over the city of Bruges, diving through the roofs and under the water of the canals revealing a view never seen before of the hidden parts of the city. The clip ended.

"Wow!" Katja said. "That's amazing.

"That's for sure. They're carrying out a similar scan of the old center of Bruges, mapping beneath where the Waterhalle was, and following the route of the original canals," Wim said. How's this going to help you find the witch?" Duke asked.

Wim grinned excitedly. "Okay. As well as having access to the 3D data around Bruges, I also worked on the software for the display at the Historium, which takes you back to the golden age of Bruges. Now, we don't have film footage or photos from the seventeenth century, but we do have an enormous number of digital stills of the various drawings, oil paintings, and sketches going back centuries. I have a friend who works in the Belgium Security service. He's given me some high-end video and analytical image processing software. I'll use it to merge all the available historical visual information online with the 3D mapping and animation from the Historium."

"I've seen that used by the FBI to stitch together cell-phone camera footage and CCTV images. They use the information to track down criminals using facial recognition software. That's a powerful piece of kit," added Duke.

"Yes. The computer power I need to render a 3D Scape is way beyond what's available to me on a laptop. I'm going to have to use the entire university computing network and throw in some cloud storage as well."

"Will they allow that?" Chandler asked.

"I've negotiated an hour's window at midnight tonight." Roxie and Katja hurried into the laboratory with Hoog, carrying bags of hot waffles and flasks of hot coffee.

"Did we miss anything?" Roxie asked cheerfully.

"Just the health and safety briefing on the use of the VR goggles," Chandler said. "Turns out it's all too easy to accidentally let go of the elastic as you put the goggles on and injure yourself." He rubbed a red mark on one side of his face. Roxy handed him a paper bag. "Here, there's a hot waffle in the bag. Hold it on your face. It'll help to bring the swelling down." Chandler took the bag. "Funny."

Wim looked around. "Okay guys, we're getting near the witching hour." He handed two sets of VR goggles to Katja and Roxie and one to Hoog as they sat down. "I just need to log in, and we're good to go." He grinned. "We're going to be drawing so much processing power I wouldn't be surprised if the lights dim."

Roxie slipped the goggles on and settled the sound buds into her ears. Wim logged in to the university network and started the program "Right, I don't know how successful this'll be, but here goes." Wim tapped some settings on the tablet, and inside the goggles, the darkness twinkled with pixels, glittering like digital snow. A low hum filled their ears as the software began to execute trillions of instructions a second, downloading terabytes of images. As if their eyes were adjusting to the dark, in front of them, something began to form. Shadowy shapes rose all around them, and they found themselves in a 360-degree evolving landscape. And then they were flying across Bruges, the ancient buildings of the city spread out below them, soaring over and around the town hall in the Burg, over the rooftops toward the Belfort before plunging in a dizzying spiral around the tower and down to the Market Square.

Then off again, racing along the surface of the Groenerei Canal and plunging below the surface into the murky depths…bursting out into the sunshine and skimming across Minnewater Lake --- sweeping above the water and between the arches of the lover's bridge.

"Sorry guys, just a little bit of showboating to demonstrate what the software's capable of. Now I'm going back to Market Square, and using the historical data to take us into the seventeenth century." Their point of view soon became the market. The picture sparkled, and the buildings took on a different hue as they began to alter their appearance. The software gradually absorbed the texture of oil paintings, sketches, and drawings---weaving them together, manipulating the polygons, blending and colorizing them until they became a seamless whole. Gradually the square took on more and more detail as the computer layered thousands of different viewpoints painted by artists over the centuries.

"Okay. I'm now going to narrow the visual field down to the year 1634 and try and pinpoint anything to do with the witch burning," explained Wim.

Everybody looked around the VR landscape as it rippled through the years. And as they traveled back through time, the square became populated with frozen figures from the past. Captured by a multitude of artists down through the centuries.

"This is incredible, I feel like I could reach out and touch them," Roxie said.

"They'll come a time when we'll be able to add digital feedback, so it actually feels that way," Wim said, his voice sounding out of place amongst the people coming and going within the historic market.

Suddenly there was a massive change in the 3D surroundings. Hundreds of people, frozen in time, crowded the market. The reason all too evident.

The gruesome sight of the flaming pyre in the background was the magnet attracting the ghoulish onlookers.

Chandler's voice cut into the silence. "Can we move through the crowd?"

Wim replied, "Give me a second."

The viewpoint shuddered briefly as terabytes of information shifted and reformed. And then they were traveling through, above, and around the crowd.

"There...the coach at the back. Can we get closer?" Roxie asked.

Again, the image flickered as they changed perspective and moved in on the coach, and the man that stood next to it.

"That's Count Brandt Van Zwart, look at his expression, he's relishing it," Hoog said.

"Well if we're right, this is the day that the order of IGNIS started," Katja said.

The viewpoint pulled back through the stationary crowd and then stopped.

"There! At the back of the crowd. There's a woman, wearing brightly colored beads, African American looking," Roxie said, her voice catching in her throat with excitement.

The computerized viewpoint moved nearer the woman. The software struggling to bring more detail to the view. It got within fifty feet of her.

"That's got to be Marja," Katja said.

And in that split-second, Marja turned and disappeared into the crowd.

# THIRTY-SIX

**BRUGES, BELGIUM – 1634**

MARJA LOOKED AROUND. The crowd was glassy-eyed at the horrendous spectacle taking place in front of them. The flames roared around the shuddering figure strapped to the burning post. Her skin crackling in the intense heat. Marja shook her head to clear it of the visions she had just witnessed. A vision from the future. Though she had the power to foresee the future, she couldn't control it. Only observe the myriad of possibilities and use her power to try and produce a particular outcome.

But this was different. Someone had reached back into her time. She'd been aware of the market surroundings shimmering as they took on a different form...then she'd seen a group of people wearing strange devices around their heads. It was a shock when she realized they were looking for her. All around, the crowd's movements slowed, until they were frozen in time. She quickly hid behind a group of people and a cart laden with fruit. She waited until her surroundings rippled again, and the crowd burst into movement before hurrying away from the Market Square.

Pushing through the throngs, she looked back and caught a glimpse of Count Brandt Van Zwart as he stood alongside his carriage. He gave her a nod. He was the first in the new order of IGNIS and a vessel for Cathelyne's soul.

As long as the burning of witches continued, so their order would grow. She reached the edge of the Market Square and headed into the Waterhalle. As usual, it was bustling with traders and crew, all busy unloading their wares to be stored in the loft above the unloading dock. It was where the elders had appeared and dragged Cathelyne away. Since she had witnessed the hanging of the sorcerer Frederick Olfert, she had felt different. The way he had fixed his eyes upon her during his death throes produced the strangest feeling within her…as if she was more than one person.

And now, years later, as she had watched Cathelyne being led to her fate in the Market Square, the full force of the sorcerer's power had been unleashed within her. As she guided Cathelyne's soul free from her body and into the Count, Marja had witnessed the floating corpses and heard the dying screams of Helga as she breathed her last breath. And as she felt her power grow, she became aware of the depths of evil the count had plumbed. The five corpses floating in the Waterhalle were only some of the many innocent girls he had slaughtered in his pursuit of pleasure. She lost track of the number of tortured souls that swirled around inside her head that night. But when they had quieted, her purpose had been made clear. Cathelyne, the girl they had burned as a witch was not dead. Though her corporeal self had been destroyed, her soul lived on within the Count. His power and status would be used to avenge the evil of the witch burnings throughout Europe with the formation of a new order. The order of IGNIS. As Marja began to exert her power and the order grew, she had a vision of the future. A future where women grew more powerful as each year passed and the order flourished. Free from the tyranny of hate they suffered in the seventeenth century and beyond. She recognized that the latest vision, an intrusion from the future into her past, needed to be prepared for. The group that had reached back into her time had no idea of the power she was able to command, and now she had hundreds of years to prepare for any risk they might pose.

# THIRTY-SEVEN

**BRUGES, BELGIUM – Present Day**

THEY RAN THROUGH the dark. Eyes gleaming in the perpetual twilight that they inhabited. This was their territory. They missed the freedom of the outside world and the human companionship they had become used to back in the heat of Louisiana. Brother and sister, weighing in at over one hundred pounds and nearly a meter high, they were heavily muscled and terrifying to look at. A mix of Cordoba fighting dog and great Dane specifically bred to protect their human companions to the death. They raced down the narrow path that ran alongside the canal. They could see and smell their prey as it scuttled ahead of them. With their superior speed and powerful teeth, the rat didn't stand a chance. Within seconds they were tugging at the squealing animal, tearing it apart and gorging themselves on the warm blood that filled their jaws, and dripped from their muzzles. They swallowed the remains of the still warm carcass and looked back the way they had come. Their ears pricked up at a sound. A deep rumble, followed by the crash of brickwork.

They sniffed at the air that drifted down toward them. Their noses twitching as 300 million receptors gorged on the stench of something further down the tunnel. Within seconds they were hurtling toward it. Their eyes glowing in the dark, saliva glands filling their mouths with drool in anticipation of the feeding frenzy that was to come

# THIRTY-EIGHT

MARSHA LOOKED DOWN at the people skating on the ice rink far below. From her vantage point at the top of the Belfort, they looked like ants. She looked across the skyline. Her eyes sweeping between the three prominent landmark towers, St. Salvator's Cathedral, the Church of Our Lady, and St. Anne's Church. The Belfort was closed to tourists for the day, but she had the keys and the access to come and go as she pleased. For centuries this had been the place she sought out when she needed to utilize her ability as an oracle. Looking out over the ancient city produced the most potent effect on her abilities. Her mind drifted back through the centuries to a time when she had watched the carilloneur playing the hand keyboard.

She stared across the city spread out below. Letting her mind float free. The sky darkened on the horizon. A vision of obsidian mirrors whirled about her, their surfaces flickering bronze. As she concentrated, the mirrors aligned, each glittering facet reflecting an alternative future stretching out ahead of her. By channeling her will, she could see the least destructive outcome that would occur from following one particular path.

Like the view from the top floor of her offices in New Orleans, the cityscape of Bruges filled her mind with possibilities. And then she saw something. One of the mirrors darkened for a moment, revealing something shadowy behind it. A portent. An alternate future that could not be avoided. She'd seen them before. The last one had been the effect Chandler Travis, the English detective, would have on their lives in Louisiana.

She'd tried to warn Roman back then, but he had failed to take her warnings seriously until it was too late. This time she wouldn't let that happen. She focused on the shadowy vision behind the surface of the mirror, trying to decipher what it foretold. The other mirrored facets spun away as she used her powers to concentrate on the remaining one. She reached toward it. As if caressing the future, teasing out the truth from the smoke and mist that swirled around her. Just like before, there was a link between the past and their future. She saw bodies, carcasses stretched out before her, and felt an overwhelming sense of death. She stared at the mirror, trying to get a feeling of the period she was looking at.

She relaxed and let her eyes defocus from the mirror. And then she was floating above the city, and as she watched, it began to change. Buildings disappeared below her, there were no cars, fewer canals, and far less people. The Waterhalle was there, as was the Basilica of the Holy Blood. Ships were anchored alongside the Burg waiting to unload their goods, and the market was teaming with people. Marsha knew where she was in history. The seventeenth century. Back when she had been given the power to save the souls of the persecuted. The period where she had used her powers to formulate the order of IGNIS.

And then she was back in the present overlooking the market and ice rink below. The shadowy figures behind the mirror were now just pale reflections of a recent reality.

She tasted the stench of death and tried to coax the secret of its source from the many possibilities swirling through her past and possible futures. But it was to no avail. She was too drained from using her power to support Roman's transition into his new identity. She would have to wait until she was stronger and try again to see what it was that could be threatening her future.

# THIRTY-NINE

WARD SETTLED INTO his chair in the catacomb room beneath the station. Half a dozen oil filled radiators had been brought in, and the temperature was almost warm. He still ached, but was glad to be out of the hospital, determined to close the cold case he'd stumbled onto. The six screens in front of him covered all angles on the market ice rink. He'd checked that they were all working and made sure there were no blind spots. He bit into a garlic prawn and followed it with a few chips from a small bag he'd bought from the fries shop at the corner of the market.

It was getting dark, and the rink was busy. Parents and children venturing onto the ice as the last rays of the sun slipped behind the Belfort. He sipped at a mug of coffee and adjusted the focus on one of the cameras. Hoog had managed to persuade the chief to spare some resources so he could monitor the rink. This was the third day he'd been watching, and he was beginning to think that the pusher had moved on. And then he saw him. Sporting his trademark long blond hair and tatty beanie, he was entering the rink.

137

The details in the case notes had been slim, but one of the tourists thought that they'd heard someone call him Blades. Whether this was as a result of his prowess on the on the ice or an ironic nod to cutting drugs he didn't know. Ward checked that the hard drive was recording and leaned forward, following the man as he moved confidently up and down the ice. For a few minutes, nothing much happened, but as night fell, a couple of students came onto the ice. They stumbled about trying to keep their balance, laughing and holding onto each other.

Blades swept past them, and they nodded. Ward tightened in on him, watching as he circled back around toward the two students. One of them reached into his pocket and pulled out a ten euro note. Blades swept past, and in a blur, the exchange was made. It may only have been ten euros, Ward thought, but throughout the evening, it would soon mount up. He went back to the frame of the exchange and printed out a date-stamped picture.

"Okay, let's see who's next," he watched as Blades circled around the rink. Ward had to admire his style. He may have been a scumbag pusher, but his skill on the ice was impressive. He watched him hurtle backward and execute a triple Lutz, starting on one leg as he picked up speed before spinning three times through the air and landing faultlessly on one leg as the other swung in an arc through the air. Ward wondered if he had ever been a professional skater, and if so, what had precipitated his descent into drug pushing. Ward looked at his watch. It was six o'clock, and the rink was getting busy. He followed Blades around the rink through the cameras. Within an hour, he had filmed and printed out well over a dozen drug exchanges, some of them with teenagers, others with tourists and students. He certainly had enough. Ward picked up his phone and tapped a number.

"Hi Hoog, I've got him. Signed, sealed and delivered." He listened. "Okay, I'll see you outside the rink in fifteen." He pocketed his phone and headed out of the dank catacomb and jogged up the stairs.

# FORTY

HOOG AND KATJA leaned against the side of the rink. Hoog chewed on a waffle, honey dripping down his sleeve.

"You're leaking," Katja said, pointing at his sleeve.

"I'm pretending to be a tourist. It's a honey trap," Hoog said, wiping at the sticky trail on his sleeve.

"On expenses I imagine."

"Of course."

"Where's über cop?" Katja looked around.

"Here he is." Hoog nodded at Ward making his way toward them. He came to a halt beside them, out of breath. Katja handed him a bag of fries. "Hoog thinks we need to blend." Ward took the fries. "Fine by me, I can never have enough fries."

Katja looked out over the rink. Their target was still showing off, sweeping round the rink, palming off his product to a group of students that huddled down at one end of the rink.

"Looks like he's still in the game."

Ward looked up from his smartphone. "Good, every move he makes is in glorious HD."

Katja looked down at the mosaic of feeds on Ward's smartphone screen. "Impressive."

"Yes. Now we just need to arrest him," Ward said.

"You cover the main exit from the rink. We have a couple more officers spread around the other exits, but he won't get far wearing skates," Katja said.

Ward slipped his phone inside his jacket and zipped it up. "What now?"

Hoog reached behind and checked his gun was secure. "Katja and I will take him down, but it'll be your arrest."

"Thank you."

"Okay. Let's go."

They went over to the rink entrance and began to strap their skates on. Hoog pulled his second boot on and turned to Katja. "I'll go clockwise, you go anti…we'll hit him from both directions at the same time. That way, even if he sees one of us, he'll still go down."

Katja cinched her boot tight. "Couldn't we just arrest him as he leaves the rink?"

Hoog slipped his foot into a skate. "Once he leaves the rink he could dump the drugs or palm them off to an accomplice. This way we nail him for dealing and possession." He looked at her. "You getting cold feet?"

Katja stamped her feet to settle the skates. "Naa, it was you I was worried about."

Hoog shook his head. "Sweet. Okay. We'll do a couple of circuits to warm up then go for it."

Katja straightened up. "He's been on the ice for hours, he'll be tired, we'll have the edge."

They stepped onto the ice and pushed off. Hoog passed Katja on the first circuit. The rink was busy. Some drunk students flailed around, trying to keep their balance. Hoog saw Blades sweeping around them without missing a beat. He didn't look tired. Maybe he was using his own product to give him a boost. He locked eyes with Katja as she passed him for the second time and then increased his speed. Hoog saw Blades from across the ice; he seemed to be going faster.

Hoog put himself on a collision course as Katja rocketed toward Blades from behind, he altered his course to pass Blades on his left. If Katja hit him from the right-hand side, they would slam him into a death spiral that would force him into the barrier at the side of the rink. But that's not what happened. Seconds before they were to take him down, he made his move. His reflexes were astonishing. In a heartbeat, he rotated his right leg and transitioned from facing forward to looking backward. Hoog barely had time to flick a warning look to Katja before Blades executed a flawless Lutz, bringing his leg up in a deadly sweep. Hoog felt the wind from Blade's razor-sharp boot as it scythed past his face while Katja threw herself onto the ice to avoid serious injury. Blades sped on as Hoog slammed to a halt beside her.

"That bastard knew we were coming." He helped Katja to her feet.

"How?" Katja asked, as they both headed after the blond pusher.

"I don't know, but he's not getting away." Blades was streaking toward the exit, traveling too fast for either of them to catch him.

Hoog slid to a halt. A small child was pushing a puck with a hockey stick alongside his father. Hoog grabbed the stick and hurled it through the air towards the fleeing pusher.

"Police! Stop." Hoog yelled.

Blades flicked a look back at him and gave a wry smile. A millisecond later the hockey stick smashed into his chest, knocking him down onto the ice. Within seconds Hoog and Katja were by his side, pinning him down. His eyes bulged, and he began to scream.

"Don't exaggerate," Hoog said.

"We're barely touching you." Katja echoed. Then she saw what he was looking at. Through the frozen ice template covering the drain hole, the leathery face of a corpse stared up at her with cold, dead eyes.

# FORTY-ONE

MARSHA SAT WATCHING and waiting in the large candlelit cellar beneath the house in the Groenerei. It was ideal for her purpose, because it also gave access to the overarched canal system that ran beneath. From there, Roman's precious hounds were able to roam unfettered day and night, enjoying the pursuit of the terrified rats that inhabited the damp passageways leading off from the main canal. She looked over at the large trough where he lay. His metamorphosis from a cellular level sludge to a living organism was nearly complete. They 'd started from the basic blocks of life, growing artificial meat in a petri dish and manipulating the DNA with gene editing. The scientific progress and sacrifices they had made over the centuries were finally paying off. Once he was fully formed, she would complete his rebirth. The regrowth from his physical DNA was one thing, but without his memory and soul, he would just be an empty husk. That was where her skills came into play. She alone held his soul and memory within her, and soon she would pour his psychic essence back into the body she loved. She heard a deep guttural sound, like someone clearing their throat after waking from a long sleep. There was a soft sucking noise. And then he sat up.

His skin was livid and sore looking. The fibrous tissues of his muscles newly formed. His eyes stared at her, trying to focus through the mucus that still clung to his face. She went over and gently wiped his skin clean with a soft cloth, clearing his eyes and nose. She marveled at the speed of his change, watching as his hair, beard, and mustache developed in front of her eyes. He shuddered and looked at her like a newborn baby. His mouth moved, but he had no words. It was time. She laid her hands against his head and concentrated. Searching the memories that swirled through her mind until she found Roman's.

The channeling began. He trembled beneath her fingers as his past lives flowed into his mind. Gradually his face relaxed. His eyelids blinked and then his eyes blazed with recognition as they fastened on her. She removed her hands from him and held a cup of water to his mouth. He drank it down greedily, then spoke.

"I'm hungry," he said.

Marsha smiled. "It's been a while. I have plenty of food in the main house."

Roman shook his head. "Not food. You."

He stepped out of the trough and held her tight. His strength was staggering. He started to undress her, never taking his eyes from her face. And then they were naked, and he was inside her. Her body arched with pleasure as lust consumed her. She held him tight as they rode each other for what seemed like an eternity. And then it was over.

He was back.

# FORTY-TWO

"…YOU WERE ENDANGERING members of the public!"

It was eleven o'clock in the morning, and Hoog and Katja were listening to an angry Chief Pieters as he went over the events of the previous evening. He paused in the middle of his tirade.

Hoog sounded exasperated, which he was. "It was a calculated risk. He was more likely to have injured someone making his escape than during our intervention."

Pieters wiped his face with a handkerchief. A vein pulsed in his forehead. "Calculated risk! What would have happened if you'd hit someone with that stick you threw?"

"I've had a lot of practice with a Kylie," Hoog said. Pieters shook his head. "Who's Kylie?"

"Not who, what. It's an aboriginal heavy throwing stick."

Pieters held up his hand. "Enough! As far as I was concerned, Ward was conducting low-level surveillance on a suspect flagged up in a cold case. Not taking part in some drug pusher on ice pantomime."

Hoog gave a tight smile. "Taking a drug dealer out of the system could save hundreds of youngsters from heading into a crack cocaine habit further down the line. As I said, it was a calculated risk." Pieters held up his hand. "Okay. We'll hand the operation over to the FEDs and Europol and let them sort it out. At the end of the day, you may even have prevented a public relations disaster."

Hoog asked, "The body under the ice?"

"Yes." Pieters sat down behind his desk. "It's a good thing we found it before a member of the public saw it, and it ended up splashed all over the news."

Hoog shook his head. "I'm not a coroner, but that body looked like it had been around forever."

"Well let's hope so. Do we have any idea where it's come from?" Pieters asked.

"There's a possibility that it was within the drainage system and ended up snagging below the drain hole," Katja said.

Pieters nodded. "Well let's see what Kruger has to say. Until then, I think we should assume Marsha Brochell to be a person of interest within our investigation. We still don't know if she's over here, but there are enough similarities between the recent torso case in the US and our ongoing investigation. Hoog and Katja, you should focus on tracking the origin of the bodies. Katja, you can work with Roxie on the historical link in your own time. I'm not convinced there's much merit in it, but after your success in the UK linking historical evidence with a contemporary investigation, I'm not going to discount it entirely. Any questions?"

"I think on the surface that sounds like a good plan," Roxie said. "But?" Pieters asked, sensing Roxie's hesitation.

"Our case started back in 1888 and ended up in the middle of a modern-day conspiracy. As I'm sure Detective Hoog will agree, the first step in a criminal enterprise isn't held hostage by temporal restrictions. Pieters looked from Chandler to Duke. Duke shrugged. "Don't look at me."

"A simpler analogy would be serendipity," Hoog said. Pieters looked at him blankly.

Hoog went on. "The way a lot of things line up to produce an unexpected and positive result. In this case both involving the past, present, and future."

Pieters smiled with relief. "Okay. That sounds like a good thing."

"There you go," Duke said.

"So, what do we know about this Brochell woman's past?"

Roxie explained. "From what we were able to find out during our previous investigation, Marsha Brochell had the uncanny knack of aligning herself with people at critical moments in their lives. Times when the right decision would make them a fortune. John Palmer Sturridge, sold his sugar cane business a week before the civil war broke out, and saved himself from losing a fortune. Jessie Livermore, the legendary stockbroker, shorted Union Pacific Railroad on a hunch in 1906 after the San Francisco earthquake, then shorted the market again during the 1907 panic making over three million dollars, and again in the 1929 crash, after which he was worth over a hundred million dollars, a billion dollars in today's money."

Pieters looked over, his face displaying the consternation he felt. "So we're saying this Brochell woman's a psychic?"

"Either that or she has an uncanny level of business acumen," Chandler said.

"Her ancestors were involved in witchcraft, vodoun, and shamanism. Marsha Brochell's great grandmother was Leatrice Brochell, one of the first vodoun queens to practice in the city of New Orleans," Duke said.

Pieters ran his hands through his sparse hair. "I don't understand. If this Brochell woman is so smart, why would she come over here and get involved in planting corpses? It sounds like she's able to make money with her…" Pieters made air quotes. "'Business acumen' so why take the risk?"

Chandler looked at Roxie before speaking. "As Roxie said. We have to look at how far back her agenda goes. In particular what her real objective is."

Hoog's phone rang. He tapped it before speaking. "Hoog." He listened. "You're sure? Okay. Thank you." He slid the phone into his pocket. "That was Kruger, he's finished the post mortem on the bodies. The cause of death for the first one we already know." "Blood loss?" Chandler asked.

"Yes. But when it comes to the second body things get a little different."

Chandler leaned forward. "How different?"

Hoog paused as if searching for the right words. "As far as Kruger has been able to determine, the body under the ice rink died over three hundred years ago."

# FORTY-THREE

THEY STOOD IN the cool of the mortuary as Kruger talked through his findings. The body lay glistening on the steel table. It's leathery face a shining black travesty of human skin. Duke looked down at it.

"I've seen this look before," Kruger said.

"What are you thinking? The Grauballe Man, the Huldermose Woman or the Tollund Man?" Duke asked.

The effects of various soil conditions on a body and the resulting preservation of the subject was his specialty. He'd given lectures on the subject in London and struck up a friendship with Chandler as a result. They'd discovered a shared interest in Jazz and conspiracy theories which had led to them working together out in Louisiana when the bodies of five Victorian women had surfaced in Spirit's Swamp.

Kruger looked surprised at his knowledge. "Spoiled for choice really. They found over five hundred preserved bodies in a similar state in Denmark alone."

Chandler suddenly became animated. "An English glam rock band called The Darkness did a song about the Tollund Man." Roxie shook her head. "How do you manage to link everything to obscure pop songs?"

"It's a gift. 'The Curse of the Tollund Man' was released in 2003 on the *Permission to Land* album. It topped the UK album charts…" Chandler trailed off.

Kruger shook his head. "Tollund man died of hanging around 375 to 210 CE, and from a criminology perspective is certainly the oldest person ever to be fingerprinted. whereas according to radiocarbon dating..." Kruger put his glasses on and picked up a printout. "And using tooth enamel as the mitochondrial source, we're able to accurately date this specimen to within three years."

Roxie leaned forward. "What's the spread?"

Kruger handed her the paper. "I'd say between 1630 to 1633."

"Jeez, where has it been since then?" Roxie asked.

Kruger shrugged. "I don't know. But the similarity of his appearance would suggest the same sort of conditions preserved him as they did the Tollund man."

"Acidity in the ground, lack of oxygen, and low temperature," Duke said.

"Exactly. I've taken some samples and sent them to toxicology. I'll let you know if they flag anything up."

"I don't suppose you have any idea how he died?" Roxie asked.

Kruger shrugged. "Well, in this case, the Tollund Man can help us out." He pointed to the corpses distended tongue and some marks around the neck. "I would guess he was strangled by an exceptionally strong man or hanged. The distended tongue is typical of a hanging. He could, of course have been garroted with a rope."

Kruger pointed at the leathery corpse. "This guy was killed when the witchcraft trials were in full swing across Europe. I contacted your latest best friend, Professor De Vries up at Sint-

Janshospitaal Museum, and we did a little bit of checking through the known victims of the witch hunts around that time, and he came up with a name. Frederick Olfert."

"For sure, he was hanged as a sorcerer," Katja said.

Kruger nodded. "Chances are, Olfert was hanged because he had a clawed hand. It can be caused by some kind of nerve disease, and was also known as Spinsters claw." Kruger moved around the body and carefully lifted the arm. The remains of the hand were locked into a claw shape with each pair of fingers forming a fleshy hook. He lowered the arm slowly down to the table. "Do you have any idea how the body ended up in the drainage system beneath the ice rink?"

"That's what we're trying to find out," Chandler said.

"The drainage system is pretty extensive. It could have come from anywhere," noted Katja.

Roxie looked down at the leathery corpse in front of her. "Could I have a fluid sample from him?"

"Of course. Any particular reason?" Kruger asked.

"Well, I'm not looking for some weird kind of souvenir." Roxie grinned. "But there's a chance we could trace where it's come from by analyzing the fluid in the body and comparing it to samples from within the canal system."

"That could work. Oh, there's one more thing that might be of interest to you." Kruger pointed to some puncture wounds on the leathery shoulder of the corpse. Chandler looked closely at the scratched skin. "Bite marks? Human or animal?"

Kruger held a small steel ruler over the marks. "I'd say animal, I can do some tests, but I'm pretty sure we're looking at a dog for this, and a big one at that."

***

They gathered outside the hospital, the temperature felt warm after the chill of the mortuary.

"What's our next move? Duke asked.

Roxie looked around the group. "I'm hoping the engineers that found the original torso ran tests on the water to check for any signs of pollution from the beer pipe before they did their inspection dive. They'll probably have historical readings from other canals around Bruges. I'll get them to test the sample from our latest victim, and maybe we'll get a match from one of their earlier results."

"That should narrow down our search area," Duke said.

"Yes." Roxie looked at Hoog and Katja. "What's your next move?"

"The ice rink," Hoog said. "We'll check the area in case there's evidence that the body could have been planted there from outside the rink."

Duke looked at his watch. "Okay. Why don't we meet up back at the station around five and we'll compare notes."

"See you then," Hoog said.

Hoog and Katja set off across the market toward the ice rink while the others made their way to Woolestraat before heading back to the Kartuizerinnenstraat police station.

# FORTY-FOUR

KATJA AND HOOG stood in front of a food stall and watched as two officers finished rolling up the police tape surrounding the rink. Katja handed Hoog a coffee and took her cup from the stallholder.

Hoog toasted her. "Thanks. I read that the author of the Jack Reacher books…"

"Lee Child?"

"Yes. I read he drinks nineteen cups of coffee a day while he's working out his plots. How many do you think we'll need to solve this one?"

Katja took a sip from her mug. "I imagine we'd need some kind of espresso drip feed."

"For sure."

"What's your plan?" Katja asked. "I don't fancy crawling through the sewers to find where our bog man came from."

"Well you're lucky, Bruges isn't like Paris. They're not big enough for you to take a tour through them."

"That's a relief," Katja said.

"But there is an underground canal system and tunnels dating back to the construction of the Provincial Court. It was built over the site of the old Waterhalle after it was demolished in the eighteenth century. The Kraanrei was arched, cutting off the water supply to the city center,"

Hoog said. "Yes. I've seen some of the original pillars from the building in the garden of the Arentshuis Museum."

"Right. At that point in history, large parts of the Dijver and Spiegerei canals were overarched and ran underground."

"So, they're still accessible?" asked Katja. "Maybe. Why do you ask?"

"I think if you had two large, conspicuous dogs that you wanted to keep out of sight, the overarched canals might be ideal."

"It's possible I suppose," Hoog said distractedly, as he sipped his coffee.

Hoog looked at the tourists milling around the stalls and skating on the ice. It all seemed so normal. And yet only hours earlier he'd been staring at a three-hundred-year-old corpse frozen in the ice. Katja stared at him over her cup.

"Are you still with us?"

Hoog shook his head. "Sorry, I was miles away. But yes you could have a point...if there's access to the canals beneath the court, and links to the drainage system, it could have been used to plant the corpse."

"It's possible," Katja said.

Hoog shot her a look. "Do you think there any blueprints showing the course of the old canal and any links it might have with the modern drainage system?"

Katja finished her coffee. "If there are, they'll be in the reference library over at the Burg. Also, Wim has access to the ground scanning radar, lidar, and x-ray data the production company are collecting for their documentary about the hidden world beneath Bruges."

"Okay, let's check the blueprints first. Then give Wim a call," Hoog said.

Katja and Hoog sat at one of the long desks inside the archives in the ancient building that sat on one side of the Burg. The government buildings and the entrance to the Basilica of the Holy Blood formed a magnificent vista for many tourists making the pilgrimage to see the City's religious and architectural sights.

Molly, the archivist at the reference library, placed another pile of dusty plans on the desk as Katja and Hoog pored over the book in front of them.

Molly looked at them with a keen eye. "They take a bit of deciphering. Sometimes you need to use them in conjunction with Google maps to orientate yourself."

Katja had been a university student with Molly before they'd graduated and gone their separate ways. Molly liked nothing better than ferreting around amongst the old ledgers, books, and plans stored in the archives.

"I already did a bit of that, but it gets a bit confusing," Katja said.

"Yes. Sometimes it's just a rough approximation. What have you got so far?"

Katja tapped the set of plans they were studying. "We're trying to trace the route of the arched section of the Kraanrei Canal. According to the blueprints and the old plans, it runs underground from the Burg to Jan Van Eyck Square. The street above it goes from Kraanplein to Biskajersplein Square, then runs behind the basilica and under the Provincial Hof, the site of the original Waterhalle."

Molly looked at her. "Looks like you have a fair idea of its course."

"As much as we can guess at," Katja said.

Molly studied a large-scale drainage plan spread across the other end of the desk. "This is the oldest plan we have of the drainage system, but there's no combined plan of the old and new systems," she paused.

"You said Wim might have some ground penetrating radar data from the documentary footage?"

"Yes," Katja said. "But I like to go down the old-fashioned route first."

"Me too," agreed Molly. "There's something about a drawing on a piece of paper that gives me more confidence than data on a computer. I somehow feel that a plan or sketch drawn in the seventeenth century is less likely to be a fake. Though there are exceptions." Katja looked across the table at her. "What do you mean?" Molly pointed to a large map on the wall. "One of the best-known maps in Bruges history. Drawn by Marcus Gheeraerts in 1562. It's an amazing piece of work, originally etched onto ten separate plates. But some might say it was an early form of fake news." Hoog looked up from the plan he had been studying. "Really?"

"Despite the incredible detail in the workmanship, it is still a piece of art, and also reflects the political situation and trading problems of the times."

"Go on," Hoog said. Molly traced her fingers along the route of the various canals and streets of the City. "If you compare this to a satellite picture, you'll see how it's really too good to be true. Even the shape of the city is a perfect egg, rather than the dented avocado it really is. Also, the size of the streets, canals and rivers are exaggerated. Even the sea is portrayed as more accessible than it really is."

"Why did Gheeraerts exaggerate those details?" Katja asked.

"The city council gave him the commission and they must have been aware that the River Zwin was silting up."

"They were trying to give the impression that Bruges was still a great place to trade. By making all the roads, and rivers with their tributaries look bigger than they really were, they were encouraging people to trade with them," Hoog said.

"Now do you see where I'm coming from?" asked Molly. "Fake news. That's incredible. But hopefully, we won't need to use that particular map to find our way around," Katja said.

"Enough of the history propaganda, is there a way to access the arched section of the Kraanrei?" asked Hoog. Molly unrolled an architectural drawing across the table.

"This is a schematic of the drainage system as far as we know.

There are various sections where they've used the underground section to run the new drainage pipes through. There are also inspection covers, which allow access to the various sewage intersections."

"So, is the underground canal passable by boat, or only on foot?" Hoog asked. Molly shrugged. "I'm not entirely sure. I think some kids went down one of the manholes on a spelunking expedition a few years back and made it as far as the Jan Van Eyck Square exit."

"Spelunking?" Molly grinned. "Exploration of caves or underground structures. It derives from the Latin word for a cave, though some say it's the noise a stupid and unprepared caver makes when he falls into the water."

"Sounds like it might be navigable," Hoog said.

"We should check that documentary footage with Wim. I don't fancy getting stuck below ground somewhere that's been used as an open sewer for hundreds of years," commented Katja. Wim sat in front of his laptop skimming through the data files as Hoog battled with the filters on the lab's old coffee machine. Katja smiled as she watched him struggle.

"You should hook up with Chandler. He sees everything after the nineteenth century as the devil's work. He probably uses coffee beans passed through a yak and grinds them with his teeth." Hoog pressed the dispenser button on the machine, and it groaned into life. Spewing a thin gruel of pale brown liquid into the cracked cup beneath it.

"Looks lovely," Katja said, wrinkling her nose. Wim looked up from the screen. "When you guys have finished your barista training, I have the files."

Wim clicked on an icon marked *Kraanrei.*

"They were mainly scanning the Principal Hof, the Basilica and other historical buildings. The ground radar collected information beneath the structures as a side effect. They didn't bother rendering any of the data they didn't need. I've used the university computer to compile the information you're interested in."

Hoog took a sip of his coffee and winced. "That is awful." He put the cup down and spoke to Wim. "Good work. How much of the area did they map?" Wim clicked open the file and the screen filled with raw data. "I managed to isolate about half a kilometer of the canal between the Jan Van Eyck Square entrance up to the Basilica before it joins the Dijver canal. You'll need the VR headset."

Hoog and Katja picked up the headsets and slipped them on. Wim clicked a file. "Okay, let's see what we've got. This is going to be a bit random as the algorithms sacrifice detail if the areas are too dark to process."

The large screen on the lab wall flickered to life, and inside the headsets they found themselves standing beneath the Jan Van Eyck Square. They looked behind them at the semicircle of light as they left the archway beneath the square behind.

Hoog looked around through his headset at the confines surrounding him. "That's going to be a tight fit for the boat when they collect their water samples."

"The clearance depends on rainfall and the Minnewater reservoir," Wim said.

They looked around as the screen grew dark. They were floating above a stretch of murky water surrounded by narrow, crumbling walkways running beside the canal. A group of small black rats scuttled along the walkway before plunging into the water.

"Oh my God, look at the rats!" Katja said. "Yuk."

"They'd probably say the same about us," Wim said with a smile. Above them stretched curved, brick archways, dank, and spidered with moss. Tendrils of vegetation had forced their roots through the smallest of cracks. Occasionally they would catch sight of a dim circle of light leaking from a manhole cover the street above.

"I've linked up GPS to the program to get an idea of where we are in relation to the surface topography," Wim said.

"We're beneath Kraanrei Street at the moment, passing the Poortersloge. The lodge was a meeting place for the rich and important members of society. Where deals were done. A meeting place for the society of the white bear. Back then they believed a bear was the oldest citizen of Bruges.

If I can find the legend...here it is." Wim tapped on his laptop. "Back in the ninth century, Baldwin the First kidnapped Judith, the daughter of a French King, and though he married her, the king banished them to the northern part of Flanders. They found themselves in the forest that would become the City of Bruges, where they were attacked by a white bear. Baldwin killed the bear, and legend says that the bear crept out of his skin and became the first citizen of Bruges."

"I think I've met some of his ancestors in the local beer cellars," Katja said.

Wim tapped his laptop. "Okay, the computers finished rendering. Here we go."

The view in their immersive headsets filled with dank canal brickwork disappearing into the darkness.

"Where are we now?" Katja asked.

Wim looked at his laptop. "Still under the Kraanrei, we should be crossing the Kraanplein soon." The canal widened out slightly as it swung to the left. "They used to unload the ships here."

He tapped his laptop, and an ancient wooden crane filled the screen, like a giant hamster wheel with a ship's prow jutting out where cargo hung from ropes.

"That's wild. They used men walking in the wheel to hoist the cargo up," Katja said.

"Yes, this was back in the thirteenth century. The picture was painted by Simon Bening, who was considered to be the greatest miniaturist in Europe at that time."

Katja and Hoog's goggles went dark. "What's happening?" Katja asked. Wim tapped some keys, and a string of codes flashed up on the screen. "Damn. Someone in the university has dumped my data stream."

"They can do that?" Katja asked.

"Yes, the university has data priority over my feed."

"What do we do now?" Katja asked as she flicked a look at her text messages.

Wim shrugged. "Wait till it frees up. Shouldn't be too long. I'm sure you have stuff to do, I'll text you when it's clear."

"No problem. Erika's left me a voice mail." Katja listened for a few seconds and then slipped the phone into her pocket. "Okay, I'm going over to see her now. Text me when it's up and running again, and we'll come back."

"Okay I'll sort out some decent coffee." "Thanks," Hoog said.

# FORTY-FIVE

KATJA COULD SEE Erika sitting at a large desk strewn with old manuscripts and open books. She called out to her and headed across the dusty floor of the storage vaults beneath the Museum.

"Where's the fire?" Katja said.

Erika looked up. "That's a phrase that is remarkably apt given what I've found."

Katja looked at the table. "And what's that?"

"The Poortersloge was also known as the Burghers Lodge." "I know. It was where the important people did their deals," Katja said.

"Yes." Erika opened a leather-bound manuscript filled with columns of Flemish text. "This is a ledger of various deals and the people involved at the White Bear Society meetings, as well as details of the hierarchy of the society."

"You'll have to translate. My Flemish is rubbish."

Erika traced her finger down the columns on the page. She halted. "Recognize that name?"

Katja squinted at the spidery letters. "Count Brandt Van Zwart?"

"Yes. Seems back then he was one of the top dogs—or bears—in the society."

Katja looked at the manuscript. "I don't suppose that's particularly unusual, after all, he was a count."

Hoog appeared at the entrance to the storage vault. "Thought you might be needing supplies." He held up a tray of coffee and waffles.

"My favorite," Erika said. Her hand snaking toward a waffle.

Katja took a coffee. "Thanks. Erika's found some more info on Count Brandt Van Zwart."

"Go on." Hoog took a bite from a waffle.

"Apparently he was a top dog in the White Bear Society."

Hoog swallowed his waffle before speaking. "It was a bit like a Masonic lodge, where the important people did their trade deals."

Erika smiled and took a bite from her waffle. She chewed and swallowed, wiping sugar from her lips before continuing. "Yes. But that's not the reason I called you over. I found some minutes from one of the meetings." She opened another book at a page marked with a museum bookmark. "Seems the society was concerned that trade deals were being done outside of the White Bear Society, by a secret group formed from its own members."

Katja looked at the book as she took a sip of coffee. "Go on."

"The society had reports of cargo ships being set on fire, and people being murdered to get traders to toe the line."

Erika studied the text. "Unimaginatively, it was known as The Black Bear Society."

"You think they ran some kind of protection racket from within the group?" asked Katja.

"I'd say it was highly likely. And here's the interesting part." Erika traced her finger down the page. "The society believed that Brandt Van Zwart was its leader."

Hoog put his coffee cup back down on to the tray.     "What did they do?"

"He was thrown out of the White Bear Society," Erika said.

"There seems to be no end to his skills. Painter, murderer, extortionist," Katja said.

"Yes. Though nothing was ever proven, they must have had enough evidence to suspect him. Apparently, traders had been disappearing for some time. Having recently done favorable deals with him," Erika said.

"You think he was getting them to drop their prices and then having them killed so he could keep their cargo?" Hoog asked.

Erika shrugged. "I doubt we'll ever know for sure, but the evidence is stacking up. Count Brandt Van Zwart shows all the signs of a murderous psychopath."

"And given how much leeway the rich and influential had back then he must have really gone overboard to be thrown out of their club," added Katja.

# FORTY-SIX

**BRUGES, BELGIUM – 1633**

COUNT BRANDT VAN Zwart stood in the shadows outside Sint-janshospitaal. It was just before midnight, and the streets were quiet. A shroud of mist clung to the surface of a canal in the distance. He heard the sound of the leper's rattles long before they appeared. A small group of them materialized by the gates and approached him. They wore the traditional heavy gray hoods and ragged cloaks of their kind. He held up his hand for them to halt. The stench as they drew near him was overwhelming. A tall man detached himself from the group. Their spokesman, he imagined. He stifled his revulsion at the state of his companions. An ear missing, fingerless hands and rotting flesh hanging off faces. Ironically, this was one of the reasons lepers could move freely through the city. No one was going to approach them unless it was someone seeking to help them. The tall man nodded to the Count.

"My name is Joseph."

"Do you speak for all?" The count asked.

"Yes."

The count forced himself to make eye contact with Joseph's rotting flesh. "I understand that money is not what you seek?" Joseph looked back at his friends. "We're past earthly possessions. We get what we need from the hospital."

The count clicked his fingers, and a shape detached itself from the shadows, a woman wearing a hooded cloak, her face showing the early stages of leprosy. She shrugged her hood off, revealing a mane of lustrous dark hair. Even now she was still beautiful.

"One night with each of you," the count said.

Joseph turned to look at his companions. The other lepers nodded.

"Agreed. What exactly do you need us to do?" Joseph asked.

The count spoke softly. "I have some people who are proving reluctant to agree to my terms. I need you to convince them."

The lepers headed along the banks of the Kraanrei and past the moored ships of the traders. Two of them carried burning torches in their hands. They halted next to one of the boats. A battered old merchant ship, typical of the type favored by traders operating under the Hanseatic League's control. Joseph read the name on its bow. *Sint Van Brugga*. He waved at them to move back.

"This is it Peres. Cut the mooring lines. James, ready the torches." A thickset man moved over to the mooring ropes and began to hack at them with a knife. Once they were loose, Peres and James hurled the torches onto the deck of the ship while the others threw jugs of oil after them. Within seconds, the drifting boat was engulfed in flames. Joseph signaled to the men. "Go!"

The men moved back along the Kraanrei away from the burning ship. And then the screaming began.

James turned to Joseph. "I thought we were just burning cargo." Joseph looked back at the burning ship, his jaw tightened as he saw men on fire desperately throwing themselves into the water.

"So did I," he said grimly.

# FORTY-SEVEN

ROXIE HAD BOOKED a taxi to take them all to Roland and Dieter's small lockup and office on the outskirts of Zeebrugge port. The engineers were leaning against an old VW van drinking coffee from their flasks as the taxi turned up. Roxie had suggested to Duke and Chandler that it would make sense to go to the engineer's premises to save time in case they found that they needed any extra equipment. After a brief discussion, Roxie gave Dieter the sample of fluid from the corpse found beneath the ice rink. Dieter rummaged in a bag he'd taken from the back of the van and fed the sample into a handheld mass spectrometer. He tapped some buttons and watched the readout.

"Okay, the sample's logged in. We should get the results pretty soon."

"Is it standard for you to measure the water quality each time you get a call out?" asked Roxie.

"Yes. That way we have a default reading. Then if we find something that needs rectifying, we have a comparison before and after treatment."

"So the day you were checking for the leak in the beer pipe you already had a previous reading to compare it with?" Roxie asked Dieter. Roland appeared alongside her, picking up on the conversation. "Yes. We thought it was unlikely there was a leak because the readings were clear, and the E-sniffer wasn't showing anything either."

"E-sniffer?" Duke asked.

Roland held up a small device with an LCD display.

"Ultra-high-speed gas chromatography. It's used it for all sorts of stuff. Detecting gas leaks, chemical threats, food, and beverage quality. All kinds of shit. It could probably tell you what you ate for breakfast."

Duke shrugged. "So, if the pipe had been leaking beer, you would have picked up traces of that within the vicinity?"

"Yes."

Roxie frowned. "So why did you still dive in the canal?" "Because no matter what some gadget tells me, I always believe in physically checking it myself." There was a soft beep from the machine.

"Okay. We have the sample logged. Now what?" Dieter asked. Roxie looked over. "Can you compare that reading with sample readings you've taken from the other canals?"

Dieter nodded. "Sure, how far back do you want me to go? I have a year's worth of readings in the memory, if you want to go back further than that, I'll need to go into the cloud and pull it down from the server."

"Let's see if we get a match from your recent data first, then we can dig deeper."

Dieter looked at the display. "Okay. What sort of comparisons are we looking for here? Are you interested in some kind of pollution? Microorganisms, chemical profiles or ambient air chemistry?" Dieter looked at their blank faces. "The reason I'm asking is that I can set the filter parameters on the equipment to skew the results toward what you're actually looking for."

Duke gave a grim smile. "You already met our headless friend."

"Damn thing scared the shit out of me," Dieter said.

"Turns out he's not the only one," Duke said.

"You've found another one?" Dieter shook his head.

"Damn. So that's what the police were doing at the ice rink."

"Yes. If we can get a match from one of the canals you've taken readings from that will narrow down our search for its geographical source," Duke said.

"Okay. So, you're looking for a reading to give us a match between the fluid from the latest victim and our historical readings from the canals around Bruges."

"Yes. Are there any areas of the canals you haven't measured throughout the course of your work?" asked Chandler.

Dieter thought about that for a moment. "Well, there are some areas where the canal has been built on over the centuries…"

"Is it possible to access those parts?" Chandler asked.

Dieter scratched his ear. "The Dijver canal goes underground next to the Basilica of the Holy Blood and reappears at the Langerei Canal between Spinolarei and Spiegelrei at Jan Van Eyck Square. The Speelmansrei Canal also disappears from beside the concert hall and re-appears next to the Zilverpand shopping center, but I don't think that's navigable by boat."

"Could you take us to where the canal goes underground at the Jan Van Eyck Square?" Roxie asked.

"I don't see why not," replied Dieter.

"Good. So if nothing comes up on the historic chromatography data, we can take samples from there," Roxie said.

They drove through the storage yards, past stacks of metal containers and towering cranes and were soon speeding down the motorway toward Bruges. As well as their diving equipment and measuring instruments, the van was towing an inflatable big enough to carry five of them along the canal. Dieter and Roland sat up front, and Roxie sat between Duke and Chandler in the back. The engine was noisy but willing, and within half an hour they were entering the outskirts of Bruges. The VW van was from the 1960s and sported bright orange paintwork. It drew admiring glances and waves everywhere they went. The van was fitted with the original single speaker transistor radio, and the static-filled AM signal drifted in and out. Somehow it managed to cling on to a radio station playing "Black Magic Woman" by Santana, which pleased Chandler no end.

Chandler watched in awe as Dieter skillfully navigated his way through the swarms of tourists, horse-drawn carriages, and suicidal students on bicycles, hurtling across the bone-shaking cobbles, totally fearless; cocooned in the bubble of immortality that encases the young. Absorbed in the music flowing through their earbuds, they seemed to belong to a different species entirely.

Chandler didn't think there had ever been a time when he'd felt that immortal. Maybe it was the things he'd seen as a detective or working the streets as a constable on the beat. From his experiences, Chandler knew only too well how the most mundane tasks such as mowing the lawn, crossing the road or climbing the stairs could all too easily end in tragedy. He'd heard a new buzzword recently. Micromorts, a measurement people used to describe how dangerous a particular activity was. So, for instance, hang gliding, parachuting or mountain climbing would be classed in hundreds of micromorts. He was pretty sure that cycling through Bruges wearing headphones and texting, without any hands controlling the bike, would rank in the thousands on the micromort scale.

Dieter hit the horn and said something in Dutch that didn't need translating for his meaning to be clear. A fresh-faced student on an old bike gave him a peremptory wave as he cut across in front of them.

"Idiot," Dieter said, giving a shrug to Chandler. "Students. They think they own the road."

Roxie peered out of the side window as they eased past a stationary horse and carriage. "I've gotta' take a ride on one of those."

"Don't worry, we'll have plenty of time for the sights. I'll need to get some coffee and waffles inside me before we climb the Belfort though," Chandler said.

They crossed the Sint-Jansplein, and Dieter pointed toward an old building. "You could start at the Chocolate Museum and then move on to the Belgium Fries Museum before you do the Belfort." Roxie's face lit up. "Cool, then I need to find a gym."

Dieter grinned. "It's not far now. Nothing in Bruges is far, that's what the tourists love about it. If you walk too far, you hit the canal at the outer ring, then all you do is walk back toward the Belfort."

"What does Bruges actually mean?" Roxie asked.

"It's been called many things, initially Bruggas back as far as 840, but it's mostly derived from the old Dutch word *brugga*, meaning bridge," Dieter said.

Chandler turned to Roxie. "The rivers were seen as living beings with enormous spiritual significance back in the sixteenth century. The estuary from the North Sea was known as The Golden Gate, and the Zwin River ran into Bruges where it fed into the canals filled by the Reie, the main river. Back then they believed that the interconnections of the canals and rivers formed a link, or bridge, to the spiritual underworld." Chandler gave a wink to Dieter.

"Great, that's all I need to know before I go for a paddle in an underground canal," Roxie said. Then she saw his smile. "You're messing with me, aren't you?"

Chandler shrugged. "Maybe."

Roxie punched him on the arm as Dieter pulled up in a large square.

Chandler looked past the statue of Jan Van Eyck at something infinitely more modern. A vast breaching whale, forty-foot high and constructed from five tons of plastic waste collected from the beaches of Hawaii. The colossal art installation was a response to the liquid city theme of the 2018 Bruges triennial. It was an impressive and sobering sight.

Dieter broke into Chandler's thoughts. "Okay. There are life jackets in the back if you want to fight over the sizes, while we get the boat unloaded."

Dieter and Roland climbed out and began to unload the inflatable from its trailer. Chandler and Duke went around to the tailgate of the van and opened it. Roxie looked inside at the garish yellow hi-viz life jackets.

"Not really my color, but better than nothing." She shrugged a jacket on while Chandler and Duke rummaged through the remaining jackets.

Duke managed to squeeze into one by removing his own jacket, and Chandler donned the remaining jacket. They headed over to the edge of the square to join Dieter and Roland, who had already lowered the dingy into the canal. Roland was busy adjusting a pair of oars.

"If you climb in one at a time that will be safest," Roland said. Chandler helped Roxie down the small wooden steps that gave them access to the dingy. There was a smaller archway to the left of the main arching passage. The canal water level reached the top of the main passage, and there was a meter's clearance in the smaller canal archway.

Roland waited for everybody to get into position, so the boat was balanced, before speaking. "Okay. There's not much clearance on this side so I won't be using the engine yet. Once we get inside, I may be able to start it up, but I don't want to gas ourselves down there. Everybody comfortable?"

They all nodded.

"We'll be traveling underground as far as Kraanplein, then continuing beneath Vlamingstraat, under the Provincial Court, beside the Burg and the Basilica of the Holy Blood before we come back out into the Dijver Canal. It's only about half a kilometer."

Duke looked at the slimy roof of the semicircular arch that led into the dark canal. "I don't wanna' be a wiseass, but couldn't we get the samples by lowering a bottle through a manhole from a nice dry street above here?"

"You're not a wiseass. But if we do it this way and get a positive reading, then we're in the right place to follow it up," explained Roxie.

"Unfortunately, that makes perfect sense," Duke said.

Dieter untied the rope that held them to the steps, picked up a small paddle and with a nod to Roland they set off. They all crouched down as the dingy slid beneath the low arch leaving a pale fingernail of light behind them as they moved deeper into the canal tunnel.

# FORTY-EIGHT

**BRUGES, BELGIUM**

BACK AT THE university, Wim greeted Hoog and Katja with a tray of steaming mugs.

"The coffee from the faculty restaurant is much better, trust me," Wim said, as he put the tray down on top of the workbench.

They'd read Wim's text and left Erika at the museum to drive back to the university. Wim seemed excited and nervous at the same time.

"What's up?" Katja asked.

Wim handed out the mugs and sat down in front of his laptop.

"I finished rendering the remaining data from the scans. And I got the data stream back half an hour ago. I thought I'd take a peek so you wouldn't waste any time on the boring stuff."

"From the look of you, it doesn't look like you've been bored," Katja said.

Wim chucked them the 3D headsets. "That's an understatement." Wim tapped some keys. "I edited out most of the canal stuff which left me with this."

Katja slipped her goggles on.

"Where are we, geographically?"

"Well, since leaving Jan Van Eyck Square and heading beneath Kraanrei, we've crossed over Sint Janstraat near what used to be the old hospital, then down Leperstraat, running alongside the Market Square, under the Provincial Court, between Woolestraat and the Burg, heading toward the Basilica of the Holy Blood—which is when it gets interesting He tapped his keyboard. The screen and the goggles filled with the dark waters of the canal beneath the streets.

"Pretty much the same old, same old. But do you notice something different?" asked Wim.

"No rats?" asked Katja.

"Precisely. And the reason for that is coming up."

Suddenly a flicker of yellow circles appeared on the screen, blinking in the dark, before materializing. They were looking at two large and familiar shapes crouched in the gloom of the tunnel. Wim pointed to a timecode readout on his laptop. "The most recent scans were taken within the last three days."

"Jesus, no wonder there aren't any rats," Hoog said. "I think we may have found the missing hounds."

Wim froze the image and zoomed in. One of the hounds had a dead rat hanging from its jaws.Hoog stared at the hound. "We need to let Chandler and Roxie know that they could be down there. Are there any access points from the streets above?" Wim tapped the keyboard and the screen filled with a changing vista of the underground canal.

"There must be a number of ancient buildings with cellars below the level of the canal," Katja said.
Wim adjusted the picture and started the video stream again. "It gets worse."
Hoog looked at him. "How much worse?"
Before Wim could reply, the answer to Hoog's question became obvious. They were standing in a stygian 3D view of the canal beneath the streets.

172

The waterway curved away to the left leaving a dark area of the earthen bank stretching away into the gloom. Wim altered the view moving around the area and sharpening the detail.

"Oh my God." Katja walked around the videoscape as if she was treading on ice. Under her feet, gleaming in the pale light that spilled down into the canal from the manhole in the street above, were the blackened husks of fifteen or more grotesquely preserved human bodies." Hoog pulled the headset off. "How do we contact them?"

"If they're below the streets they won't have a phone signal," said Katja. Wim thought for a second. "I know a way around that." Hoog looked up. "How?" Wim went to the end of one of the workbenches and opened a large drawer. He lifted out a small quadcopter painted  in camouflage colors. The name Charlie was stenciled on the side of it in white letters.

"A drone?" Hoog asked.

Katja looked at it. "Who's Charlie?"

Wim grinned. "My dad was a big fan of Apocalypse Now."

Katja remembered seeing the classic film during a retro night showing when she'd been a student at Ghent University.

"If the drone can track them down, we can warn them," Hoog said. Wim began to adjust some settings on the drone. "I can set the drone to send a video clip when it comes within range of a Bluetooth device. I'll tell them to head back and that you're on your way." Hoog looked at the diminutive drone and shook his head. "How does it find its way without access to GPS below ground?"

"I've been using this drone as an AI test bed for years. It's smarter than a fox. It has all kinds of proximity avoidance and defensive capabilities. It'll use stored GPS data to navigate and just keep on going until it locks onto a signal." Hoog nodded. "Okay, let us know if you make contact of any kind. Let's go."

\*\*\*

They left the university and ran toward the parking lot. They picked up the E40, past Aalter and headed toward Oostkamp. Katja looked over at Hoog. "Do you think the dogs are still down there?"
Hoog flicked her a look. "I don't know. But better safe than sorry." Katja looked through the windshield at Wim's quadcopter drone ahead of them. It waggled at them before zooming off toward Bruges.
"I hope Wim makes contact. I'm worried about them." "Don't be. The dogs will probably be more scared of them."
Hoog said, trying to lighten the mood.

Katja looked at him. "That's the sort of thing an animal lover would say. But I still wouldn't want to run into them."
Hoog looked into the rear mirror. A battered Mercedes SUV was closing up on them fast. "What's this guy playing at?"
Katja looked behind. "Looks like he's in a hurry." "Aren't we all. Stick the Christmas decorations up."

Katja reached down and picked up the magnetic blue light, opened the window, and stuck it on the roof of the Audi. Hoog turned the light on. "That should slow him down."
It didn't. There was a bone-jarring crunch as the SUV smashed into the back of them. Hoog yanked the wheel as the Audi went into a spin. He steered into the direction of travel and mashed the accelerator. The powerful engine howled as all sorts of computer activated traction systems tried desperately to regain control. Hoog managed to straighten up for a second, and then the SUV rammed them again. Their world became a kaleidoscope of cars and scenery spinning past the windows.

"Jesus!" Katja shouted as she clung onto the grab handle above the door. Hoog swerved around a car, missed a truck by inches, and ended up in a four-wheel drift before sliding to a halt in the safety lane. Steam drifted from beneath the hood, and the acrid smell of burnt rubber filled the car.

Katja jumped out and watched the SUV vanish into the distance. She leaned back into the car and reached for the radio. "We just got rammed by a Mercedes SUV, license plate AG16 TFS, silver gray, maybe two or more passengers, driver, male, sharp featured with dark hair, all wearing gray hoodies. Headed toward Oostkamp on the E40."

The dispatcher's voice crackled over the speaker. "Copy that.

Do you need assistance?"

Katja twisted her neck and looked at Hoog. He shook his head. She pressed the handheld mic. "No, I think we'll make it to the city center, but we'll need a replacement car."

"Okay. Copy that." The dispatcher signed off.

Hoog started the car and checked the display. "We're starting to overheat."

Hoog pulled out onto the slow lane, eyeing the instruments as he accelerated back into the middle lane. "I think the radiator's leaking. If we turn the heater on, we may be able to make it back to town." Katja turned to Hoog. "How do we find out where they are in the canal?"

Hoog thought for a moment. "There's only about half a kilometer of the canal running under the streets, if we get access at the midpoint, we can use Wim's idea to track them."

"Bluetooth?"

"Yes."

"They were planning to start at the entrance in Jan Van Eyck Square, so we need to get access further down the Kraanrei."

The traffic started to slow as motorists began queuing for the turn off into Bruges. Katja put the blue light on, and they used the safety lane to get ahead of the traffic before crossing the Katelinjstraat Bridge. To the left of them, the lake in Minnewater Park glimmered in the sunlight. Hoog slowed the car as they continued down Katelinjstraat into Mariastraat crossing over the canal. The Audi began to shudder, and there was a shrieking noise from under the bonnet. Hoog coasted to the side of the road.

"The engine's fucked."

"What do we do now?"

Hoog climbed out of the car. "We'll get a carriage."

Katja got out and slammed the door. Hoog opened the trunk of the Audi and rummaged around in the tire well. He pulled out a crowbar and closed the trunk.

"We'll need this," Hoog said.

They walked down to the Market Square where a group of carriages stood waiting. The horses standing with one leg cocked while their drivers chatted and smoked beside them. Hoog nodded to one of the drivers and climbed into his carriage. He flashed his badge. "Take us to Academiestraat. Quick as you like."

"For sure. I give you a ten percent discount for being a public official," said the driver. He climbed into the carriage, shook the reins, and the horse trotted across the square.

The driver began his tourist spiel. "The Belfort has 366 steps and was built in 1240 and it was rebuilt in 1280 after a big fire. The upper part was built between 1483 and 1487 when they added a wooden spire decorated with the image of Saint Michael, but it caught fire after being struck by lightning in 1493, which destroyed the bells. They rebuilt the spire, but it caught fire again in 1741—"

Hoog looked at him and shook his head. "Why are you telling us this?" The driver shrugged. "Just saying, some people never learn."

He shook the reins again, and the horse trotted past the Historium before exiting the square.

"Look, we just want to be dropped at Academiestraat. You don't need to give us a guided tour. We live here for Christ's sake," Hoog said.

The driver tapped his nose and gave a wink. "That's my point. If I didn't give you the tour, I would be taking money under false pretenses. I don't take any chances with the feds."

Hoog muttered beneath his breath. "Give me strength."

Katja stifled a smile with her hand. She was still wired from the SUV ramming them and the carriage driver's chatter had helped distract her from the near-death experience.

"If you want to pick up the pace I promise not to give you a ticket. We need to get to Academiestraat as fast as possible. People's lives are at stake," Hoog said.

The driver nodded. "Ya. I'll do my best." Hoog turned to Katja. "You alright?"

"I'm okay. Just a bit shook up. What do you think it was all about back there?'

"I don't know. Maybe I gave the wrong person a parking ticket."

"That would be a bit of an extreme reaction," Katja said.

"We live in an extreme world. Korean missiles, Trump's wall, the Eurozone, Brexit, need I go on?"

"You don't think it's connected to a current case?"

"The drugs bust? It's a possibility, but what would it achieve? The investigation is being handled by the feds and Europol. They can't force all of them off the road."

# FORTY-NINE

THE MERCEDES SUV sat idling next to the rubble-strewn building site behind the façade of a house being refurbished on Vlamingstraat. Five men were squashed inside the SUV. Their heavy shoulders and muscular arms jostled for space. Their leader, Rudi, a sharp featured individual with rat-like teeth and eyes that darted around on constant alert, sat in the driver's seat.

He smacked the steering wheel with the palm of his hand, punctuating his speech as he derided the men.

"Have you any idea what that bitch is going to do to us if we don't finish this and fast!" He rubbed at his wrist exposing a small tattoo of a bear.

"We did our best, Rudi. He had the reflexes of a snake."

Rudi turned to look at the man speaking. "Karim. How hard is it to squash a car with this tank?"

The largest of the men on the back seat reached over and squeezed Rudi's shoulder with one large hand. With a weaker man, it would have been a squeeze of encouragement, but the power of the man's hand pinned Rudi to his seat.

"Take it easy, Rudi. He got away, but we know what he's looking for. His friends are at the canal right now, maybe even beneath our feet. They will all meet up, and when they do, we'll be waiting." He removed his hand.

Rudi massaged his shoulder. "Okay, Marco, but if you— we— screw this up, there will be no more chances. That bitch gonna' burn us good."

"She's only one woman," Marco said.

Rudi gave a grim smile. "Oh no my friend, she is more than that."

# FIFTY

**BRUGES, BELGIUM – 1633**

THE COUNT SAT at the head of a long table in a room at the Poortersloge. A group of nervous-looking traders listened intently to what he had to say.

"As you are aware, one of our fellow traders lost his ship and some of his men in a tragic accident very recently."

One of the traders spoke up. "It wasn't an accident."

The count smiled and looked at the man. His name was Lucha da Ragusa, a Venetian silk trader—a very successful one. Lucha leaned across the table, fixing the count with a stare.

"Some men were seen throwing burning torches onto the deck shortly before it caught fire. They were lepers." He slammed his fist on the table. "Since when did lepers have anything against traders?"

The count shrugged. "Well they have nothing to lose, maybe someone offered them something in exchange for their nefarious acts?" Lucha sat back down. "What do you suggest we do about the situation?" The count spoke, "You are all members of this society because I can get you a better price than you would normally get from within the White Bear Society. But profit is not without risk. Whether it be from discovery by the legitimate society, or from profiteers, or pirates who have no code, and no boundaries."

Lucha shook his head. "It doesn't make sense. Maybe we should ask the lepers who're hiring them?"

The Count's mouth closed into a tight line. His eyes were glacial.

"That won't be necessary. I will look into the situation, and deal with it."

The count looked around the table at the tense faces that surrounded him.

"I promise you that there will no longer be any further disruption to your trade, your ships, or the crew within them." He paused. "Of course, extra protection comes with extra costs. I think we agreed on twenty Ducats?"

The men at the table muttered amongst themselves before falling silent. They looked to Lucha, and each slowly nodded. Lucha reached into his pocket and produced a small velvet pouch that clinked. He threw it to the count who caught it effortlessly.

"Twenty gold ducats as agreed," Lucha said.

Slowly, each of the seated figures produced a pouch from their pockets and slid it across the table.

The count smiled and slipped the coin-filled pouches into a leather bag in front of him.

"Now we are agreed, let us discuss the terms of trade and start making money."

# FIFTY-ONE

**BRUGES, BELGIUM – Present day**

BRANDT VAN ZWART moved the bundles of euro notes into a line in front of him on the table. He was sitting next to Marsha in Le Pelican, a closed beer cellar in Eekhoutpoort, in a passageway that led off from Eekhoutstraat. Its entrance lay behind some unassuming wooden doors. The Fonteyne brothers, two muscle-bound Walloon bouncers, made sure it didn't get too noisy after dark and kept the nearby residents happy.

The street had inherited its name from the Abbey of Eeckhoute, which was demolished in the nineteenth century. The only remaining relic of the abbey was a statue of St. Augustin on the gate that led to the passageway. The beer cellar was situated in the original catacombs that had stretched out beneath the abbey, and its vaulted ceilings gave it a church-like atmosphere. Adam Blackburn had bought the property and opened it as a beer cellar in the 1930s.

Over the years Adam and Roman Blackburn had traveled back and forth between Louisiana and Bruges. In Louisiana, he was a Blackburn, while in Bruges he was Brandt Van Zwart. Two identities, one person. Bar staff came and went, as did the various criminals that kept their underworld operations running; drugs, trafficking, prostitution, and protection rackets. The only constants were Marsha and her companion. The players in the underworld asked no questions. They just took the money, did the job, and when it was time to go, they went. But her latest group of unsavory characters had a problem.

The five men that sat opposite Brandt Van Zwart bore the story of their life in every line on their faces. And right now, they didn't look happy.

One of the dealers, Marco, a wide-shouldered Walloon, twisting his greasy blond dreads like a nervous tic, spoke first. "Point is man, they took Blades out. We used to get a lot of trade kickbacks through him, and now he's banged up. What's going on? I thought we had the feds under control. This is a piece of shit. You need to sort this or else." He slammed his hand down on the table, making the solid oak vibrate.

Brandt Van Zwart looked at Marsha. He didn't need her spiritual powers to work out what had gone wrong here. The appearance of the body under the ice rink and the police raid on Blades had damaged their lucrative drug network. Like most major cities, the underworld's supply of drugs from the pushers, and the kickbacks keeping the feds off their backs, worked like a well-oiled machine. If a dealer got out of line, became greedy, or skimmed too much off the top, steps were taken. The police would be tipped off, and the resulting arrest would become a feather in the cap of the local forces.

But the two feds that had taken Blades down weren't part of an official investigation. A young officer had been given some cold cases to clear up, with no real chance of success. Something to keep him busy. But against all the odds, he'd managed to piece together similar reports of Blade's activities from tourist's complaints stretching back for years. He'd mounted video surveillance, and the two officers had come at Blades from out of nowhere.

There had been an instance before the present chief of police was installed when the link between drugs and police corruption had broken down. With the death of the previous chief, order had been restored. Chief Pieters was fully aware of the checks and balances that existed between crime and the law. A situation in part reflected by the affection he held his wife and children in, along with his own lif

Brandt Van Zwart was convinced that this was a one-of, a fluke. If it wasn't, then the situation would be remedied. The Walloon was staring at him. It was obvious he wanted answers, reassurances from him that would quiet his primeval thought processes. Zwart realized he needed to send him a message. He gave a smile that didn't reach his eyes, sliding the piles of notes across the table one by one as he punctuated his words with the actions.

"Okay, why don't we call this month's cut zero. You keep all the money from your deals until we sort out the problem. How does that sound?"

The Walloon shrugged, gave a smile revealing yellowed fangs and a gold filling. "Sounds okay to—"

Zwart slammed a fist into his nose, rocking him back in his seat and sending a spurt of blood onto his shirt. Brandt was out of his seat and reaching over to grab him by the throat before he had time to blink. He moved his face down closer to the choking Walloon.

"Don't you ever threaten me like that again. Understand?" He threw the Walloon back into his seat. "Everybody okay now?"

The Walloon spat some blood onto the pile of notes in front of him. "Shit man, I think you busted my nose." Zwart looked at him. "I hope so. Are we finished here?" The other men turned to look at the Walloon's bloodied nose, then slowly nodded.

"Good, we'll meet up at the end of the month and see how the land lies, right?"

The Walloon fixed Zwart with a hard stare but said nothing. Zwart threw him a handkerchief.
The Walloon wiped the blood from his face, took a bundle of euros off the table, and walked out. The rest of them did the same before following him out.
Once they had left, Brandt Van Zwart turned to Marsha.
"What now?"

Marsha reached out and took his hand. "You do know you would make the world's worst diplomat?"

"Maybe, but Marco needed talking to in his own language, the language of force."

"They have no idea we allowed Blades to be taken for our own reasons. Now when something happens to Chandler and his friends, everybody will assume they were the victims of a drug cartel revenge attack," Marsha said.

"Exactly. A series of coincidences that combined to cause a tragic outcome for the valiant forces of good against evil."

"Yes. The appearance of the body beneath the rink was unfortunate. But it won't affect our plans," Marsha said.

She looked at Zwart. No matter how many times he had been brought back, he was still the ruthless character she had chosen to possess all those centuries ago. Of course, she had been able to mold and control his inner soul, to refine and improve his abilities to survive in the modern world. But she felt her body quiver with the knowledge that he still could possess her heart and mind, not to mention the physical side of things. Had he become the sophisticated man she sometimes wished for, would that not dilute the excitement he was able to induce within her during their more intimate moments? She saw him staring at her. He had a look in his eye; a look she knew only too well.

He wanted her, and he wanted her soon. She gave him a smile. "Everything is in place. They've split up to try and track us down. But it will end badly for them, and then we will be safe once more."

"Good." He reached for her and led her through the bar and upstairs toward the bedroom in the flat above the bar. He pushed her gently back onto the bed and began unbuttoning her blouse. She fumbled for his belt, while he kicked off his shoes.

Soon they were naked and pressed against each other until the heat of their bodies became too great for her to bear.

She pulled free, straddled him with one powerful thigh, and within seconds he was inside her. It was the second time they had made love since his rebirth, and for both of them, it felt like the first time all over again. And as the overpowering waves of her climax swept through her, she knew one thing for sure. She would do whatever it took to ensure the man beneath her lived forever.

# FIFTY-TWO

HOOG AND KATJA jumped down from the carriage and headed along Academiestraat, past the Poortersloge and into the Kraanrei leading away from the Jan Van Eyck Square.

"There's one," Hoog said, pointing at a steel manhole set into the pavement at the rear of the lodge.

Hoog bent down and levered at the edge of the cover with the crowbar he'd taken from the Audi. He gripped the edge of the heavy metal cover, heaving it clear and sliding it across the pavement. He recoiled at the stench from below. "That's revolting."

Katja sniffed the air above the hole. "Didn't they recently upgrade the sewers?"

Hoog grunted. "Yes, but the canal system isn't connected to the sewers, or it shouldn't be."

He knew from experience that there were still people who treated the canals as somewhere convenient to dump their trash under cover of darkness. There was also the occasional dead dog, cat, or worse found floating in the canals. The smell was accepted by the tourists as part of the unique character of Bruges and a way of life for the residents. The odd putrid whiff as you stepped out of an expensive restaurant on a cold winter's evening was a way of letting you know that no matter how rich you were, your nose was as poor as the next man's.

Hoog lowered himself carefully down into the hole. The metal ladder was slippery and treacherous, and he needed to concentrate.

Katja clambered down after him.

Halfway down Hoog handed her the crowbar. She used it to reach up, hook the manhole cover, and drag it back into place with a dull clang.

"Let's hope a delivery van doesn't park over that," she said.

"Don't worry, that's not the only manhole cover on our route," Hoog said, playing his flashlight on the rungs as Katja made her way down to join him. They swung their flashlights around and listened. Nothing.

Katja checked her phone. "No Bluetooth devices in range." Hoog looked at his. "Me neither."

He looked back in the direction of the Jan Van Eyck Square. There was a faint glow of light spilling in from the narrow gap between the archway and the canal. He felt sure he would have seen or heard anybody between them and the entrance. The lack of a Bluetooth hit reinforced his feelings.

"They're probably halfway down the tunnel by now."

Katja nodded, swinging her flashlight around and pointing into the gloom. "I agree, we would hear them talking if they were anywhere near. This place is like a giant echo chamber. A really smelly one. It's like every bad smell you've ever tried to get out of your nostrils has decided to have a party down here."

Hoog headed along the narrow path to one side of the canal. "That smell may be our friend."

Katja looked at him. "What makes you say that?"

"If the dogs are down here then it might help mask our smell." Katja doubted if that was the case and said so. "I admire your optimism."

"Not my dashing good looks and snake hips then?" he said with a smile.

"No. We have around six million receptors in our noses, whereas a dog has three hundred million. Also, the part of its brain that analyses smells is forty times greater than our abilities. To put that into perspective, it's around a hundred thousand times more acute."

"I love it when you talk statistics."

"Really, well here's some more. If you made the same analogy with a dog's vision, we could see for a third of a mile, and they could see three thousand miles.

Hoog looked at her. "Are you telling me we're not going to be able to hide behind a shitty smell?"

"Some dogs can detect certain odors in parts per trillion. So, what do you think?"

Hoog looked at her. "I think I picked a bad day to splash on the Paco Rabanne."

"Is that what that is?"

Before Hoog could reply there was a beep from his phone. "I've got a hit from a Bluetooth device."

There were another couple of beeps.

"I have two hits as well. What's the range of Bluetooth?" Katja asked.

"Wim said the maximum range was two hundred meters, but that was dependent on conditions." Hoog took his phone out and held it up. The sound of two more beeps echoed off the roof. "If the drone made it to them, and they picked up Wim's

message, they should be on their way out by now."

"Let's hope so," Katja said.

They headed further along the canal system. The light from the entrance behind them grew fainter until only the light from their flashlights and the occasional manhole cover above was visible. The sound of metal scraping across stone echoed down the tunnel. "Turn your flashlight off."

Hoog whispered.

Hoog pulled Katja into a rough stone recess in the wall behind them. They pushed back into the shadow and watched as five figures clad in dark clothing clambered down the steel ladder onto the canal path. Along with their black outfits, they were all heavily armed and wore night vision goggles.

Hoog realized that crouching in the shadows was not going to help them. The men only had to look around and they'd be seen. He needed a distraction, and he needed it fast. He slowly reached down and picked something up. There was a soft splash, and the leader whirled around, his gun pointed at the water, watching the ripples spread across the surface.

"It's only a rat Rudi," one of the men said with a laugh.

Rudi uncocked his gun and waved them onward. "If you see his dogs you are not to shoot unless they attack. Understood?"

The men mumbled a reply as they headed off into the darkness.

Hoog waited until the men had disappeared around the curve of the canal before speaking. "Who were they?"

Katja shook her head. "I don't know, but I think I recognized one of them from the SUV that rammed us."

Hoog gave a grim smile. "We have to stop them before they reach Chandler and the rest of them. They won't stand a chance against those guys. We need to get ahead of them."

"I agree, but how do we do that? Hoog grinned.

"That's easy."

# FIFTY-THREE

DIETER AND ROLAND paddled the dingy along the canal. They'd decided against starting up the motor given the confined space they were traveling down. They were using their headlamps and had left the last glimmer of natural light far behind them. Roxie looked up at the dank, moss-covered roof of weathered bricks above them. The gurgle of water echoed all around them. The mass spectrometer gave a soft ping.

Dieter studied the readout. "Got a partial match with your sample." He held out the device for Roxie to see. "Here, have a look."

Roxie peered at the LCD screen. "What am I looking for?"

Dieter tapped the top line of two readouts that showed a range that resembled a share price chart. "See how these two peaks are similar?"

Roxie looked at them. The peaks and valleys of the readout mimicked each other to a lesser degree. But the similarities were obvious. "So, the water quality is starting to match the sample we took from the body?"

Dieter pressed a button on the device and looked at the screen.

"Yes. If we keep taking readings, I'm hoping it will eventually match your sample. If not, then we are in the wrong canal."

"How accurate are these devices?" Roxie asked.

"They're used to detect counterfeit drinks and medicines. They can distinguish between over forty different counterfeit brands of whiskey...through sealed glass containers."

"Impressive," Roxie said.

"I heard that ten percent of food and drink is fraudulent. That's over forty billion dollars a year," Duke said.

Roxie sniffed. "Do you smell that?" She covered her nose with her hand.

Roland stopped paddling, and they drifted toward a curve in the canal ahead. They approached a black mound that seemed to flow down from the wall toward the canal in the corner. There was a beep from Dieters spectroscope.

"We have a match."

Roxie looked at the ominous black mound. "I think I could tell you that with my own device." She said tapping her nose.

The boat drifted to the edge of the canal and bumped against the side. Roland secured the boat with a weight on the path. "Okay. Be careful when you get out. Make sure to distribute your weight evenly."

"You sayin" I'm carrying too much weight?" asked Duke. Roland looked flustered for a moment.

"I'm joshing with you man. Anyways, I've fallen out of more boats than you've had Belgian beers. And I ain't falling into something that smells this bad, no siree."

Chandler played his flashlight over the dark mass in front of them. There was no doubt what they were looking at. Dead bodies. A lot of them.

"Holy crap," Duke said.

Chandler moved nearer to the mound. He looked closely at the eerily preserved bodies heaped in front of him. Like the body beneath the ice rink, they all had leathery skin and a waxy appearance.

Duke pointed his flashlight up at the roof. "Looks like they came through when the brickwork gave way."

"Are we under a church?" Duke asked.

Roland pulled a waterproof street map from his pocket and studied it. "We won't get any GPS down here, but from a rough guess I'd say we're somewhere between the Provincial Court and the Basilica of the Holy Blood."

Roxie looked over the charnel pile, "So these bodies could be from a cemetery?"

Dieter shook his head. "There aren't any cemeteries within the city."

Chandler turned to look down the canal. There was a high-pitched whirring sound. Like an angry wasp. A big one. And it was getting nearer.
"What's that?"

They turned toward the sound. Something black glided toward them. One by one, their phones started to beep as messages came in.

Roxie looked at her screen. "Someone's sending media files via Bluetooth."
Dieter squinted down the dark canal tunnel.

Roxie pointed her flashlight at the approaching object. "It's a drone. That must be the source of the files. There's no other way of contacting us down here."

The drone hovered in the distance, a red light winking in the dark.

"Oh shit." Roxie stared at the video file as it played.
Chandler and the others crowded around and watched it play on her phone. The terrifying images of the hounds and the dead rat hanging from one of their jaws reached its end, and they were left looking at Wim talking to the camera.

*"Hoog and Katja are on their way, but it might be best if you head back the way you came and whatever you do, stay on the water. We don't know where the dogs are. Also, someone tried to run Hoog and Katja off the road on their way into Bruges. Their car's pretty much a write-off. Hang in there, see you later."*

"What the hell?" Duke said.

A burst of machine gun fire filled the night.

Pieces of brickwork exploded from the roof and ricocheted around them. They heard the hard crunch of feet coming toward them.

Five men appeared out of the darkness. The drone rocketed toward them. A blaze of stroboscopic light flaring out from the machine, overloading the men's night vision goggles, while a stream of smoke jetted from the drone, further adding to the confusion as it swooped past the dazzled men and sped off. A sound bite from *Ride of the Valkyries* echoed down the tunnel as it disappeared into the darkness. Hoog looked after it. "Wim wasn't joking, was he? That drone's smart."

The leader barked a command. "Switch your flashlights off and put your hands up. Now!"

Another volley of shots hit the roof above, showering them with brick dust.

"Do what he says," Duke said. Dieter and Roland held their hands up as high as the narrow passageway allowed. They looked terrified. Rudi gestured to his men to stay back as he came nearer, his gun swinging between Duke and Roxie. He stopped opposite Duke.

"How many are you?" he asked.     "Enough," Duke said.

"Funny guy," Rudi said, slamming Duke in the belly with the butt of his gun. Duke staggered back but didn't go down. Roxie held onto Duke's arm, gave it a squeeze.

"How many?" Rudi repeated.

"There are five of us down here and more on the way. We're police officers."

Rudi smiled through tobacco-stained teeth.

"There's no way of communicating while you're down here, so if you are expecting backup it's not coming." He ratcheted his weapon.

Roxie shook her head. "I'm afraid you're a little behind the times. Nowadays we use TTE signaling."

Rudi stared blankly at her, then shrugged. "The fuck…?"

Roxie continued as if speaking to a small child. "Ultra-low frequency radio waves. They're able to penetrate hundreds of feet of rock. Or in this case a few meters of brick. I'm sorry, do you guys use feet or meters, I'm never really sure."

Rudi looked worried for a moment. Then he said. "Really, so where are your transmitters?"

Roxie looked at him. "The drone was streaming pictures of you and your men back to police HQ. I imagine you have a few minutes before they arrive. Why don't you put your guns down, take the silly goggles off, and hand yourselves in? You've obviously mistaken us for somebody else. Maybe some friends of yours that you've fallen out with. In a big way, judging by the number of toys you've brought along." Roxie stepped toward him.

"What is that anyway? A Kalashnikov? Where did you steal that from, a museum?" Rudi ground down on his anger.

"Maybe you should hear what the nice man has to say?" Duke said, gently pulling Roxie back to join them.

Something splashed in the canal alongside them. Rudi fired a volley of shots into the water.

"They're just rats, they won't bother you," Roxie said.

The men behind Rudi looked nervous. Marco came forward. His square head and deep-set eyes more aggressive looking with the sticking plaster across his nose.

"What are we going to do?" Rudi looked around. "What we came here for. Nobody's coming to save them." Rudi raised his weapon then froze, his eyes wide, staring into the dark.

His men started to back away, feverishly crossing themselves and mumbling something in their mother tongues. Roxie looked behind her. There was just enough light to make out what Rudi and his men could see all too clearly through their NVGs. Two of the blackened, leather-skinned corpses were walking toward them.Rudi opened fire, and everyone hit the ground. The two corpses kept on coming, their slick bodies peppered with holes from the impact of Rudi's bullets.

Roxie could see what Rudi and his men couldn't. Hoog and Katja using the corpses as shields.

"Flashlights!" Roxie shouted. They all fired up their flashlights and pointed them at Rudi and his men, searing their eyeballs through the NVG's. Rudi ripped his goggles off, followed by his men.

Hoog and Katja opened fire, spaced shots aimed with deadly accuracy, at the approaching men. Then there was silence. Hoog and Katja dropped the corpses onto the ground with a dull thump. Katja moved over to the fallen men on the ground and collected the guns before turning to Hoog. "Good shot. Body mass but nonlethal. Impressive." "I do my best," Hoog said.

There was a low moan from Rudi and the dull glint of steel in his hand. Duke kicked a knife from his hand, sending it skittering across the path and into the canal with a splash.

"There ya go," Duke said. Dieter threw up on the path. Roland shrugged. "I think he ate something his stomach disagreed with last night." He handed Dieter a handkerchief. The engineer nodded his thanks. "I should steer clear of seafood." Katja and Hoog circled round the injured men, cuffing them with handcuffs and zip ties.

"How did you get past the men?" Roxie asked.

"One of Hoog's bright ideas. I've swum in better quality water that's for sure. But compared to hugging a corpse that now seems like no big deal." She sniffed her sodden clothing. "I am so charging the department for new clothes."

Chandler looked at the pile of corpses. "So this is where our friend at the ice-rink came from."

"Wim downloaded a lot of recent data the documentary team recorded but didn't use. We saw the hounds down here. It was Wim's idea to use the drone to get in contact with you via Bluetooth," Katja said.

Chandler turned to Roxie. "That's another drink I owe King Harald Bluetooth." Katja looked at Roxie. "What's he talking about?" Roxie said. "It's a long and not very amusing anecdote involving how I met Chandler and a close encounter with alligators and some creepy women out in the Louisiana swamps." "Okay, something to revisit when I've caught up on my boxed set of 'The Wire.'" Katja said. Hoog smiled. "You really are on the cutting edge." Rudi groaned on the ground.

Hoog went over to him. "Don't worry, we'll have you patched up and ready for your trial in no time. Of course, sometimes the paramedics just don't have enough morphine to go around. So, what I'm wondering is, which one of you needs morphine the most. Because whoever it is, needs to start talking. What are you all doing down here, and why do you want us dead? I'm guessing some of you were responsible for the state of my car?" Hoog looked at Rudi. He saw a small tattoo of a black bear on his wrist. He looked around at the other men.

"Nobody wants to talk? Okay, we'll see if the dashcam in my car can clear up any misunderstanding. We have two counts of attempted murder to start with. And I'm guessing a search of your houses will turn up some more stuff that will add to your sentences. Am I right? The way I see it, there'll be a whole new Europe by the time you get out." He looked at Marco. The big man gave an imperceptible nod. Hoog shot him a look of acknowledgment. If he could get Marco to roll over on Rudi, then there was a chance he could play them off against each other and find out what was going on. Hoog straightened up. "Okay, let's get you out of here, and once you've been treated for your injuries, we'll have a more comfortable chat down at the station."

# FIFTY-FOUR

THEY SAT IN the catacomb incident room below the station. There was nothing they could do until Rudi and the rest of his gang were patched up and released back into police custody. It was an ideal time to compare notes and work out a strategy for    the next part of their investigation. A couple of gas heaters and some dehumidifiers kept the chill and damp at bay, and the substantial amount of coffee and waffles they'd recently demolished couldn't help but improve the situation. Roxie and Katja had set up a large oblong whiteboard between two easels at one end of the room. Various notes and printouts were fixed to    the boards. The board on the left was *Brandt Van Zwart, 1634,* while the right bore the legend *Ongoing Investigation.*

Hoog took a slug of coffee. "I think Katja and Roxie should start, and we'll pitch in as we go along."

Chandler and Duke nodded, and Ward gave a thumbs up, his mouth full of waffle.

Katja stood next to the 1634 part of the whiteboard.

"Okay, some of what we know in the cold-case side of this   investigation is conjecture, but we have enough historical details to make an educated guess."

She tapped the board on which there was a printout of Count Brandt Van Zwart's Bio and picture. "We believe that the artist, Brandt Van Zwart may have been responsible for an unknown number of murders, principally of young girls who he lured into sitting for his paintings."

She tapped copies of the six paintings from the Groeninge Museum as she spoke. "Using X- ray analysis, we have established that he was in the habit of painting them in the nude, before painting clothes onto them, after which they were subsequently murdered. Apart from this girl."

Katja tapped a printout on the board. "Cathelyne Verpoort, a young prostitute who refused to pose naked." Katja continued, "She was working in the Waterhalle the night the bodies of five girls were found in the water. The elders appeared, and she was arrested. It's highly likely the count was seeking revenge over her refusal to pose naked and had set her up."

"There are elements from that period that echo the exploits of Jack the Ripper in the late nineteenth century," Chandler said.

"Yes. Prostitutes, evisceration, and conspiracy theories galore," added Roxie.

Hoog moved nearer the white board. "We have a commonality in some parts of our case. The torso in the Dijver canal and the similarity of its ante-mortem injuries to those found on torsos recovered in Louisiana, along with evidence of exsanguination. Then there's the seventeenth-century corpse beneath the ice rink, which may be linked to the recently discovered bodies beneath the Kraanrei."

"We're waiting to hear from Kruger on the DNA and carbon dating analysis, but my gut feeling is that our second originated from there and wasn't part of any deliberate act by the people connected to the first torso," Katja said.

"We recently got word from Kruger about the first torso. He got a DNA hit from CODIS. Christian York, born in America, a few charges of petty theft, after which he moved to Paris. He dropped off the radar a few months back, but his DNA was all over a dead woman whose body was found with a broken neck in an alleyway. According to the police, it looked like a mugging that went wrong," Hoog said.

199

"Well we won't feel too bad for him then. But it's still a murder case," Katja said.

"Why do you think you were targeted by Rudi and his men?" Ward asked.

Hoog ran his fingers through his hair. Found something small and wet, which he studied with distaste, before dropping it into a metal bin under the desk. He felt like he'd never be clean again after swimming in the canal and close dancing with a corpse. "We're hoping that Marco, the one with the nose job, will help us on that score. All of them have a record of drugs involvement, and we believe that Blades was also a member of their gang."

Ward looked worried. "Do you think they were planning to murder you as retaliation for messing with their drug business?"

Hoog shrugged. "I don't know. But somebody tipped them off about our movements. They were right behind us on the motorway, and they knew where to find Chandler and his crew."

"Maybe it's not what we've done that's started this backlash…maybe it's something we haven't done yet," Roxie said.

Duke scratched his chin. "What could that be?" He looked at Chandler who was staring at the whiteboards with a glazed expression.

"Here we go. He has his Hercule Poirot expression on," Duke said. Hoog looked at Chandler. "Why doesn't he wear a Sherlock Holmes expression, Poirot's our man."

Chandler wasn't listening. He was in a world of his own. A world of connections, coincidences and possibilities all whirling around in his head. He looked at the whiteboard. "We're missing the pinwheel." Katja looked blank.

"You lost me," Duke said.

"Okay, what's a pinwheel?" Hoog asked.

Roxie stared at Chandler. She had a dim memory of what he was talking about, but couldn't put her finger on it.

Chandler smiled and started pacing. "When we were in London, I took Roxie to the trooping of the color."

Roxie nodded, it was coming back to her. A hugely colorful event, with massed bands marching in front of the queen. She remembered they'd all worn freakishly large bearskin hats. Chandler continued. "One of the key components of the parade is known as the pinwheel. It's impossible to do a ninety- degree turn with four hundred marching guards, so they perform a counterclockwise spin wheel maneuver, which is when the entire massed band pivots around its own center. It's a tradition passed down through generations. But technique apart, it all hinges on everybody following the lead of one man. The senior bass drummer, the timekeeper. He's the center of the pinwheel, the one who everybody takes their cue from."

Hoog looked around. "I don't want to be the stupid one here, but what is your point?"

Chandler picked up a pen and drew a circle between the two investigations on the board. Then drew spokes between the various names and pictures in front of him, talking as he joined each line toward the center.

"The torsos in Louisiana, the torso in the canal, the burning at the stake of Cathelyne Verpoort." He moved to the other side of the board. "The seventeenth-century body beneath the ice rink, and the others beside the canal. The dogs we saw down in the canal. Roman Blackburn and his resemblance to Count Brandt Van Zwart." He paused.

"And something that has been demonstrated to be better than surveillance…a remarkable prescience. An ability to know things were going to happen and to be in a position to take advantage of that situation. "He drew a line from the sugar plantation owner John Palmer Sturridge to the center, and then another from Jessie Livermore and Adam Blackburn to the center of the board. It now resembled a spoked wheel with a black circle in the center. He hovered his marker over the empty circle and looked around the room. "Anyone?"

201

Duke spoke first. "Marsha Brochell. She's the only one who might be able to predict our every move. Much as it pains me to acknowledge the possibility of her mumbo jumbo, the evidence is growing."

Chandler wrote 'Marsha' into the circle and stepped back.

"She's linked to everything, all eyes are on her, nobody makes a move without looking to her. Don't you see, Marsha's the timekeeper. And if she truly is immortal, she could have been controlling things for centuries. If Marsha's in Bruges, then everything that happened between the seventeenth-century, up to now, and the things that are about to happen were, are, and will be, orchestrated by her."

"If she really is psychic it would explain how she knows our every move. The future is her country," Roxie said.

Hoog rubbed his eyes. They'd been troubling him since his swim beneath the canal.

"I'm really not looking forward to writing this case up. We're going to have to dance round an awful lot of coincidences to avoid using the 'W' word."

"Which word's that?" Katja said with a knowing grin.

"Exactly," Hoog said.

"If Marsha ordered the attack on us by those men, then they must know her, and what her plan is," Duke said. His phone gave a ping. He looked at the screen. "The security company in charge of the Museum just sent me the footage from their CCTV."

Roxie opened up her laptop. "You can access it from your provider on here."

Duke leaned over and tapped his details into the browser. His account loaded and he hit the link. The footage began to play as they all gathered around. Roxie speeded it up with one eye on the timecode.

"After midnight, right?" Roxie asked.

Duke nodded. "Yes. And we're only interested in the one night."

The black and white footage flicked past. There was a flurry of movement as the workmen at the building site loaded up their trucks and left for the evening. Only a couple of cars and a white truck remained as the sun went down and the lights lit up the outside of the museum. Roxie moved it forwards.

"There." Chandler pointed at the white truck. Roxie hit play.

A man carrying a heavy black holdall was standing in front of the metal gate leading into the building site in front of the museum. He was wearing a long duster coat and opening the gate with some keys.

"I'm guessing he's not looking for his horse," Duke said.

The man opened the gate and went through, leaving it wide open behind him. Roxie paused the footage and tightened in on the back of the man's head. The top of a wetsuit was clearly visible above the collar of the duster.

"He's pretty skinny, ideal for wriggling through a drain conduit," Roxie said. "And he's wearing a wetsuit."

She hit play, and they watched as the man headed towards the small white truck. He pointed a key fob at the truck, and its lights flashed once. He slid the side door open, heaved the black holdall inside, and closed the door.

"Go back a bit," Chandler said, "as he puts the bag into the truck."

Roxie edged the footage back slowly and watched Chandler.

"There," Chandler said.

Something glinted in the dark. Roxie paused the video and zoomed in. A semi-circle of glass flared into the frame as something dangled from a tube outside the bag.

"It's a pressure gauge," Chandler said. "That's our man."

"Well, it was either that or someone on their way to an S and M club." Katja joked.

"We need to see his face," Duke said.

Roxie restarted the video. The man went around to the driver's door and climbed in. The headlights flared into the camera as he started the truck up and drove towards the open gate.

"Damn! We can't see his face," Duke cursed.

"Hold on, he's stopping," Chandler said.

The truck drove out of the gate and stopped. The man jumped down from the cab and walked back to the entrance, closing it and locking it behind him. He went back to the truck and climbed back into the cab.

"There!" Duke yelled in triumph. "Finally."

Roxie froze the picture as the man looked out of the windscreen. She tightened in on his face. A sharp-featured individual with rat like teeth. The gang leader. Rudi.

They stood looking at the freeze frame.

"Sonofabitch," Duke said, rubbing at his stomach. "I won't forget that mother."

"Why do you think he went to all the trouble to get out and lock up?" Roxie asked.

Chandler had thought about that. "Well, I'm guessing that most security systems would only check the footage if theft were reported, or discovered. By closing the gate and locking up, there wouldn't be a trace of anything that would merit anybody checking the recording."

"Smart little weasel," Duke said.

Chandler looked at the freeze frame. "Well, that's a result. We have lots of questions, and he can answer some of them. With the right incentive."

"I'll give him some incentives," Duke growled. "Some questions need answers. Why were there bodies in the overarched part of the canal, why was a torso planted opposite the police station?"

Who authorized the attack on Hoog and Katja?" Chandler said.

"We know he was responsible for planting the torso, so he has to know who killed the American, and why the torso was left the way it was."

"He knows he's going down one way or the other. If Rudi didn't kill the American he's not going to take the fall for someone else," Duke said. Hoog finished chewing a waffle.

"Now we know where the dogs were last seen, we should be able to track them down." Hoog stood up and stretched. "We'll reconvene tomorrow morning, Kruger should have more information on the bodies by then."

"Sounds like a good idea. I'll see you all tomorrow." Ward gave them a wave and headed out.

Chandler, Roxie, and Duke ambled past Hoog and Katja.

"Don't hit the clubs too hard," Hoog said to Chandler with a smile. "I think I'll skip that. See you tomorrow," Chandler said as they headed up the stone stairs leading out of the catacomb. Hoog and Katja watched them go.

"Are you going straight home?" Hoog asked.

"I don't know. I'm still a bit wired," Katja said. The silence hung there. And then she said, "I could probably force a beer down. You?"

"No force necessary. Any particular preference?"

"You choose," Katja said.

"Okay. I'll surprise you," Hoog said with a smile.

"You usually do."

They switched the lights off and headed up the stairs.

# FIFTY-FIVE

HOOG AND KATJA were on their second beer, and the tension was draining out of them. Neither of them was a habitual drinker, but back when Katja had been working in Bruges, and they were more involved with each other, they'd shared many a happy night drinking in the multitude of beer cellars, and drinking haunts that Bruges had to offer. Le Pelican was somewhere that he hadn't been with Katja before, and he had chosen the venue for various reasons. It was neutral, no memories or regrets to cloud the evening. He studied the clientele occupying the tables dotted around the rough stone floor. As a policeman, he could never stop analyzing the people in a room. After all, the world was a different place now, and what had once been a cozy environment amongst people you knew was now somewhere where anything could happen.

He took a sip of the excellent Abbot, a Hoppy House beer. Good though it was, it would have to be his last. Tomorrow was going to be a challenging day. By now news of the arrest of Rudi and his gang would have spread through the criminal underground and people would be on high alert.

"I'd forgotten how good it is to have a beer in this city." Katja's eyes gleamed in the dim light.

"Yes, it's been a while since I've had an accomplice." Hoog felt the years peeling back to a time when they'd been far less worried about the morning after, a time when they had each other's backs and could cover for each other if need be.

He caught himself reaching out to stroke her wrist like he'd done back then and managed to stop before he made contact. The investigation was complicated enough without an emotional layer on top.

He wondered how Chandler and Roxie operated as a couple. No matter how well trained you were, if there was an emotional link, it was always going to affect any split-second decisions out in the field. His thoughts were jolted back to the present by Katja's voice.

"What are your thoughts on tracking these people down?"

Hoog looked at her. It took a second to work out what she meant.

"Whoever they are," Katja added.

"I think Chandler's right. Marsha has her fingers in everything. Once we find her, I'm sure we'll be able to join the dots."

Hoog wondered if that was ever going to happen.

"If Marsha really is an über witch, how do we, mere mortals, defeat her?" Katja said. She laughed. "It's okay, I get it, you don't want to believe in witches. But I have a plan B. We burn her with a Taser. It's not a bonfire, but it's the best we've got," she paused. Hoog took a slow sip of his beer. "The human race has always needed to put people into boxes. The Christian church created prejudices against people in the witch box—women with different beliefs. Back then they would have burnt meteorologists for claiming they could predict the weather."

"That's for sure. Witchcraft's been around in one form or another for forty thousand years. They were people who believed that nature was more powerful than human beings and should be treated with respect," Katja said.

Hoog looked at his beer. "I think most people would have a hard time disagreeing with that, considering what's been going on with the world over the last few years."

"Well, über witch or not. If she's behind this, she's going down."

207

# FIFTY-SIX

THE BONIFACIUS WAS a beautiful sixteenth-century guesthouse overlooking the Groenerei Canal. It was a triumphant mix of the old and new and was luxuriously appointed, lacking nothing in the way of modern comforts. Chandler had chosen it for the view and its age. As predicted, Roxie had been blown away by its antiquity when she first arrived. Chandler had only felt slightly guilty at the cost, but given the fact that it was cutting into Roxie's UK holiday to help with the investigation, he was able to sleep easy.

Only that night he wasn't.

Roxie looked over at him as he tossed and turned beneath the luxurious sheets and soft, down-filled pillows. "Trouble sleeping?" she asked. Chandler cricked his neck and sat up. "Yes. And I don't know why. I'm knackered after today. I should have gone out like a light. Perhaps we should have gone for that drink with Hoog."

"I think it will do them good to have some time alone together," Roxie said.

Chandler looked over at her. "Why do you say that?"

Roxie got up on one elbow. "You do know they used to be an item."

Chandler shook his head. "No, how long ago?"

"A couple of years. Katja said things got a bit messy, and she got a transfer to Antwerp."

208

"And now she's back," Chandler said.

Roxie settled a pillow behind her head. "Yes. She had some problems relating to the general public, so her boss in Antwerp thought it was a good idea to have Hoog take her under his wing. Lend her a bit of his Zen-like abilities to deal with irritating situations."

"And I'm guessing her boss over in Antwerp didn't realize they'd been in a relationship."

"No. And she didn't think to mention it."

Chandler grunted. "Right. So, you think she still carries a torch for him?"

"Yes, she told me about their relationship and why they split up, but I sense they still have a connection. Speaking of which…" she said with a mischievous look in her eye. "Is there any way I might be able to connect with you to ease your tension?"

Chandler looked at her. With the moonlight spilling through the window behind her and that angelic smile playing across her face he didn't think she needed to ask the question.

"Maybe a little later when my head's a bit clearer."

Roxie looked at him, her female intuition coming into play.

"You still getting those dreams?"

Chandler adjusted the pillow, so they were both sitting at the same level. "Yes. But they're not even dreams. It's more of a sensation, like part of me is somewhere else."

"I don't want to bring up quantum entanglement at this late hour, but you do have messed up DNA, which could be alive and kicking out there in the wild."

"I know, I'm sure it'll pass," Chandler said.

"Blackburn's dead and resting in pieces within the alligators of Spirit's Swamp so you shouldn't have any remaining connectivity," Roxie said, reaching across and smoothing a piece of wayward hair from his forehead. His skin was cold and clammy. Chandler shook his head, trying to clear it of the dislocation he was feeling.

He'd felt fine while he was in London, but since arriving in Bruges, something had changed. "I suppose you're right. It's just my overactive imagination."

Roxie looked across at the old black-and-white postcard of the Simon and Garfunkel *Sound of Silence* album cover propped up against the bedside lamp. "You know they advise people not to have any electronic devices in the bedroom at night as it interferes with sleeping patterns."

Chandler looked at her. "We don't have any. I always switch my phone off, and you know I don't get on with computers."

Roxie pointed to the postcard.

Chandler's father, a policeman himself, had set puzzles for his son throughout his life. She felt sure that part of Chandler's skill at solving crimes during his time in the Met had come from those earlier challenges. When they'd cleared out his father's London flat, Chandler found the postcard. He'd carried it around ever since. On the back of the postcard, there was a list of random words:

**Whistle, Honest, Hope, Surprise, Business, Coup, Receipt, Bite, Finger.**

The meaning of which Chandler had failed to solve. It obviously meant a lot to Chandler on an emotional level, so she had to tread carefully. "Maybe seeing that every night before you go to sleep is overstimulating your brain? I know it drives you mad when you can't work out the crossword clues. And you have been carrying it around for months." Chandler smiled. She was right of course. It was the last thing he looked at before turning in, other than her. Perhaps he was hoping that his subconscious mind would work out the significance of the random words while he slept.

Chandler picked up the postcard, reached over Roxie, and placed the card against her lamp. "Maybe it's better off over here."

"Thanks for that," Roxie said with a smile.

"My dad used to say that's a bit of a Toyah, whenever he couldn't solve a problem. And that's what the postcard is to me, and has been for some time."

Roxie wrinkled her nose, which only served to make her cuter than she already was. "Toyah? Is this another of your obscure references to something?"

"Yes, back in the day one of his favorite artists was Toyah, she had a big hit with a song called 'It's a Mystery' in the eighties."

"Well, it's going to have to stay a Toyah for now, okay?" Roxie said.

Chandler pulled her closer to him, felt her cool, moist lips caressing his, and the hardness of her breasts pressing against him. He pulled away for a second. "I fell in love with you the moment I saw you in Louisiana. How about you?"

Roxie cocked her head. "When you started talking about the history of Victorian London, you were so passionate." She kissed him again. "And you know how much I love old things."

"Hey, less of the old. There's still life in this old dog." Chandler flipped over on top of her, felt her body envelop him, and her legs wrap around his back. As she began to move beneath him, his head began to clear.

# FIFTY-SEVEN

HOOG LOOKED MOURNFULLY at his empty glass. Most of the tourists had departed the cellar, and only die-hard locals and a group of noisy Australians huddled in a corner were left. Hoog looked across at Katja. Her eyes were fixed on something at the far end of the room.

"Somebody, you know?" Hoog asked. Katja dragged her eyes back to him.

"I don't know. But there's a guy at the end of the room that is the spitting image of..." Katja shook her head. "No, it's late, I've had a few beers. I'm just suffering from a bad case of predictive imagery." She waited for Hoog to reply. And when he did, it wasn't what she was expecting.

"I did have an alternative motive for bringing you here," Hoog said. "What do you mean?" Katja said, suspiciously.

"The guy at the end of the bar. It's exactly who you think it is."

"What?" Katja asked. "The psycho Count. From the painting, the artist back in the seventeenth-century, Brandt Van Zwart." Hoog smiled. "Not quite, but he is related to him."

Katja shook her head. "This is Belgium, there are probably millions of people that look like that. It doesn't help that everyone, including dogs, have a beard or a mustache these days." Hoog got up.

"What are you doing?" Katja asked.

But Hoog was already headed toward the other end of the bar. He reached the table where a tall man with dark hair, a neatly trimmed mustache, and a short beard was sitting with a couple of other men.

"Hi, sorry to trouble you, but my friend's a bit of an art geek, and she thought she recognized you from somewhere. You're an artist, right?"

The man stared at Hoog and pushed his hair back off his forehead.

Hoog caught the flash of a small tattoo of a black bear on his wrist. "No, one of my ancestors was an artist a long time ago, he was a Count, and a bit of a dog apparently. Maybe she saw one of his portraits. He was no Breughel, that is for sure."

Hoog shrugged. "No problem, sorry to disturb."

Hoog turned and headed back to where Katja was sitting.

"Well?" Katja asked.

Hoog sat down. "He seems to know about the count and his ancestry, but that doesn't really tell us anything other than he's part of the same bloodline."

"It's a start," Katja said.

A server materialized next to their table and placed two glasses of champagne in front of them. "Compliments of the house."

Hoog thanked her. "Who exactly is the house?"

"The owner, Brandt Van Zwart, you were just talking to him."

"Ah, yes of course. How long has he been running the place?"

The server thought for a moment. "Well, I've only been here for a few months, but I think it's been in his family forever. He's only recently returned from abroad. Apparently, he comes and goes."

"Thank you," Hoog said, and raised his glass in the direction of the far end of the room. He saw a hand wave in return. The server smiled and moved off.

213

Hoog took a sip of the champagne and stared over at the table where Brandt Van Zwart sat.

"Something bothering you?" Katja asked.

"He had a tattoo on his wrist, a black bear."

Katja shrugged. "That's no big deal, it's more or less the emblem of Bruges, it implies a connection to the earth and great wisdom."

"I know, and I may be jumping to conclusions here, but Rudi had the same tattoo," Hoog said.

"Probably just a coincidence, and I know how you like them." She thought for a moment. "Having said that, Erika found some manuscripts that detailed an alternative to the White Bear Society. A secret faction within the normal society, but hardcore. They used blackmail, threats, and extortion to get themselves a good trade deal by threatening the merchants. People were killed, ships set on fire. There were suspicions that Count Brandt Van Zwart was working both ends of the deal and selling protection to the same people he was targeting." Katja said.

"Brandt Van Zwart may not have inherited his ancestor's artistic abilities, but perhaps he's continued the criminal side of things. I seem to remember he was in a bit of trouble a few years back," Hoog said.

He drained his glass and stood up. "I think we need to take a look into his background and see what he's been up to for the last year or so.

Katja finished her drink and followed him out through the door and into the cold night air. They headed through the arched passageway of Eekhoutpoort and into Eekhoustraat.

"Where are you staying?" Hoog asked.

"In a friend's flat in Woolestraat, it's a little quirky. But it's free."

"Okay. You want me to walk you home?"

"You think I need protecting?"

He knew she was teasing him. "Normally no. But there's been two attempts on our lives this week, so I'm thinking, why risk them getting third time lucky."

Katja thought for a moment. "Can't do any harm."

214

They set off down Eekhoustraat, past the teashop where they'd eaten earlier in the week, then turned left alongside the Dijver canal. The large Christmas globes in the trees reflected off the canal's surface, and the Belfort's octagonal upper tower was visible in the distance. Hoog had been told it was one of the most photographed spots in Bruges, and he could believe it. No matter how many times he saw the view, it still took his breath away. Tonight, it was spectacular. There was a full moon, and the water was a mirror of stillness. The reflections of the ancient buildings alongside the canal stretched down into the watery depths, giving it an eerie feel.

"Do you want to take a selfie?" Katja asked. A humorous smile on her face.

Hoog shook his head. "I think I already have a few of those, but it is unusually atmospheric tonight."

"Why do you think that is?" Katja knew Hoog could always be relied on to give the most complicated of answers to a simple question. She didn't have long to wait.

"Snell's law of refraction. The relationship between the angles of incidence and refraction, when light passes between two different isotropic media, such as air and water."

"Ah, that explains it. I was wondering." Hoog looked at her.

"You have no idea what I'm talking about do you?"

"I vaguely remember something about critical angles, water air boundaries, and 48.6 degrees. "Hoog laughed. "Not bad. A full moon and no wind or boats certainly help though." He looked back toward the bridge. "I thought we were headed to Wollestraat?"

"We are. I just fancied a walk along the canal. I could do with a bit more of a walk to clear my head. That champagne was the good stuff." Hoog shrugged. "Why not."

215

They walked beside the Dijver canal along the cobbled walkway and through the canopy of trees. They turned right down Nieuwstraat and then into Oude Burg, past Martin's Brugge into Hallestraat, alongside the glowing windows of the tourist shops ringing the base of the Belfort and into the Market Square. They stood looking out across the square at the new Sissy Boy clothes shop that occupied the old post office. Even a UNESCO world heritage site wasn't immune from change, Hoog mused. It was after ten, and the market was quieter now. With the horse and carriage tours no longer running, and the stalls and ice rink closed, it was populated by groups of friends heading out to beer cellars and back to their hotels. An old lady slowly walked her dog. It lingered around the rubbish bins, on the lookout for the detritus of dropped chips, prawns, and waffles.

The ice rink was deserted, and the stalls were all closed up. A few stragglers, muffled against the chill, dragged their suitcases behind them as they headed for the hotels in the side streets leading off from the square. "Okay, well, thank you for the police escort," Katja said.

"Not so fast. It's only a few minutes away. I'll see you to the door." Katja shook her head. She wasn't going to shake him off. "Okay, c'mon then." They headed around the Belfort and down Wollestraat. Katja stopped.

"What is it?" Hoog asked.

"It's nothing. It's just, I told Roxie about us." It came out in a rush.

"Us?" Hogg said.

"Just that we'd been an item a few years back. I think she'd worked it out anyway." Hoog smiled. "No worries. As you say, she worked it out. Women know things like that." They continued walking. Katja halted outside the entrance to the Torture Museum. "You're staying here?" Hoog laughed.

The Torture Museum was a popular attraction for thousands of tourists and had initially been a prison back in the fourteenth century when it was known as Oude Steen, or Old Stone. There was a set of wooden stocks in front of the entrance, and a glass door leading to flats above the museum on the right.

"Very tasteful," Hoog said.

Katja laughed. "I did say it was quirky."

She fished out her keys and immediately dropped them.

They both bent down to pick them up and banged heads.

"Ouch," Katja said, and burst into laughter. "I'm so wasted." Hoog rubbed his head and smiled. "I've always said that." He bent slowly down and scooped up the keys. "Let me."

He opened the door and handed her the keys. "You okay…" He pointed at the narrow flight of stairs that led up to the top floor.

She switched the light on and bent down to kiss him on the cheek. He turned his head and kissed her on the mouth. The kiss went on.

Katja pulled back. "Fuck…are you sure?" Hoog shrugged. "I am if you are."

She turned and headed up the stairs.

He followed up behind. "You always did look good, even on your way out."

She flicked a look over her shoulder. "That line never grows old."

Hoog winced. "I wish I could say the same about me. These stairs are a killer."

He reached the top of the stairs and paused as Katja flicked on the lights in the sitting room. The apartment was a typical Bruges house that had been converted and now occupied two floors of the original building. A precarious wrought iron and wood staircase spiraled up to the second bedroom.

Katja opened a door that led off to another bedroom from the sitting room. A large double bed occupied the center of the room, and there was a small window through which the Belfort was visible. She walked back into the sitting room, opened a cupboard, and pulled out a bottle of wine.

"Nightcap?" she asked.

He went over and took the bottle from her, placed it on the table and led her through into the bedroom. "I'd rather be awake for this." She shrugged off her jacket, kicked off her shoes, and began to unbuckle his belt. "Always the gentleman."

His hands slid under her blouse, and she melted into him. He drank in the smell of her hair, scooped her up, and placed her on the bed as he stepped clear of his trousers and pulled off his shirt.

She stroked his chest as he began to kiss her. Whatever his exercise routine had been during the two years she'd been away, she thought, it had certainly paid off.

# FIFTY-EIGHT

KRUGER RANG THEM the next morning. He had something
to show them and was being his usual mysterious self about
his
findings. With the number of corpses now standing at fifteen,
Kruger's normal workspace couldn't accommodate them. So,
he
had been allocated premises out of the city, in an old abandoned
airfield in Ursel.

The airfield was designated as a reserve NATO airbase but
was rarely used except by the local flying club. One of the old
hangars had been converted into a temperature-controlled area,
and a row of portable ref refrigeration units filled the space with
a low humming sound. Chandler, Duke, and Roxie had arrived
first.

Chandler stood looking across the floor. He rubbed his hands
together and wished he'd invested in a more substantial parka and
a heavy sweater. He'd seen a winter clothing stall as they'd passed
the market on their way to the hotel that could have easily
fulfilled his needs. But he'd put off the decision for no good
reason, apart from his British habit of frugality. He saw Roxie
smiling at him.

When they'd left the hotel for a wander around the Market Square, she'd bought a long, down-filled
parka with a mock fur hood, which she was thrilled with. Needless to say, she looked stunning in it.

"You okay, Mr. frugal?"

"I will be once I get something hot inside me." He said with a grin.

The hangar was fitted with twenty or more metal folding tables instead of the regular mortuary equipment, and Chandler was reminded of the only time he had been to an aircraft investigation site. But in this case, the bodies were all grotesquely preserved.

"This takes me back," Duke said, looking around.

"Yes. It's a bit like the old refrigerated warehouse in Louisiana," Roxie said. "I'm missing Chilly already."
She wondered how Duke's cheery deputy was faring back in Louisiana. She felt a pang of nostalgia and wondered if, or when, she would be returning to America.

Kruger came toward them carrying an iPad in his hand. From the dark rings around his eyes, it looked like he'd been up all night. "Hoog and Katja are on the way. They were held up while they checked on the condition of the drug dealers who attacked you yesterday. Apparently, they'll be released into custody this afternoon." He picked up a thermos and poured himself a mug of strong black coffee. He took a swig. "I thought we'd wait until they turn up. Don't want to have to repeat everything. I told them to bring hot coffee and more pastries. I've consumed half my body weight in caffeine and pastries while I've been working out here. I think it's the cold. But I should be used to that."

"What did you make of the scene at Sint-Jansplein?" Roxie asked.

"Pretty gruesome. Looks like there was a landslip beneath the property. The original house dates back to the seventeenth century but was demolished and built over at some point before being turned into the Sleepy Owl restaurant."

Kruger flicked through some pictures on his iPad as he held it up for them to see. A heap of bodies forming a slope spilling out over collapsed brickwork, and a gaping hole in the floor of the building above.

"What about the manager of the restaurant. Does he know anything about the previous owners?" Chandler asked.

Kruger shook his head. "No. They had no idea what was under the house. All they knew was the house basement had been tanked to prevent rising damp."

"Any idea how the bodies could have ended up there?" Chandler asked.

"Not so far. It could be that the original house was built on a mass burial site that nobody knew existed." Kruger said.
Brakes screeched outside as a car slid to a halt.

Kruger smiled. "I didn't think Hoog could resist an empty runway."

The hangar door swung open, and Hoog and Katja walked in. Hoog looked as tired as Kruger.

Chandler wondered if anyone on the team had got a good night's sleep.

"Sorry we're late. But I come bearing gifts." Hoog placed a large plastic bag on an empty table and unloaded some cups of coffee before pulling out a selection of pastries wrapped in wax paper. Once the team had sampled Hoog's offerings, Kruger began. "Okay. All in all, we have fifteen bodies, and that includes the two that suffered multiple gunshot wounds." He shot a meaningful look at Hoog. The detective raised his hands. "It was them or us. Kruger shook his head and continued. "So, my first job was to establish that we were dealing with a cold case here, rather than a contemporary crime."

"Isn't that obvious from the way they look? Or would a recent victim look the same in these conditions?" Chandler asked.

"Difficult to say. I haven't had to investigate anything like this during my time as coroner." Duke swallowed a mouthful of pastry.

"I don't think any of us has seen anything like this before, although the torsos we found out in Spirit's Swamp wouldn't have won any beauty contests."

Kruger took a sip of his coffee. "I'm sure." He put his coffee down. "First off, some of these bodies date back to the seventeenth-century."

The team looked at each other.

Katja spoke first. "At this rate, we're going to have to open up a new museum."

Kruger looked at his iPad, studying his notes. "I started to put them in chronological order to see if there was some kind of a pattern to their time of death."

Katja looked over at the bodies. Their black skin gleaming in the harsh fluorescent overheads. "And was there?"

Kruger looked down at the screen. "The dates ranged from the seventeenth century up to the nineteenth century. It's probably best if I walk you round the bodies while I explain."

"That sounds like the world's worst guided tour," Roxie said. "That's for sure," Hoog said, taking a slug of his coffee. They worked their way past the steel tables and their grim contents, while Kruger laid out his findings. "Starting with this one, he's pretty much the same age as the corpse you found under the ice rink, maybe a few years older." He moved to the next one.

"This one is older still, separated by a decade or so. This next victim is only a few years older, so a retrograde step."

Roxie flicked him a look. "What do you mean?"

Kruger said. "Let me have my fun before the big reveal. Believe me. It'll be worth it. Okay. Next one did well, he lived twenty years longer."

He moved down the line of waxy figures, reeling off their varying life spans, before reaching the last of the bodies.

Chandler stared down at the body of the man on the table in front of him. Trying to work out where this was all leading. He was used to orchestrating the Poirot moment, and it was beginning to frustrate him that he couldn't make the intuitive jump with the facts that Kruger had laid out for him. "So, what's going on here?" he eventually asked.

222

Kruger turned the iPad round to show them what was on the screen. The display showed the blocky skyline of a DNA readout. "I ran a check through CODIS using mitochondrial DNA, looking for any familial hits, along with carbon dating to establish their ages and time of death."

"Go on," Chandler said.

"I got two matching results. One from the traces of DNA you found in the troughs beneath the house in Louisiana, which Roxie matched to the late Governor Roman Blackburn, and another from Brandt Van Zwart, the owner of Le Pelican beer cellar."

"That's seriously weird, even for this case. And why was Brandt Van Zwart even in the database?" Roxie asked.

"He was arrested a few years back after a drug dealer was shot and killed outside his beer cellar. At the time, it was suspected that Brandt Van Zwart was running drugs from the premises, and the victim was the head of a rival gang trying to muscle in."

"So what happened?" Roxie said.

"The case was dropped, because of insufficient evidence," Kruger said. Roxie nodded. "Which is why his DNA was in the database.

But if he was innocent, it should have been deleted."

"Yes. But we got lucky, somebody messed up," Kruger said. "So, the DNA of these corpses match Blackburn, and Brandt Van Zwart's DNA?" Roxie said. "How's that possible? Brandt Van Zwart's bloodline stretches back to the seventeenth-century, and we only know about the Blackburn's from the nineteenth-century onwards."

"You're saying we got a whole heap of dead Blackburns and one live Brandt Van Zwart, all sharing the same DNA. How does that even begin to make sense?" Duke said.

Roxie looked around the hanger at the bodies on the steel tables.

"Another weird thing, why aren't there any women?"

Kruger looked around at the bodies. "This investigation has a knack of throwing up more questions than answers."

"What about our Tollund man lookalike, the sorcerer?" Chandler asked.

"It's possible he may have been buried first, and the others buried alongside him as a matter of convenience," Kruger said. "His DNA doesn't match anybody. But if we go with your friend professor Vries' story, the only DNA he might be linked to would be the slave girl he transferred his powers to…"

"Marja Nalangu, or if we believe in transmigration, Marsha Brochell," Katja said.

Kruger said. "Yes, but we don't have DNA from either of them in the database."

"We found some souvenirs from Bruges in the old Rafetti house out in the swamp. Mugs and pictures of the Belfort made from lace. If Blackburn's ancestors are somehow linked to Brandt Van Zwart, that might explain how they got there," Chandler said.

Kruger turned to Chandler. "I imagine even psychopaths feel the need to go on holiday sometimes." He paused, then, "The evidence that was found beneath the house out in the swamp…flatworms, artificial meat, multiple blood samples of chimeric DNA. It all points toward some sort of fixation with longevity, maybe even a search for immortality. Planarian flatworms can surpass the Hayflick limit.…"

"Talk me through that last bit…the worm and the Hayflick thing," Katja said.

Kruger held up an apologetic hand. "Sorry, the Hayflick limit is the point at which cells no longer divide because of damage to the DNA, like shortened telomeres; telomeres are a part of our chromosomes that gradually get shorter with age. The planarian flatworm doesn't have that problem. Cut one of them in half, and a few weeks later it regenerates into two separate entities. One scientist called it immortality under the edge of a knife."

"So, you think Blackburn and the women out in the swamp were aiming for immortality. Using their victims' blood in their experiments?" Katja asked.

224

"We think so," Chandler said. His mind flashing back to the undeveloped fetuses they'd found floating in glass tanks beneath the Rafetti house. "But the secret of whether or not they were successful died with Governor Roman Blackburn. Unless Marsha Brochell turns up to enlighten us."

"So how did Roman Blackburn end up with the same DNA as Brandt Van Zwart, a man whose bloodline stretches back to the seventeenth century?" Katja asked.

There was a pause while Kruger waited for someone to speak. Roxie broke the silence. "This may be a bit off the wall, but given the physical similarities between Roman and Brant Van Zwart, could it be possible that we're not looking at two people with the same DNA, but rather one person with two identities."

"That would make perfect sense if it weren't for the fact that Blackburn's a long time dead," Duke said.

"Could it be some sort of genetic manipulation?" Katja asked.

Kruger shrugged, "I don't know much about the intricacies of gene manipulation, but it is possible for cells to mutate for various reasons. Giving birth, radiation, illness, interbreeding," Kruger said. "Anything that weakens or disrupts the genetic process can have an effect. But that's a disruption, it doesn't explain how two different bloodlines could wind up having the same DNA."

"So, it's a Toyah," Roxie said.

"A what?" Kruger asked.

"Never mind," Roxie said, I'll tell you later. Let's hear what else you know about these bodies." Kruger looked at their expectant faces. "I would say that what we found this week is the result of something that began back in the seventeenth century. Something that caused the death of all these men. The torsos you found out in Louisiana were victims of Blackburn's experiments and died from loss of blood. These victims," he gestured to the macabre display of bodies around the hangar, "they died because someone gave them the wrong type of blood." It took them another coffee and a waffle to absorb the significance of Kruger's findings. And now they were drilling down to the detail.

"I did a check on a few more things, but one thing stood out," Kruger said. Chandler couldn't help himself. "Blood groups?"

Kruger gave him a nod. "Well done my friend. As you know, antigens within the body determine blood type, such as A or B. Those with Rhesus antigens are type D, then we have Rh- positive and Rh-negative, and of course the most common one, type O. Around thirty-six blood groups have been classified, and from them, over 340 blood group antigens have been found." Kruger paused. And then continued. "Fathers and sons can have different blood groups, so I was surprised to discover that all of these men shared the same blood group. AB negative."

"The rarest," Chandler said. "Though of course, they wouldn't have known that, as blood groups weren't classified until the eighteenth century."

"Precisely," Kruger said. "Which is both the reason and the cause of their deaths." There was a silence as they digested what Kruger had said.

"Wow," Roxie said. "I'm glad I hung in for the lecture. Do you want to hit us with the punchline?"

Kruger held his iPad up with the DNA readouts. "Because they were all AB negative when they were given a blood transfusion, it was usually one of the more common blood groups. A, B, AB, or O. This would have produced an acute hemolytic transfusion reaction, a condition when the immune system sends out a mass of signals that rip the blood cells apart, triggering an uncontrollable clotting cascade, causing blood to clot in the veins and resulting in death."

Chandler looked over at the waxy face of the nearest corpse. He gave an involuntary shiver, and it wasn't just because of the temperature in the hangar. "If the results of the experiments they were conducting back in the seventeenth century and beyond were passed down by the survivors, that could explain how Blackburn ended up in the swamp continuing his experiments with the Rafetti sisters. Kruger went on. "Fathers and sons can have different blood groups, so I was surprised to discover that all of these men shared the same blood group. AB negative."

226

"The rarest," Chandler said. "Though of course, they wouldn't have known that, as blood groups weren't classified until the eighteenth century."

"Precisely," Kruger said. "Which is both the reason and the cause of their deaths." There was a silence as they digested what Kruger had said.

"Wow," Roxie said. "I'm glad I hung in for the lecture. Do you want to hit us with the punchline?"

Kruger held his iPad up with the DNA readouts. "Because they were all AB negative when they were given a blood transfusion, it was usually one of the more common blood groups. A, B, AB, or O. This would have produced an acute hemolytic transfusion reaction, a condition when the immune system sends out a mass of signals that rip the blood cells apart, triggering an uncontrollable clotting cascade, causing blood to clot in the veins and resulting in death."

Chandler nodded. It all made some kind of sense. "So they were trying to live longer by getting transfusions, but because they didn't know anything about blood groups it was killing them."

"That's both weird and kind of sad at the same time. Do you think they ever succeeded? Found someone with the right blood group?" asked Roxie. Kruger shrugged. "Maybe sometimes they did, and they lived a bit longer. But then the next time it was the wrong blood group, and they died. That would explain the differences in ages."

"So, all of these men died because they were searching for immortality?" Katja asked.

"It could be. But if Marsha is the über witch, she's already immortal," Roxie said. Hoog's phone rang, and he flicked a look at the screen. "It's the chief." He tapped the screen.

"Chief?" He listened. "Okay, I'll pass that on. No, the victims are all hundreds of years old, so it's definitely an archaeological case. Okay, we'll be back at the station within the hour." He ended the call. "The chief wants us back to interrogate Rudi and the other gang members."

He looked at Katja. "He suggested that you and Roxie might like to check the site back at Sint-Jansplein, in case we missed something, now that we have more details." "Looks like the chief's cutting us a bit of slack," Roxie said. "We'd better get back there before he changes his mind. You know what he's like," Katja said.

Hoog reached into his pocket and pulled out a key fob which he dangled in front of Katja. She made a grab for it, and he whipped it away. Then handed it back to her with a grin. "Be careful, we're only allowed a new car every month, cutbacks. I'll catch up later and fill you in on the results of the interrogation," Hoog said.

They thanked Kruger and made their way out of the chill of the hangar and into the weak winter sunshine outside. Hoog stood next to Chandler and Duke while Katja and Roxie took Hoog's new patrol car and headed back to Bruges. Erika had left Katja a voicemail about some further information she'd uncovered in the Groeninge archives. She'd sounded pretty excited, and Katja wanted to head over there first and find out why.

Katja and Roxie walked down the stone stairway that led to the archive depositary beneath the Groeninge Museum. Erika was hunched over a large table strewn with what looked like charcoal sketches.

Erika hailed them with a brief wave of her hand. "Glad you could tear yourself away from your chilly guests."

Katja smiled at Erika's sense of humor and moved over to the table. "What's got you so excited?" Katja asked her.

"The email you sent me with the information on the bodies you found by the canal, along with their timelines. When I read their cause of death, something rang a bell."

Erika carefully held up a charcoal sketch in one gloved hand. It was a picture showing the inside of old Sint-janshospitaal. But more importantly, it showed a man with a series of quills, forming a tube with silver joints giving blood to someone that resembled Brandt Van Zwart in a hospital bed. To one side stood a dark -skinned nurse in a nun's habit overseeing the procedure.

"Oh my God!" Katja exclaimed. "When was this drawn?"

Erika turned the sketch over and showed her the faded inscription on the back.

*'1750 Marja Nalangu, Sint-Janshospitaal.'*

Katja read it with mounting excitement. "According to Aart, Marja Nalangu was the Negress slave that witnessed the hanging of the sorcerer Frederick Olfert, who, before he died, granted her his powers." Erika nodded. "Apparently, but for her to end up as Marsha Brochell required quite a journey it turns out."

Katja thought back to her time with Aart as they'd walked through the Museum. "Yes, Aart gave me some context to the witch hunts back in 1634, and one possible explanation as to how Marja could have transitioned from an über witch in the seventeenth century, to Marsha Brochell, a Vodoun queen of New Orleans in the nineteenth century. And it was terrifying."

Erika put a hand on Katja's shoulder.

"Yes, Aart he told me about the self-immolation story. It's a part of witchcraft lore I'd never heard of." She looked at the picture. "The hospital dates back to the twelfth century, and it was last used in 1977."

Katja pointed to the crude quill and silver tube. "A procedure like this wasn't in any way safe until at least the start of the twentieth century."

"Yes. As was demonstrated quite clearly by the number of victims Kruger has just examined," Erika said.

Roxie walked around the table, glancing at the various manuscripts and sketches, talking it through, putting it all together.

"If Marja was our über witch back in 1634, channeling the souls of witches burnt at the stake into those that persecuted them to fuel the growth of the IGNIS order, and Count Brandt Van Zwart was the first to be possessed. They have a special bond...more than lovers." Roxie paused, and Katja picked up the story.

"But there's a problem. As the years go by, Count Brandt Van Zwart gets older. But Marja..."

Erika smiled. "Marja's immortal."

Roxie stared at the sketch. "She was trying to keep him alive forever, using her power combined with the blood transfusions and the experiments out at Spirit's Swamp."

"When you were investigating what the Bloods were up to in the old house out in the swamp, didn't something come up about Anglamakerska?" Katja asked.

"Babymakers...yes. It was originally some kind of foster home for unwanted children. Back in those days they had a bad reputation as it was more profitable if the babies died in their care rather than paying for the cost of bringing them up. We thought Blackburn and the Rafetti sisters were using stem cell blood from umbilical's as part of their experiments. But there was no real evidence to prove anything like that. The torsos turning up in the swamps from the victims they used as human blood pumps were the only real proof against the Rafetti sisters and Blackburn," Roxie said.

Katja picked up a photocopy of the sketch. "This is in the seventeenth-century, nothing was known about blood types, transfusions or stem cells back then."

Erika took the picture gently from her. "Blackburn and Marsha were in business, together weren't they?"

"Yes. Advising businesses on decisions about their future. A kind of corporate astrology I suppose," Roxie said.

Katja looked around the room before speaking. "Maybe back in the seventeenth-century she could see into the future, but without enough detail for her to understand what she was looking at?" Erika thought for a moment. "So she could see the blood transfusions but not understand the level of complexity involved." Katja nodded, her mind working overtime. "So all those bodies...they're just failed experiments. Attempts to keep Brandt Van Zwart alive?"

Roxie shook her head. "But that doesn't make sense. Where did the other bodies come from?" Then she got it. "She's not only losing the man she's in love with, but she's also losing a son..."

"Are we talking *Oedipus Rex* here?" Katja asked.

Erika sat down. "You're right. It's the only thing that makes any sense. Incest is still legal in some countries today. Back then no one would have known. She gave birth to sons who each went on to become the father to the next in line." Roxie said. "So, she kept on going while simultaneously carrying out experiments on her partners and sons. That's messed up."

Katja shrugged. "That's an understatement. But as an über witch with the power to channel the souls of witches burnt at the stake into other human beings, a little bit of incest down through the centuries is no big deal."

"Yes. After all, it's no weirder than our belief in the immaculate conception," Erika said.

Roxie frowned. "So this could still be going on?"

"Yes. After all, as I said, it's not even illegal in some countries. And back when she was doing it, there was no way it would ever come to light," explained Erika.

"But why was she doing all this?" Roxie asked.

Erika gave a sad smile. "For the strongest reason in the world. Love. The thought of living forever and watching your partners die over and over again was unbearable."

"So the only way she could stop that happening was to make her partner, husband, son, whatever, immortal," Katja said.

"Exactly. And she would stop at nothing to achieve it."

Katja thought about this. "Maybe she's already achieved her plan. If Brandt Van Zwart and Roman Blackburn were one and the same, he could travel the world adopting a different identity in each country..."

Erika looked up from her notes. "Yes. Blackburn in America and England, Brandt Van Zwart in Bruges and other cities. One person, two passports."

"But Blackburn died in the swamp," Roxie said.

Erika looked at her. "A Blackburn died...but what if there's more than one?"

# FIFTY-NINE

RUDI SAT HUNCHED over in the corner of his cell. The hospital had patched him up and given him a shot of painkiller. Compared to the drugs already in his system, it was minimal, and after the medics had carried out a tox screen, they'd upped his pain killers to compensate. The pain had receded to a dull ache. The bullet had glanced a rib and gone through some flesh, it stung, but he'd had worse. He chewed a fingernail and considered his options. He and his men had failed catastrophically.

Their instructions had been clear. Take the three visitors out, and make it look like retaliation by the drug network behind Blades. They were meant to have been on their own and an easy target. It had all gone to plan until Hoog, and his bitch, had shown up. After his recent disagreement with Marco, he wouldn't be surprised if the Walloon didn't try and save his own skin by cutting a deal with the feds. Even with witness protection and a new identity Rudi doubted he'd survive very long with Marsha on his trail. Her visits to Bruges were always punctuated by savage acts of violence against anyone who stepped out of line. And this extended to the local law enforcement officials as well.

Pieter's previous boss, De Klerk, had discovered that to his cost. He'd been burnt to death, along with his wife and children, in his own home after gas had been poured through the mail slot and the doors nailed shut. Since then, the drug business had run smoothly beneath the radar, benefitting both parties. Until now.

The arrival of the English and American visitors had coincided with an officer setting Blades up followed by a successful arrest. Rudi felt sure that Pieters would have to explain how this happened on his watch. His role in planting the American's torso in the canal was part of some bigger plan that Marsha had not made him aware of, though he felt sure it was linked to whatever had happened in Louisiana.

She'd returned to Bruges without Brandt Van Zwart, and no one had dared ask about him. And then one day there he was. His old self, tho' "old" was a relative term, as he was looking younger and healthier than ever. Rudi wondered what it was that he took. Whatever drugs they were, he needed to get hold of some. Life hadn't been easy recently, and his habits were starting to catch up on him. Zwart was still as unpredictable as ever, something the Walloon found out the hard way. The body beneath the ice rink and the pile of ancient corpses discovered under the Sleepy Owl restaurant were something else entirely.

Again, it wasn't something he was going to ask her about. She gave instructions, not answers. He'd seen more than enough to know what was permitted and what was not. He just did what he was told and took the money. He looked around the confines of his cell and felt uneasy.
The power structure of the Bruges criminal underworld was changing. Both within his realm, and Marsha's. Something wasn't right. Not only were they facing attacks on their day-to-day business, but Marsha and Brandt Van Zwart's past were also under investigation. How this was a threat to their business, he didn't know. If Marsha was starting to lose her grip on things, perhaps it was time to bail. If all her energies were taken up with protecting herself and Brandt Van Zwart, maybe it was time to turn things around.

With money and connections, there were plenty of countries in Europe he could disappear to. He was snapped out of his thoughts by the sound of rattling keys, and the door to his cell swung open. A swarthy officer nodded at him. "Looks like someone wants a chat with you, Rudi."

He got up slowly from his bed, pain lancing through him as he straightened up. The thought of warm sun and wine in a foreign city suddenly seemed very attractive indeed.

# SIXTY

HOOG SAT ALONGSIDE Chandler and Duke in the small interview room. Rudi sat opposite them. His ribs were tightly bandaged, and he moved with obvious pain.

Rudi looked at the three men. "What is this? Good cop, bad cop, and Englishman?"

"This is just a little chat in case we can come to some sort of agreement, a sort of beneficial exchange of information if you like. After all, we don't really have to try hard to charge you with anything. In fact, our main problem is we have too much on you. It would be nice if we could break it down into bite-sized chunks, and spread it around amongst your friends. Or…maybe we charge the head of the snake," Hoog said.

Rudi glowered at him.

"I'm not suggesting you're a snake, but if there were one involved, you'd be nearer the tail than the person we're after." Rudi said nothing.

Hoog said, "All we need from you, is a name, an address, you know the deal."

Duke leaned nearer to Rudi. "Okay, you're looking at several counts of attempted murder, GBH, illegal possession of firearms, drugs, and I'm sure we'll find more evidence when we search your premises."

Hoog produced some printouts and laid them out like a card shark. Starting with a picture of Rudi c losing the gate and climbing into the van outside the museum.

"This is the night you placed a human torso in the canal opposite the police station." Hoog placed two close-ups of the pressure gauge and Rudi's wetsuit visible beneath his long duster coat.

"Quite a clear picture, I think you'll agree. But as it turns out, we don't really need these pictures, because of course, your DNA is all over our vertically challenged friend. Now what's interesting is that there are no other DNA traces on the torso. So, I guess that means you could be looking at first-degree murder?"

That got Rudi's attention.

"I didn't kill anyone," Rudi said.

"Not for want of trying," Duke said.

Hoog laid out two more pictures, the SUV ramming Hoog and Katja's car, and a drone shot of the armed gang in the canal tunnel.

"I've no doubt some of your friends would be more than happy to corroborate your involvement at these recent crime scenes."

"I want my lawyer," Rudi said.

"You have every right to a lawyer, but of course we haven't charged you with anything yet, so you should look at this as a window of opportunity," Hoog said.

"A window that could slam shut on your fingers real fast," Duke snarled. "Okay, let's start again," Hoog said.

"You tell us the names behind the drug network you're involved in, who your suppliers are, the pushers on the street, and who's pulling the strings. You tell us who ordered the attack on our car and the attempted murders at the canal. And most importantly, you tell us who's responsible for the torso victim, and why you planted it opposite the police station." "What's in it for me?" Rudi asked.

"We'll put you up in witness protection until we've shut down your operation. And then provide you with a new identity," Hoog said. "Unless you help us with information, you're looking at a charge of first-degree murder, which on top of all the other charges will probably mean a life sentence," Chandler said.

Rudi sat silent for a moment. "What about Marco, you going to offer him the same deal?"

"Marco will have to make his own choices," Hoog said.

Rudi shifted in his chair. Tried to ease the dull ache pulsing through his ribs as the drugs began to wear off.

"If you give me protection, he'll know I've ratted him out."

Hoog shrugged. "He's not going to be around to bother you for a long time. And when he does get released, he won't be able to find you anyway."

Chandler looked at his watch. He hadn't heard from Roxie since she'd driven off with Katja. The interrogation was going too slowly. Rudi needed to be aware of the consequences if he didn't make a deal with them.

"Do you know what the worst thing we could do to you right now?" Chandler asked.

Rudi shook his head. "Well you want to charge me with first-degree murder and supplying drugs, so, no I don't know what could be worse."

"We could let you go," Chandler said.

It didn't take Rudi to work that one out. "No. I've got rights," he bleated. Duke smiled. The only way you would get anywhere with people like Rudi was to either scare them or outsmart them. "Of course, you have rights, as we have the right to release you without charge pending inquiries."

A look of fear flitted over Rudi's face as he worked out the odds against his survival once released.

"How do I know you'll protect me?" Rudi said. Hoog looked at his texts. Nothing from Katja. "You have my word," He said. Rudi sighed. "You may be able to protect me from Rudi, but no way on earth will you be able to protect me from her."

Chandler looked up from the notes he'd been making and swapped a look with Hoog. "Who are you talking about?"

Rudi shook his head. "No names. All you need to know is it was her that ordered us to take you out. It felt like there was some bad blood between you. She wanted to make it look like it was a revenge attack for arresting Blades."

Hoog thought back to the recent interrogation with the terrified skater. He wasn't saying anything about anybody. Whoever was running the operation had a tight grip on the gang members working for them.

"You need to tell us where she is. If she's as powerful as you say, then no one is safe until she's locked up," Chandler said. Again, he saw fear in Rudi's eyes. "I can't tell you that." "What if we made it look like Marco gave us the information, that way we could keep you out of it."

Rudi shook his head. "She'd know. She always does." Chandler gave Hoog a look. They weren't getting anywhere, and he was becoming increasingly worried about Roxie. He slid another picture across the table towards Rudi. "Is this her?"

Rudi didn't have to say anything. The expression on his face was one of sheer terror. Chandler picked up the picture of Marsha Brochell and studied it. Whatever information they were hoping to get, it wasn't going to come from Rudi.

# SIXTY-ONE

THE SICK MAN lay on a small wooden cot inside one of the cubicles within the hospital. Trailing from his arm was a series of quills connected by joints made from silver. One end led from his arm, while the other was attached to Hans Groot, a young artist, sitting next to the bed. Blood pulsed between the two, its flow darkening the walls of the quills.

A nurse approached him. Her dark skin glowed beneath the veiled wimple of her habit. Hans knew her as Marja. She had saved his life after he was wounded during the battle of Lauffeldt two years earlier. She'd brought him back to the hospital, bandaged up his wounds, and nursed him through the fever that had followed. Though he believed she possessed special powers when it came to healing, he kept those thoughts to himself. They lived in dangerous times.

"Are you well?" she asked.

"A little tired," Hans replied. "Do you think I am helping?"

Marja looked at Groot. He should have been a good supply of blood. He had already lived a long and healthy life. She had felt the vitality within him when she had used her powers to bring him back to health. The recipient of his blood was from the lineage of Count Brandt Van Zwart.

The color of his skin, once a dark yellow with livid purple spots, was starting to change color, and the spots were fading. The blood exchange was helping.

"Yes. He is getting better." Marja said.

She reached over and gently stroked the man's arm. He moaned softly. She removed the quill and held it up high to stop the blood leaking out. She took the other end from Groot, before pressing a white cloth to the small wound in his arm. Groot rubbed at the skin on his arm to ease the ache. The staff at the hospital had worked hard to save his life, and he owed them and Marja a great debt.

"Do you think you can save him?" Hans asked.

Marja looked down at the young man lying on the bed as his eyes flickered open, and he smiled up at her. She turned to Groot and held his arm.

"I believe you have helped him, and now I must help you."

Hans shook his head. "That will not be necessary, you already gave me my life at Lauffeldt."

"You will live to a great age…long enough for the whole of Europe to recognize your skills as an artist," Marja said as she squeezed his arm. He felt a jolt, as if a powerful force flowed through him.

A myriad of images swirled through his mind, saturating his thoughts with their powerful colors. They kept coming until he could hardly keep track of their many facets. A myriad of different subjects and compositions swirling around him. And as they faded, he found himself looking into Marja's eyes as if in a trance. She released his arm, and he felt his strength return.

"You must go now," Marja said. "You have much work to do before it is your time."

He looked at her before speaking, seeing a deep sadness in her eyes. "Thank you. I will begin my works anew for the hospital and all those who work in here. And the work that I do will be a gift."

He stood up, nodded to her, and walked across the ward and out into the night.

# SIXTY-TWO

**Present Day**

MARSHA SAT WITH Brandt Van Zwart, looking out across the canal. The sunlight sparkled off the slow-moving water sliding past below their window. Brandt Van Zwart was playing with his beard. Running his fingers nervously through the dark tufts of hair. Marsha poured a glass of wine and handed it to him.

"The man that spoke to you is Detective Jochum Van De Hoog. Like before, when you were Roman Blackburn in Louisiana, they are investigating in parallel with the past to try and track us down in the present. They have no idea what is in store for them." He took a sip of his wine. Brandt Van Zwart was starting to become his fully formed self. The sisters had done good work out in the swamp. It was unfortunate that the burial ground of his ancestors had been breached by the rising level of the canals and the cold weather. The expansion and contraction of the ancient stonework beneath the restaurant had caused it to rupture. The police investigations would cease once they realized the age of the bodies. Pieters had explained to her that the arrest of Blades was an accident. But she was going to have to show him that there were consequences. Marsha had reminded Pieters of his wife and daughters. And he'd broken down on the phone, promising to redress the situation any way he could. He'd listened while she explained what he was going to do, and his voice had betrayed the fear he felt. But he had no choice. He'd called Katja and Roxie at the airfield and given them instructions. He knew he had started a chain of events that would haunt him for the rest of his life. But it wasn't his life he was concerned with.

# SIXTY-THREE

KATJA AND ROXIE left Erika at the Groeninge Museum and drove toward the Sleepy Owl.

"Why do you think Pieters has had a change of heart?" Roxie asked.

Katja looked over at her. She'd been wondering the same thing. "No idea. He's been a bit strange for weeks now. I gave up trying to understand men a long time ago." Roxie laughed. "You and me both."

Katja flicked her a look. "So, do you believe it?"

Roxie shrugged. "What? That Marsha's an über witch, who's been controlling things since the seventeenth century?"

"Yes," Katja said.

Roxie cocked her head on one side. "Maybe. But if we accept that, then we also have to believe in her power."

Katja hit the car's horn as a student on a bicycle cut across in front of her. "Idiot!"

Roxie nodded, then continued. "With what we already know about her from our investigation in Louisiana, Erika's findings on IGNIS, and De Vries' historical knowledge of witches, I'm starting to become a believer."

Katja turned off Vlamingstraat and into Kraanplein heading toward Sint Janstraat, her mind joining the dots as she maneuvered through the bustling streets. "Marja Nalangu, a young Maasai servant girl, is possessed by the soul of Frederick Olfert, a sorcerer hanged in 1630."

Roxie picked up the narrative, "Marja doesn't realize the full scope of her powers until 1634 when Cathelyne Verpoort is burned as a witch, and Marja channels Cathelyne's soul into the body of the artist, and possible serial killer, Count Brandt Van Zwart…"

"An all-round creep who set her up as a witch because she turned down his demands to pose naked…" Katja said.

"Exactly. He then becomes the first member of IGNIS, a kind of witch-based suffragette order that spread across Europe," Roxie said.

"Count Brandt Van Zwart was also the start of a dynasty that led to Tumblety and the ensuing Blackburn bloodline orchestrated by Marsha Brochell. Our über witch," Katya continued. "That's the bit I struggled to understand," Roxie said. "De Vries explained it to me, and Erika filled in the sordid details." Katja paused as an old lady made her way slowly across a crosswalk. "Marja used incest and experimentation to try and gain immortality for her partners…by the time she had become Marsha Brochell and Blackburn became part of your investigation, she was getting near to success." Roxie said. "It was how Marja Nalangu became Marsha Brochell, part of a bloodline stretching back to the vodoun queen Maria Laveau that blew me away."

"Yes, that made my skin crawl. She experimented with blood transfusions for centuries in Bruges to try and gain immortality for her partners and failed. But then, with her ability to curate the souls and minds of her past lovers, she heads to New Orleans and transmigrates into Marsha Brochell, whose great grandmother was the vodoun queen Leatrice Brochell…" Katja said.

"Transmigrates. That's a word Chandler's gonna' love wrapping his tongue around," Roxie said, shaking her head. "And to achieve this transmigration she used self-immolation." Roxie gave an involuntary shudder.

Katja shrugged. "Apparently she felt no pain."

"So now she's in the nineteenth-century, and starts influencing the rich and powerful with her ability to see future events. Like sugar baron, John Palmer Sturridge, and stockbroker, Jessie Livermore. Working her way through the well-heeled while our Ripper suspect and the Blackburn's keep her company," Roxie said.

"All the time carrying on with her experiments and the search for immortality." Katja slowed the car as they headed into Sint-Jansplein.

The area had been cordoned off while the police investigation was carried out, and a few scraps of police tape still lay on the cobbles. She climbed out of the car and joined Roxie, who was already looking around.

"Is it always this quiet?" Roxie asked.

Katja locked the car with the key fob. "Nope. I'm guessing the police cordon frightened people off."

They walked toward the entrance to the restaurant where a bored police officer was standing outside.

Katja showed her pass. "Okay if we go in? We're just checking a few things."

"Be my guest, it's pretty creepy down there."

Roxie smiled at the young officer. "So, you've been down there?" The officer nodded. "Yes. And I'm in no hurry to go again," he paused, looked at Roxie. "Er, unless you want me to come with you."

"Thanks for the offer, but we'll be fine," Roxie said.

The officer looked relieved and disappointed at the same time. "Okay. There's an access ladder in the garden around the back." Roxie nodded, and they walked along the side of the house until they came to an untidy garden at the back.

Part of the garden near the house had fallen away, and they could see a dark hole cordoned off with metal fencing beside the house. They made their way carefully through a wooden gate and into the garden. Scaffolding had been erected and support brackets installed to prevent any further slippage beneath the building. A steel ladder disappeared down into the hole, and there were danger signs around the scene, and warnings about the wearing of hard hats.

"Do we have helmets?" Katja asked.

"No, I'll take the risk. If there were anything planning on falling, it would have happened by now," Roxie said.

"Good point."

Katja went over to the hole where the ladder was and carefully stepped onto it. She looked around the overgrown garden and at the view stretching out over the city. She could make out the Poortersloge in the distance and the statue in Jan Van Eyck Square, with the canal glimmering below it. Roxie came over and looked down the hole.

"Want me to go first?" she asked. "No, I'm fine." Katja said. She climbed down the ladder and found herself standing in a tunnel that stretched into the darkness beside the canal in both directions. She flicked her flashlight on and held the ladder while Roxie clambered down to join her. She sniffed at the air.

"Jeez, that is skanky."

"Skanky?" Katja said'

"Sorry, slang for nasty. I don't have to ask what the smell is."

"No, you don't. We've already seen where it comes from," Katja said. She shone her flashlight around. The slope of bricks and earth was no longer strewn with corpses, only the fluttering crime scene tape stretching across the canal path.

"What's that?" Roxie pointed her flashlight down the canal at a darker shadow on the wall.

They walked along the path and came to an archway set into the wall. "Must have been the entrance to an old cellar," Katja said.

Roxie ran her fingers over the hinges and the lock. They came away black with oil. "This has been recently oiled."

Katja reached into a pocket. Pulled out two small lock picks, and started to work on the lock.

Roxie watched, impressed. "Cool...how long did it take you to learn that?"

Katja twisted the picks. There was a click. "I was a bored teenager. Hung out with some squatters for a while."

"What a badass. I bet you were popular."

Katja pushed at the door. "Not with everyone." Rust flaked down from the door jamb as it swung open. They found themselves in a rough-hewn passageway leading from left to right. They headed back the way they'd come, parallel to the canal path. The passageway ended in a pile of rubble.

"This must have led to the cellar under the restaurant before it collapsed," Katja said. "Where from?" Roxie asked.

Katja looked back the way they'd come. "Let's see."

They walked back down and past the door. The darkness stretched ahead of them.

"Why would this have been built?" Roxie asked. "I have no idea. Maybe it leads to a nunnery."

Roxie looked at her. "You're going to have to explain that one."

"Okay, back in 1498 there was a nunnery near the Reie River, while on the other side there was an Augustine monastery. A young monk fell in love with a nun, Hortence Dupont."

"Ah, daughter of the millionaire gunpowder manufacturer, one of the richest families in America...smart monk." Roxie quipped.

"Not quite. Apparently, he discovered a tunnel that connected the two buildings, and used it to visit her."

Roxie shook her head. "What could possibly go wrong?"

"Exactly," Katja said. "When she tried to run away, he stabbed her and buried the body. Their ghosts now wander the buildings. Some nights, she appears as a snowy white figure. On others, he appears with a grim face. Both ghosts disappear at midnight."

"Cute story," Roxie said.

247

"Yes. The Augustijnenbrug near the tunnel is still there, though the monastery is long gone."

Up ahead a darker patch showed up in the beams of their flashlight. Another door.

"Here we go." Katja looked at the heavy wooden door in the light from their flashlights. She pointed hers at the ground. "Look at this." Katja crouched down and stared at something in the mud. Paw prints.

"Maybe we should get some backup?" Roxie said.

"Sounds like a plan." They turned to go.

A bone-chilling sound echoed down the passageway. Roxie knew immediately what it was. The last time she'd heard it was in the middle of Spirit's Swamp back in Louisiana. It was the howl of a Dogo Argentino, and it was coming their way.

"Get the door open. Now!" Roxie yelled.

Katja fumbled with the picks, dropping one. It landed in the mud. She snatched it up and hurriedly cleaned the dirt off before sliding two picks into the lock. The howling stopped. But that didn't matter, because now the sound of heavy breathing was close enough to hear. There was a click, and Katja shouldered the door open. They stumbled through slamming the door behind them.

Within seconds, the dog was scratching at the door and whining. Katja shined her flashlight around the room they found themselves in. It was an ancient, cluttered cellar that stretched away into the gloom on either side of them. Two large dog bowls half full of water sat on the floor, and the remains of a ham bone glinted next to them.

"Someone must let them in," Roxie said. She looked back at the door as the dog scratched at the wood. She wondered if the animal recognized her smell, and then mentally slapped herself. Of course, it did. Its three hundred million nose receptors could probably have smelled her a hundred miles away.

"Are you okay?" Katja whispered.

"We need to get out of here before someone comes to let it in." "If there are two of them, and one's outside…" Katja left it hanging.

"Shit!" Roxie said.

"C'mon."

Katja headed toward a steep set of stone steps leading up on the far side of the cellar. There were piles of old furniture and what looked like an old butcher's block standing on four legs with two drawers below. On the wall behind it were racks containing rusted surgical instruments, saws, and serrated knives. Katja looked at them.

"Are those what I think they are?"

Roxie nodded. "All the trappings of a regular seventeenth- century serial killer. Let's get out of this place, it's totally creeping me out."

They headed up the steps and found themselves in a large but old-fashioned kitchen. There was a musty smell, and the air tasted stale. Roxie looked around. "My realtor would claim this had a ton of original features."

Katja wiped her hand across the wooden work surfaces. Her hand came away covered in a damp film of dirt. "Which in plain English means no one has updated this kitchen in decades…if ever."

They walked through the kitchen and entered a hallway. At the far end, stairs led up to another floor. A series of dingy paintings of Venetian landscapes, brooding canals and men in Gondolas lined the walls. Katja looked at one of them. Touched some crude initials at the bottom. "*B.V.Z.*" Roxie stopped next to her.

"Do you think this is one of his houses?"

"I think the dogs clinch it for me. I say we check upstairs and then leave through the front door. No way am I going back down to the canal," Katja said, as she slowly climbed the stairs. "I'm with you on that," Roxie said, following behind.

At the top of the stairs was a small landing and a sitting room with arched windows looking out toward Jan Van Eyck Square and the canal. Katja fished her phone out and took a picture of the windows.

"See something?" Roxie asked.

"I don't know, but these windows," Katja walked over to the glass and ran her fingers over it. "I think this is Venetian glass. They were pretty much the only people making them back then."

Roxie looked at the windows. "Are you saying someone had these windows brought over by boat all the way from Venice?"

"Yes, that's weird, isn't it? The other windows in the house aren't as old. These windows and the view reminded me of the paintings we looked at in the Groeninge Museum with Erika."

"The ones painted by Brandt Van Zwart?" Roxie asked.

"Yes. I'll send a picture to Erika and get her to compare them with the oil paintings."

Roxie looked through the window and out across the city. "It should be easy enough to track down the owner of the house."

"Yes, I'll get that sorted when we get back to the station." Katja looked over. "Did you hear that?"

"What?" Roxie asked.

"I thought I heard something." Katja looked toward the door that led out to the landing.

"All old houses creak. Especially ones sitting over a canal." Katja walked out onto the landing. Listening.

Roxie joined her.

They both held their breath. There was only the sound of the city and the distant tinkle of the Belfort's carillon.

Roxie walked over to a closed door on the opposite side of the landing and tried the handle. It was locked.

"Let's see what's behind this and then get out of here. It's making my skin crawl," Roxie said.

Katja produced her picks and set to work. There was a dull click, and the door opened. She reached around and turned on the light switch. A naked bulb hung from the ceiling casting a dim yellow light over the contents of the room. It looked like it was used as a study. It held some bookcases, a small desk, and a single bed against one wall. Some old toolboxes lay in a heap on the floor, next to which was a bundle of rope.

Katja went over to the rope and looked at it. "This is the same kind of rope that was used to tie the torso to the beer pipe stantion in the canal." Katja took a picture of the rope. "We'll get a search warrant and come back. Kruger can analyze it."

There was a noise from behind a door at the end of the room. Katja gave Roxie a look and went to open the door. She was turning the handle when the door burst open, slamming her backward into Roxie, knocking them both to the floor.

Roxie barely had to time to register a pale face in a rough gray hoodie before she was pinned down and felt the sharp prick of a syringe in her neck.

The last thing Katja saw was Roxie's terrified face, and then blackness swept over her.

# SIXTY-FOUR

HER HEAD FELT like it was going to explode. The pain was indescribable. It was as if someone was using a sledgehammer inside her skull. The forty-seven bells of the rotating carillon drum filled the night with a cacophony of sound and moments later the massive bell began to toll the hour. It was deafening. Katja counted eight strikes. She'd been unconscious for over three hours. Her eyelids felt like sheets of sandpaper as she struggled to open them. She heard a groan next to her. It was Roxie.

Katja looked around. They were roped to what looked like a pile of wood kindling at the top of the Belfort. Her ears were still ringing from the bells, and the inside of her head buzzed. The last time she'd felt like that was when someone had fired a shotgun at her during a dawn drugs raid.

Roxie turned to look at Katja. Her voice came out as a croak. "What the hell happened?"

Katja tried to move, but the ropes cut into her wrists. She looked down at her feet. Her ankles had been zip tied together. The last thing she remembered was two men bursting out of the room in the study and injecting them with some kind of sedative.

"Someone drugged us." Katja said. She craned her neck to look behind. The pair of them were roped to the bottom of the flagpole.

252

Stacks of tinder had been piled around it, and she could see some kind of metal canister behind the pile. There was an acrid smell. Some sort of fuel, or an accelerant, of some kind. She could just make out the LED numbers of a display on the ground behind them. The numbers were counting down from sixty minutes. That wasn't so bad, she thought to herself. They just needed to get help, and quickly. Then she saw the devices on the wall in front of her. A newly fitted security camera, and another device that made a soft whirring noise from the spinning vane that was part of it.

Roxie groaned again as she tried to free her hands.

"Shit!

That hurts," she said.

"That's just your circulation coming back," Katja said. "We need to get out of here. There's some sort of timer set to go off in sixty minutes."

Katja looked up at the camera. "That camera is new. We have to assume whoever carried us up here fitted it to see us."

Roxie nodded at the spinning vane. "So, whoever kidnapped us probably fitted the anemometer as well."

Roxie nodded grimly.

"If it's linked to some kind of triggering device…" Katja thought about it. "That would rule out any attempt to reach us by helicopter because of the downdraft."

They said nothing for a moment.

"They'll realize we're missing by now. They'll find our car…" Katja said.

"They'll waste time looking for us in the canal tunnels. Shit!" Roxie struggled against her bonds.

"I'd keep still. We don't know how many trips they've set up here. There could be sensors on the stairs below to prevent anybody coming up that way, and if a trip on the anemometer prevents any rescue by helicopter…what does that leave?" Katja asked.

Roxie shrugged. "I don't know, but if we were being ransomed someone would have been told where we were by now. Wouldn't they?"

Katja tested the bonds on her arms and legs. They were solid.

"Why bother going to all this trouble when they could have just thrown us in a room and called in with their demands?"

"Shit!" Roxie said, struggling against the ropes that held her. "Careful, we don't know what they've set up to stop us escaping," Katja said.

Katja looked down at the kindling that surrounded them. She remembered the words of the coachmen that had driven her and Hoog to Academiestraat, telling them about how the Belfort was burnt down in 1280, then again after a lightning strike in 1493, and again in 1741...and his final prophetic words, *some people never learn*. Was that what this was about? Was someone teaching them a lesson? She turned to Roxie.

"Do you think it's her?" Roxie looked at her. "Who?"

"The über witch, Marsha. Burning us alive so she can make us part of her cartel of reborn witches."

Roxie looked down at the ropes binding her, the stacked firewood and the camera lens staring down at them. Her shoulders slumped. "Oh my God. That's why we're here."

"The torso. It wasn't planted to stick a finger up at the police or mess with the tourist industry, it was bait...a means of getting you, Chandler and Duke involved in the investigation over here. We were meant to think it was linked to the original case or a copycat killer."

"But what about Duke and Chandler...?" Roxie said. "Aren't they in danger?"

"Maybe she has something planned for them as well." Katja swiveled around and strained to look at the LED display. There were forty-five minutes left.

"If they come to save us, they could become victims as well. The only way we can stop that happening is by getting out of here ourselves."

"But what about the sensors?" Roxie asked.

Katja slumped back against the firewood. "You may be right. I'd
be guessing whatever I did. I just thought that all the sensors are
to prevent people from rescuing us, not that anybody knows we're
here." Roxie looked at her. She had a point, maybe Marsha
hadn't thought that they could free themselves.

"She's covered the stairs and approaches from the air…but
freeing ourselves? Maybe there is a way. If only we can think of
it."

"What about the camera?" Roxie asked.

Katja looked up at it. "You're right. They may even have
sound. If they see us doing anything that threatens their plan,
they may trigger the fire earlier." She leaned over to speak into
Roxie's ear. "If we think of anything, we should talk about it
during the chimes. No way will they hear us above the
bells."

"Okay. But to be honest, with our hands and feet tied like
this I'm damn short of ideas."

Katja leaned over to her again. "We have Hoog, Duke, and
Chandler, put them together, and you have a pretty formidable
team, and they also have Wim and Ward. Between them,
they'll come up with something, but they need to know we're
up here. Even if we scream, they'll be nobody to hear us until
the Belfort opens tomorrow morning, by which time we'll just
be a pile of ashes."

"I don't suppose there's any chance of rain?"

Katja shook her head. "We had a lot of rain in November; I'm
not sure we can rely on that to save us. Besides, I'm guessing that
smell is an accelerant. It would take a monsoon to put out the fire
once it started."

"I'm guessing the tower is too high for a fire hose to reach?"
Roxie asked.

"Yes. The highest a ladder would reach is just over thirty
meters, and the tower is eighty meters high. The hose would get
us another twelve meters, still only halfway to giving us a chance
of soaking this bonfire."

255

"There's got to be another way," Roxie said.

But as the wind started to pick up and the vane on the anemometer spun ever faster, she wondered if they had enough time to think of it

# SIXTY-FIVE

THEY SAT IN the interview room after Rudi had been taken back to his cell. Hoog got up and paced the room.
"If the woman behind the attack on us is Marsha Brochell, then we have to assume she's our killer, and that she ordered Rudi to place the torso in the canal."

"Yes, she used it to make it look like a copycat killer, or something connected to the Louisiana case so you would be brought into the investigation," Hoog said.
Hoog looked at his phone, then back to Chandler.

"Have you heard anything from Roxie?"
Chandler shook his head. "Nothing."

"It's not like Katja to be out of contact." He rechecked his phone. Nothing. "Who else knows where they are?" Hoog asked. Duke and Chandler looked at each other before Duke spoke. "Only us and Pieters, your chief. The order came through him." Hoog stopped his pacing. He felt a chill run through him.

"So they're at the scene by themselves." Chandler looked to Hoog. Roxie and Katja were more than capable of looking after themselves in normal situations, but nothing about this case was normal. Especially when it involved Marsha Brochell.

"We should get over there. Now."
Hoog's phone pinged with an incoming message. It was from the station and was marked URGENT. He hit the link, and a video began to stream. The color drained from his face as he watched. "Jesus! It's Katja and Roxie. They've been kidnapped!"

257

# SIXTY-SIX

IT HADN'T TAKEN long for Marsha to carry out her plan. The firewood was taken up in canvas sacks and placed next to the flagpole at the top of the Belfort tower. A phone call to the UNESCO liaison office in Brussels was all it took to get permission to fit a camera as part of a supposed wildlife study around the ancient structure. And while the technician was up there, it was an easy job for him to link the anemometer to the detonator for the fuel accelerant. Once the wiring was completed, it was a simple enough task to stack the firewood over the fuel container. A separate motion sensor at the base of the stairway would go live when the Belfort closed for the evening.

Once the two women were in place, it would be impossible to reach them by the stairs without triggering the detonator with its two-minute countdown. Nowhere near enough time for anybody to reach the top of the building in time to prevent the inevitable inferno. Any attempt to reach the women from the air would also set off the detonator when the anemometer readout reached over one hundred miles an hour, easily achieved by the downdraft from a helicopter. Marsha smiled to herself. They would soon discover that there were consequences for threatening a dynasty she had been protecting for centuries. But their deaths wouldn't be a simple act of revenge on her part. Their dying in the ancient way would enable her to further expand her influence, and to finally achieve her ultimate aim.

# SIXTY-SEVEN

HOOG WAS STILL reeling from the horror of the situation that faced him. Both Chandler and Duke had also received the link to the video stream along with the police stations at Coiseaukaai and Kartuizerinnenstraat. The link was delivered from an anonymous IP cloaked with some heavy-duty encryption, and so far, was proving impossible to trace. Once they realized what was happening, the department had declared a maximum-security alert. The area around the Belfort was cordoned off, and a mobile command unit was soon on site.

Hoog stared at the live stream from the camera at the top of the Belfort. He was seated in the mobile command unit, and his insides were churning as he stared at the live video feed on the screen in front of him. He could see the stacks of kindling wood piled around the foot of the flag pole, and Roxie and Katja sitting against it. Their arms were zip locked together and their legs pinioned by heavy ropes. Behind the kindling, Hoog saw a small canister, probably the accelerant for the fire, and some wires snaking away to sensors of some kind. But the most frightening thing in the picture was the red LED countdown winking in the dark. Twenty-nine minutes and counting.

A police cordon had been set up around the Belfort, and a lot of disgruntled tourists were bombarding the officers outside for information. There was no way they were getting any, and the press had also been told that in no uncertain terms. A complete press blackout was essential to prevent anything being released that might cause the people behind the kidnapping from setting off the incendiary device prematurely.

Chandler and Duke stood behind Hoog staring at the screen.

"What do we do? Those bastards seem to have thought of everything," Chandler asked.

From what they'd learned by interrogating Rudi, Marco and the other members of the gang, it seemed highly likely that Marsha and members of her criminal network were behind the kidnapping. Whether it was revenge or something else, they didn't know. It was now completely dark, and officers were stationed around the base of the tower.

"What about the drone?" Duke asked. "Maybe Wim could use it to remove the device and drop it in the canal."

Hoog looked at him. "That's a good idea, but would it trigger a detonator linked to the anemometer?"

Chandler paced, desperately thinking. If the pressure was set for the downdraft of a normal helicopter, it shouldn't be tripped by a small drone. "It can't be that sensitive, or it would be triggered by any large gust of wind."

"Yes, and whoever they are, they want to be in control of our suffering." Hoog pulled his phone out of his pocket and dialed. "Wim, we have a situation. How soon could you rig up a drone with some kind of lifting hook and get it to the top of the Belfort?" He listened. "Okay. Get it in the air and get down here as quick as you can."

He turned to Duke and Chandler. "He says it's going to take around fifteen minutes to get it in position, and he's not sure if it will be strong enough to lift the canister until he actually tries. He's also going to equip it with a knife that he can drop near them. They might be able to cut themselves free." Hoog chewed his lip.

"Okay, good idea."

His officers had discovered a motion sensor at the foot of the stairs leading up to the roof of the Belfort. A stationary LED was frozen at two minutes.

"Usain Bolt couldn't get up those stairs in less than two minutes," Chandler said as he stared up at the Belfort.

"We have less than half an hour before it self-ignites." Hoog looked at the video feed, racking his brain for an answer.

Chandler suddenly clapped his hands together. "What about airborne firefighters? They could get a helicopter alongside the Belfort and do a water dump onto the roof. Once the firewood was doused, the crew could rappel down and free them."

Hoog turned to an officer standing next to the entrance. "Get on to HQ and get a helicopter over here with firefighting equipment onboard."

"Yes sir."

The officer unclipped his radio handset and immediately requested a connection with the control center. "We need immediate assistance from any helicopter capable of being equipped with a water drop or fire-retardant system, over." He listened to the feed coming into his earpiece. "Understood, be advised the site is on the top of the Belfort, with possible incendiary devices linked to various trips. On no account is the helicopter to pass over the site, it has to approach from the side. Over." There was more feedback in his ear, and then he clipped his handheld mic onto his uniform and turned to Hoog. "They have a medical helicopter on site at Sint-Janshospitaal. The fire services are headed over there to equip it with a 500-liter heli-bucket. They estimate they'll be alongside the Belfort within 20 minutes."

"Godverdomme!" Hoog swore in Dutch. The margin of safety was way too small. They had twenty-five minutes to save Roxie and Katja.

# SIXTY-EIGHT

THE STARTER MOTOR whined as the rotors on the Explorer 900 helicopter began to turn. Hélène Hecke, or Peachy, as she was known because of her red cheeks and radiant smile, threw herself into the copilot's seat with well-practiced ease. Jan Christus, the pilot, finished up his preflight checks and flicked her a smile. They'd known each other for a while, and her skills with the firefighting equipment were second to none.

"Welcome aboard, Peachy," he said, pitching his voice above the growing crescendo of noise above him as the blades began to bite. She shot him a smile. "Glad to be here. It's been a while." She adjusted her safety harness and the noise-canceling headset as she went through her own equipment checks. They were equipped with a water bucket and a fire-retardant foam jet onboard, and it was essential everything was locked down and in position for immediate deployment. Though the helicopter was mainly used for common medical emergencies, it was an essential aircraft for other forms of emergency. If there were a fire in the heart of Bruges trying to get a normal fire engine through the narrow-cobbled streets packed with tourists and horse-drawn carriages would be a logistical nightmare. A fire in the closely packed medieval houses could turn into a conflagration that could destroy the entire city. To prevent this, and because of the recent tragedy at Notre Dame, the government had equipped some of the Explorer helicopters with firefighting equipment enabling a blaze to be tackled within minutes of the machine being airborne.

Peachy looked across to Jan as he completed his checks. The rotor blades thudded as he engaged the controls, and the helicopter rolled forward across the hospital roof.

"What's this all about anyway?" she asked.

Jan increased the throttle, and they were soon airborne and sweeping over the grounds of the hospital heading for Bruges. Once he was happy with everything, Jan replied, "I got a call from Detective Hoog. A visiting civilian and his partner were kidnapped this afternoon. Some nutcase has strapped them to a pile of firewood attached to an incendiary device."

"So why don't they send in the DSU big guns to sort them out?" Peachy asked.

"Quite a few reasons actually. For a start, they're roped to the flagpole on top of the Belfort. Secondly, there are triggering devices that will activate if anyone tries to climb the tower, or approach from the air."

"So that's why we're using the Bambi bucket," Peachy said, referring to the lightweight canvas bucket they were going to fill from a water source on their way.

"Yes. That way we'll be able to douse the fire without getting too close. Providing your aim is as good as I remember?"

Peachy smiled. "Luckily, I went to bed early last night, so we're all good."

She looked below them, Minnewater Park lay ahead. The lake in front of the lock house that controlled the canal water levels in Bruges was an ideal place to drop down and scoop up hundreds of liters of water. Jan tilted the helicopter and swooped down, the trailing canvas bucket streaming beneath them. Seconds later he was hovering over the water. A family of startled swans took off, their wings beating across the surface as the bucket scooped up its load.

"Okay, good to go," Peachy said.

Jan wound the throttle up, and they lifted above the lake and continued on their way. In the distance, the hexagonal spire of the Belfort pierced the sky.

"We should be there within a few minutes." Peachy looked at him. "What do you think this is? Some kind of terrorist attack?" Jan shrugged. "It's a bit weird. Recreating burning witches at the stake, isn't it? We gave that up a long time ago."

"Let's hope it's some random guy without all his marbles," Peachy said.

"Yes. They have until the hour strikes to get them out of there. Unless something sets the device off ahead of time." Peachy looked at her watch. "Twenty minutes. We can do this."

Jan smiled and opened up the throttle. "I'll get you over the Belfort, you hit the target. We're not allowed closer than two hundred feet, or the downdraft could trigger the device."

"Piece of cake, or waffle. Either way, I'll make it a bullseye," Peachy said.

The Pratt and Whitney turbo engines howled as Jan pushed the craft toward its maximum speed of 250 kilometers an hour.

# SIXTY-NINE

INSIDE THE MOBILE command unit, Chandler's phone rang. He picked it up. "Hello?" He handed it to Hoog. "It's Wim." Hoog activated the speakerphone. "Go ahead, Wim."

Wim's voice spilled out of the small speaker. "The drone will be with you in fifteen minutes."

"That's great," Hoog said.

"I've also cut into the return video feed from the Belfort so we can put it into a loop if we need to," Wim said.

Hoog shook his head. "I'm sorry. What does that mean?"

Wim paused. "Okay, sorry to geek you. It means that I can switch their feed to an earlier loop if I need to. Your feed will still be live."

"Okay, so they won't know what we're up to?"

"Exactly. Well, not on that camera at least. I don't know if there are other cameras. These fuckers seem to have thought of everything. Okay, I'd better concentrate. Wish me luck," replied Wim. "For Roxie and Katja's sake, I hope we have more than luck on this one."

"I'm with you on that." The line went dead as Wim cut off.

265

Hoog looked at a video feed of the Market Square. Tourists were milling around. Taking selfies with the police cordon in the background. A small group of teenagers on motorbikes and scooters were enjoying hot dogs and chips in one corner of the square, while families stood around, soaking up the festive atmosphere. The ice rink was in full swing, and pop music blared from its speakers.

At any other time, Hoog would have happily watched the people enjoying themselves. But right now, he couldn't see anybody without thinking they might be watching him or his officers. He looked at the drone's camera feed as it raced toward the Belfort. It was ahead of the fire department helicopter and would soon be on site. With its onboard camera, grappling hook, and knife, Wim was hopeful of snagging the timer or fuel canister and dropping it into a canal. Or at the very least, getting the knife near enough to Katja or Roxie so they could cut themselves free. Failing that, five hundred liters of water delivered accurately would drench the kindling and prevent it from being ignited.

Wim's voice hissed through the speaker on the CCTV console.

"The drone's over the Belfort now."

The drone's camera showed Katja and Roxie looking tired but alert as they stared up at the drone.

Wim's voice said, "You'll hear them, and they'll hear you.

I'm patching audio through to you now."

Hoog leaned forward and spoke into the mic. "Are you both okay?"

On the video link, Katja looked relieved at hearing his voice.

"I've been better. They were waiting for us. We didn't get a look at them. They knocked us out with some sort of drug."

Anger washed over Hoog as he imagined how terrifying that must have been. "Don't worry. We'll get you out of there. Do you know if the device is attached to anything or could we tow it out of there?"

Roxie shook her head. "It's zip locked to the flagpole. I don't think the drone will be able to lift it."

Wim hovered the quadcopter drone closer, zooming its onboard camera into a space between the piles of firewood.

Hoog saw the faint gleam of a metal canister and some wires leading off from it. "Okay. We daren't risk moving the device. Wim's going to drop a knife so you can cut yourself free. Okay?" Katja and Roxie nodded. Hoog watched the screen as Wim maneuvered the drone above the women. A gust of wind caught the drone, knocking it off course. The picture oscillated wildly, and he saw the knife bouncing across the rooftop out of their reach. "Dammit!" Hoog swore, getting sympathetic glances from the technicians monitoring the scene. Wim's voice came over the coms link. "The drone's taken a hit, I'll need to get it back and do some running repairs. Sorry." Hoog could hear the disappointment in Wim's voice. "It's okay Wim. We'll find another way." Hoog looked at the screens. "How long 'till the fire department helicopter gets here?"

An officer pointed at one of the screens. "Looks like they're ahead of schedule."

Hoog looked at the screen. He saw a white light and a flashing red one above it heading towards the city. But something was wrong. It was way too early. Loading up a medical helicopter with fire-fighting equipment and a water dump bag took time. They'd said it was fifteen minutes away and that was barely five minutes ago.

"That's not possible," Hoog said. The officers in front of the monitor screens turned to look at him. He didn't waste any time explaining. "Can you tighten in on that?" He saw a cameraman leaning out of an open door, pointing his camera towards the Belfort. Hoog felt his heart pounding and heard the blood roaring in his ears. All his years of training and police experience hadn't prepared him for the challenge he was facing. With enough time there was a solution to everything.

But with a countdown, everything changed. Even the best mountaineer in the world couldn't scale the outside of the Belfort in the time they had left.

If the helicopter came too close to the Belfort and the anemometer, it could override the countdown and detonate the accelerant within the firewood. An approach from the bottom of the tower gave him two minutes to reach them. All of the options would lead to the same outcome. Triggering the fire. And in the middle of the resulting conflagration would be Roxie and Katja. He had to save them.

If Marsha was behind this, she'd planned for every eventuality, including helicopters. She knew ladders and hoses wouldn't reach—nothing could save them, or so she believed. But she hadn't thought of everything; she couldn't have. Something deep inside him was sure of that. Whether it was because she was an immortal and had more exposure to the past than the future, or maybe because even an über witch wasn't infallible, he didn't know. What he did know was that he was only going to get one chance.

# SEVENTY

THE TRIP ALONG the canal hadn't taken long. A simple rowboat had sufficed to carry Marsha and Brandt Van Zwart beneath the Kraanrei, and Sint Janstraat, and they were soon under Market Square. Through the manhole covers that punctuated the tunnel roof above her, she heard the wail of the police sirens and the roar of the approaching helicopter. The whole of the market and the Burg had been cordoned off. The police had thrown all of their resources at the situation. She doubted there was an officer left in the satellite station at Kartuizerinnenstraat or the new offices at Coiseaukaai. After all, they were dealing with an unprecedented attack in the heart of the City. Everything was going to plan. Up ahead the canal narrowed. The Provincial Court that dominated the square had been built on the site of the old Waterhalle. Over the years, sewer systems and underground pipes had commandeered more space alongside the canal beneath the streets, and as a result, their progress was sometimes tricky. Brandt Van Zwart slowed the boat, dragging his oars against the flow of the water, guiding the boat toward the crumbling walls of the canal and towards some worn steps covered in a mantle of moss. He tied the boat to a corroded iron ring set into the side of the wall. Marsha looked around. Traces of the previous buildings, their foundations, and weathered stone buttresses, jutted out of the dark above them. They turned on their flashlights and climbed up the narrow, crumbling stairway that led up to the basilica. The Basilica of the Holy Blood, now home to the most precious of relics, supposedly brought back from the crusade by Count Flanders in 1150. It had courted controversy and religious fervor for hundreds of years.

269

Every year on Ascension Day, the city was flooded with thousands of tourists following the procession of the Holy Blood, when the precious relic was carried through the streets. Above them in the upper chapel Basilica Museum, the vial was housed in a gold and silver shrine consisting of a gem-encrusted hexagonal case with over one hundred precious stones. But more valuable than any of the precious metals or gems was what was contained within the rock crystal vial.

A piece of cloth stained with the blood of Christ.

Usually, the relic would be locked away in the safe overnight, but Marsha had arranged for that particular ritual to be bypassed. She'd contacted Saul du Bois, a member of the Noble Brotherhood of the Holy Blood, and the person in charge of the relic's safe keeping that week. She'd told him that a photographer was updating the church website. She was familiar with his reluctance to rise early and knew that she only had to let human nature take its course to achieve her aim. It didn't take him long to work out that leaving the relic on display overnight would save him having to get up so early in the morning. With the relic already out on display, he could stick to his normal routine and meet the photographer outside the Basilica at nine o' clock.

They paused beneath a rusty iron grill, and Brandt Van Zwart played his flashlight around. Passages and tunnels had existed beneath the Burg and the Basilica for centuries.

Wherever there was power and wealth, there was the danger of an uprising by the downtrodden and underprivileged. Many of the rich and powerful had discovered to their cost how dangerous it could be not to have an escape route.

But they were breaking in, not out. She reflected on the progress they had made, the experiments that had been carried out at great cost, and risk, had reached fruition. Having a companion that would be with her forever was within her grasp. But there was still one last thing that needed to be done. One final action needed to form a bridge between Brandt Van Zwart and the immortality they both craved.

The grill made a grinding sound as Brandt Van Zwart pushed it open. Flecks of rust floated down through shafts of light as it fell back. Thudding against the stone floor above. Moments later, they were clambering up and into the secret chamber beneath the basilica.

She listened. The sirens were more muted now. And she heard the dull thud of the helicopters rotor blades in the background. She smiled. What had come to save them would soon become the instrument of their destruction.

.

# SEVENTY-ONE

THERE WAS NO other way. Whichever way he looked at it, time was running out. Using the stairs gave him two minutes once he'd tripped the countdown. Two minutes to climb 366 steps and that didn't include the ladders that provided access to the roof. It was impossible. As Chandler had said, even Usain Bolt couldn't do that. He realized everyone was looking at him. How long had he been standing there thinking? They must have seen the madness that danced in his eyes. But it wasn't madness; it was hope. He knew what he had to do.

"I'm heading for the roof."

Chandler and Duke looked at him.

"There isn't enough time. You'll be killing them." Chandler said. Hoog could see the fear and anger in his friend's eyes, and he knew exactly what he was going through.

"You have to trust me. We can't risk that news helicopter triggering the detonator. Believe me, there's no way I would put Katja and Roxie in any more danger than they're already in." Chandler looked at him. Came to a decision.

"Okay. How can we help?"

"Tell the fire helicopter that I'm up there and keep everyone away from the bottom of the Belfort." He turned around, pushed the truck door open, and jumped down. As he raced across Market Square, he saw the Buzz-Ard helicopter.

It was seconds away from the square and the Belfort. Seconds before the downdraft from its blades tripped the countdown, robbing him of any advantage and sealing Roxie and Katja's fate. But that wasn't going to happen. Not while there was breath in his body. If there weren't so many people in the square, he would have pulled out his gun and fired warning shots at the helicopter himself. He could imagine the lecture on health and safety that Pieters would have given him. But he could care less about that. They could fire him for all he cared, as long as he saved them, nothing else mattered.

He reached the corner of the square leading off to Vlamingstraat, beside the cafés with their awnings and outside tables. There was the usual bunch of teenagers sitting on their bikes chilling out, chatting to their girlfriends. He saw a boy sitting on a bright green Honda Monkey motorbike, sucking on a vape. The diminutive bike was so small it looked like a toy. The boy saw Hoog running towards him and gave him a guilty look out of the corner of his eye. Maybe he had a stash somewhere about his person. Hoog didn't give a damn. He could have had a kilo of heroin taped to his forehead for all he cared. No, what he was interested in was worth far more to him than any drug stash. He ran up to the boy and flashed his I.D. at him. "I haven't done anything man…" the boy gabbled.

"Off the bike," Hoog said. "What?" the boy grumbled and reluctantly climbed off. Hoog waved a couple of hundred-euro notes in his face. "Just need to borrow this for a bit." The boy took the notes. "Whatever." Hoog revved the bike, dropped the clutch, and left a smoking trail of burnt rubber across the cobbles as the engine howled and he raced across the square.

The helicopter's shadow slithered across the cobbles as it headed toward the Belfort. Hoog swerved around tourists as he rocketed toward the Belfort. Ahead of him, he saw officers clearing a path to the base of the tower.

Within seconds he was through the cordon and roaring beneath the arch and into the courtyard behind the Belfort. He veered left and clawed his way up the approach steps leading to the first-floor booking office and entry turnstiles. He jumped off the bike and wheeled it through the narrow gap between the turnstiles, reached the other side and climbed back on to the bike.

He looked up at the LED timer and its display frozen at two minutes. Hoog revved the engine hard and roared up and onto the bottom of the spiral staircase. The LED started its countdown as the bike bucked and jerked, its wheels scrabbling for purchase on the worn stone. The two-stroke engine howled as he fought to keep the bike upright. The noise from the bike's exhaust was deafening, and the fumes stung his eyes. The wheels jarred as they fought for grip on the ancient stone, sending waves of pain up through his spine. He looked at the timer counting down on his wrist. Twenty seconds gone and he was approaching the second floor.

Hoog fought to keep control of the bike. His elbows and knees slammed into the bricks on either side of the stairway, he ignored the pain as he clawed his way up the spiraling stone steps, to the second floor, scrabbling past the great bell. He hung onto the twisting machine as the steps narrowed. There was a screech of metal as the rear mudguard and a light cluster was ripped off against the rough stone wall. Then he was alongside the magnificent carillon. He barely gave it a glance. Dropped the bike and sprinted toward the door that led to the roof. It was locked. He looked around. Caught a glimpse of something red on the far wall. A CO2 fire extinguisher. *Thank God for health and safety*. he thought as he ripped it from its mountings, ran back to the door, and slammed the heavy canister into the lock.

The wood splintered into pieces, and the door swung open.
He saw two metal ladders leading to the roof. He climbed
awkwardly up the first one, still clutching the fire
extinguisher, and then squeezed across the roof space and
onto the second one.

He reached the top and stepped out onto the octagonal
lantern tower. The Buzz-Ard helicopter hovered overhead.
Battering him with its downdraft. Deafened by the thud of its
rotors, he could see the cameraman pointing at him as he raced
over to where Katja and Roxie were tied. He saw the LED
countdown on the side of the metal canister within the wooden
pyre.

Twenty seconds and counting. There wasn't enough
time to defuse it, even if he knew how to, which he didn't.
But, he remembered something Wim had once told him about
how geeks overclocking their computers needed extra
cooling to prevent thermal runaway.

*Would that work in the opposite direction? Could he slow
the countdown with freezing gas?*

"Hang on, I'm going to get you out of there," he shouted
against the noise of the helicopter.

Katja and Roxie stared at him with frightened eyes. "It's
okay, Wim's got the security camera on a loop, it's safe to talk."
We didn't think anyone would come," Katja said.

"I was passing," Hoog shouted, as he aimed the black
horn  of the extinguisher between the firewood and pulled
the trigger. $CO_2$ gas blasted out and swamped the ignition
countdown unit. A sheen of frost instantly formed over the
digital readout, the display barely visible beneath it.

"C'mon," he yelled. Gradually the countdown slowed, now it
was only counting down once every five seconds. It had worked.
The temperature was outside the tolerance of the electronics. He
snatched up the knife dropped by Wim's drone and began
hacking at the ropes and cable ties binding Roxie and Katja to
the flagpole. Within seconds, they were free.

They stood up, massaging the feeling back into their cramped muscles.

"Damn that hurts," Roxie said.

"Get down the ladders, hurry!" Hoog shouted.

He turned back to the hovering helicopter. It was time they got out of the way and made room for the fire helicopter. He pulled out his gun and aimed it right at the camera. He saw the cameraman say something into his headset, and the craft veered away. He looked at the countdown.

Five seconds left.

He ran to the doorway and climbed down the ladder. Katja and Roxie stood waiting on the roof below, their faces pale and drawn.

"Are you okay?" he asked.

Katja hugged him close. Her warm body molded against him like a second skin. She looked up at Hoog. "Better than that."

"Get a room," Roxie called out with a pained smile.

There was a muffled roar from above, and a lurid orange light lit up the stairwell.

"C'mon!" Hoog shouted. They scrambled down the winding

stairs to the carillon and heard a dull thump above them.

"The water dump!" Hoog yelled. Seconds later, the water exploded down the stairwell, sweeping them off their feet.

"Hang on!" They clung onto the cables leading from the carillon as the water flooded past.

Roxie looked after the disappearing water. "That would have been the end to a perfect day…"

Katja released her grip on the steel cable. "Yes, to be saved from the fire only to be drowned by the aftermath."

"Yes. Ironic for sure. Okay. Let's get you out of here," Hoog said.

# SEVENTY-TWO

**BASILICA OF THE HOLY BLOOD**

MARSHA LOOKED AROUND the musty room they had climbed into. It was filled with old paintings, religious icons, broken pews, and rotting cushions. It hadn't always been a storeroom. Back during the French revolution, it had been the escape route for the Templars.

They listened. The curators of the relic would have left by now, but she wanted to be sure that they were alone. Brandt Van Zwart opened the old wooden door that led out into the lower chapel.

They continued through the ornate archway and began to climb up the monumental staircase toward the upper chapel, where the reliquary was kept. The staircase was commonly known as *De Steegheere*. Designed by architect William Aerts in the Gothic and Renaissance style. As they hurried up the steps, passing the sweeping brick walls and vaulted ceilings, Marsha remembered the terror that had embraced the people fleeing from the advancing French soldiers all those centuries ago. They reached the top of the staircase and entered the upper chapel.

The reliquary sat in its crystal vial within the silver tabernacle in a glass case on top of the altar between two marble angels. Brandt Van Zwart had brought a padded rucksack that would hold and protect the relic. He went over to the alter, opened the case and the tabernacle, and lifted the crystal container out. Slipping it into the rucksack, he fastened the top flap, closed the tabernacle, and within seconds, they were on their way. Marsha had paid the security expert a large amount of money to make sure the cameras and the alarm system employed at the Basilica were out of commission for the half hour they needed.

Outside in the square the sound of shouting and screaming accompanied the wail of police sirens. They retraced their footsteps to where they had left the boat and were soon gliding silently back along the canal.

# SEVENTY-THREE

CROWDS OF TOURISTS and news crews swarmed around the Market Square, while above them the Explorer helicopter banked away from the Belfort. Its water bucket trailing beneath it. A stout American tourist stood gawping up at the Belfort, along with his wife and two small children, as they watched a plume of smoke rising from the top of the tower.

"What's happening, Dad?" one of the children asked, pointing up at the smoke.

"Looks like they got a new pope, son," the man said.

There was a loud rushing sound as water overflowed from the Belfort roof and plumed down through the air. The crowd cheered, but this soon changed to screams as they were drenched by the water cascading down the outside of the Belfort.

\*\*\*

Father Saul du Bois headed down Woolestraat, and past the Olive Tree restaurant before turning right down Breidelstraat and into the Burg. It was a route he followed to the Basilica every morning and repeated in the evening on his way home. Today was a little different as he had to supervise a photo shoot of the relic in the Basilica for use on the church website.

He'd been contacted the day before, and they'd explained what they wanted to take pictures of, and how long they would be. Father Saul was still irritated at the change in his routine, especially the thought of having to get up earlier to accommodate them. By the time the Basilica was closed for the night, he'd worked out a solution. Instead of removing the relic from its position in the tabernacle and locking it in the safe, he would leave it in situ. It was only for one night, and there was more than adequate security in place to protect it, that way he could rise at his usual time, let the photographer in, and be done by ten when the general public started to come in. He'd gone to bed early, nursing a headache, and had taken a couple of sleeping pills in the hope that a good night's sleep would cure it. He'd risen early and was preparing breakfast when he saw the news. Some sort of murder attempt on two police officers held hostage in the Belfort. He dimly remembered hearing the sound of a helicopter as he'd drifted off to sleep but had thought no more about it. But now he felt uneasy.

He hurried across the Burg toward the church. As a member of the Noble Brotherhood of the Holy Blood, he and those before him had safeguarded the relic since 1400. The Basilica of the Holy Blood church dominated one corner of the Burg. With its gilt façade, gothic upper chapel, and Romanesque style, it was one of the best-preserved churches in West Flanders. It had proved a huge tourist draw, and along with the Procession of the Holy Blood on Ascension Day, was responsible for a large part of the church's income. He reached the front entrance of the Basilica and opened the door with the heavy wrought iron key, one of two on the keyring he always carried. The sound of the door opening boomed around the cavernous space. He crossed himself and looked around. There was nothing out of the ordinary. As far as he could tell the only thing missing were the hordes of tourists.

Much as he knew how important they were to the Basilica's upkeep, he couldn't help but feel irritated at the occasional lack of respect they showed for their surroundings.

He looked over at the white baroque style marble altar. It was decorated with two angels, between which sat the silver tabernacle containing the relic. The overall impression within the Basilica should have produced a feeling of reverence amongst the visitors, but instead, they treated it like an amusement arcade. One of them had even asked him for a selfie with them both holding the reliquary. He shook his head in disgust at the memory.

And then, as he glanced at the tabernacle, the blood drained from his face. He was only too aware of the tricks one's mind could play. It had the ability to manufacture an image based on seeing an object in a particular place for weeks and months, even years. Like parking your car in the same spot every day…and then one day it's gone. Your brain, rather than accepting the reality, fabricates the image that it is expecting to see. Father Saul even remembered the term: confabulation, a disturbance of memory. misinterpreted memories about oneself or the world. And there it was—or wasn't. He moved over to the tabernacle and stared at it. Its curved silver surface warmed by the soft golden light from the overhead lamps. But within the tabernacle, something that had been there for as long as he could remember, was gone.

# SEVENTY-FOUR

CHIEF PIETERS LOOKED around the office. The well-worn desk, the citations on the wall, and the pictures of him posing with the mayor and the dignitaries of the town. Evidence of a successful career and a well-deserved climb from the lower ranks to the upper echelons of law enforcement. He picked up the picture that had sat on his desk since he had taken up the position of chief. A photo of him standing next to his smiling wife and their two beautiful daughters. They at least were real. But the persona he'd been inhabiting for all these years, wasn't. He'd told himself that everyone told the odd white lie. The public had to be protected, budgets kept to, the press managed, and the approval of his superiors earned. When he'd been promoted after the death of his superior, he soon learned how things were run. And more importantly, how the horrific death of Chief De Klerk, along with his wife and children, wasn't the accident everyone believed it to have been.

They'd called it *housekeeping*. And looking back, that was the moment he could have, should have, walked away. Away from the only job he was good at. A career stretching back over twenty Years. He told himself that his wife and daughters would be in danger if he didn't toe the line.

But he was lying to himself. He was too scared to do the right thing. Too afraid to stand up to them like a man and walk away from their threats and demands. Instead, he took the money and the protection they promised.

As long as he turned a blind eye to the lucrative drug trade that was operating right under his nose, then everything would be all right.

But it wasn't all right. The problem with turning a blind eye to crime was that there were police officers, who were far-sighted enough to know when something was going on right beneath their noses. And like a freshly killed carcass starting to decay, the smell kept on growing until it could no longer be hidden. Detective Jochum Van De Hoog and Officer Katja Blondell were exceptional in their fields. They complimented each other, and their success rate was off the charts. It was only a matter of time before they uncovered what he had kept hidden for so many years. But then he got a break. They fell in love. He'd seized the opportunity to sow the seeds of unrest between them. He'd called her into his office and alluded to the unwritten law of in-house relationships, how they were a danger to the other officers that served alongside them. He never told her directly that he knew, just brought it up casually, while hiding the point of the meeting beneath a layer of congratulation on her progress. Having sown that seed, he then went on to put as much pressure as he could on their burgeoning love affair with caseloads and shift patterns. And when he saw the cracks beginning to appear, he set up the offer of a transfer to Antwerp. She was at her lowest ebb and had taken the opportunity without too much opposition. And so Pieters was able to keep things on an even keel. The drugs kept running, and the money rolled in. But now they were back, not together as such, but working as a team. But it hadn't been Hoog and Katja that threatened his situation. No, he'd messed up. He'd given Ward Johansson, a keen young officer, some cold cases to keep him occupied, and it had backfired. Ward had uncovered a connection to a dealer running drugs around the ice rink over the holiday period. He'd managed to identify the gang leader, and with Hoog and Katja's help, carried out a successful surveillance operation that had brought down the dealer known as Blades.

They came down on him hard. Threatened his wife and children and promised to destroy his career as well. He didn't have any choice. He had to deliver what they wanted. He'd walked away from the mobile command unit outside the Belfort. There was no way he could watch what was destined to happen. Or live with the consequences. He'd spoken to her on the phone. She sensed what he wanted. A way out.

He'd listened to what she said. He wrote a note for his wife and children and propped it up against the photograph on his desk before leaving.

He walked down the stairs into the lower floor and the catacombs. He entered the area that had recently been flooded. There were still sheets of crumpled paper lying around. Pieces of the cold case files that had led him to where he was now. There was nothing else in the room apart from the petrol driven pump and a spare jerry can of fuel. The exhaust was vented through a hole in the temporary wooden shutter covering the shattered glass of the window. He unscrewed the top of the jerry can and upended it. He took the cheap disposable lighter from his pocket, and with streaming eyes and burning throat, flicked the lighter. By the time the fire alarms went off, he was dead.

# SEVENTY-FIVE

ROXIE AND KATJA sat opposite Hoog, Duke, and Chandler in the back of the mobile command unit. It was ten o'clock in the morning, and the ordinarily bustling square was subdued. Since the fire and the flooding of the Belfort, the day before, both the tower and the Market Square were in the midst of a major cleanup operation, and it would be several days before the area was deemed safe. They'd been up half the night dealing with the situation, and making sure that Katja and Roxie were taken care of by the paramedics after their ordeal in the Belfort. And now, after grabbing a few hours' sleep, they were back on site.

"Why do you think he did it?" Katja asked. She was still struggling to come to terms with Chief Pieters suicide and searching for answers.

Hoog shook his head. There was no question it was a suicide. The CCTV from the catacomb had left them in no doubt. Though the letter to his wife had been more ambiguous.

"I don't know. He told his wife he was sorry, and that he was looking forward to seeing her again."

Roxie took a sip of coffee. "What did he mean by that?"
Chandler leaned forward. He was relieved that Roxie and Katja were safe, but the death of the chief had hit them all hard. "Maybe he meant that when she died, they would be reunited again.  It's something commonly inscribed on headstones, 'together again once more', or some such phrase."

285

Duke looked up. "Seems to me that what Pieters did was totally out of character. If we didn't have the CCTV footage, I'd be looking for her fingerprints at the scene of the crime. You guys knew him better than us. What do you think?"

Hoog shrugged. He didn't know what to think. He'd been pretty banged up getting to the top of the Belfort and hadn't slept much during the night either. His mind wasn't in great shape, and he certainly wasn't in a position to untangle all the probabilities of the case or Marsha's possible connection to the events that had taken place on the roof of the Belfort.

"The manner of Pieters death conforms to the same ritualistic pattern followed by the members of IGNIS," Chandler said.

Duke looked at him. "You saying he killed himself because he believed he would come back by possessing somebody else?"

"Whatever reasons he had for killing himself, it must have been going on for some time. Remember how freaked out he was after we arrested Blades at the rink?"

"Yes, I thought that at the time," Chandler said. "You brought down a drug dealer, and he seemed more concerned about health and safety."

Katja took a sip of coffee. She was bone tired. The ordeal on the top of the Belfort and the cold were finally catching up with her. "Yes, that did seem a bit out of proportion."

"I don't want to bad mouth the guy, but if he was on the take, then smashing the drug ring would have pissed off his paymasters," Duke said.

Hoog sighed. He'd liked Pieters, but he had to agree his behavior had been out of character since the ice rink operation.

Katja looked at Hoog. "Do you think he was on the take?"

Hoog shrugged. "I don't know. But even if he was, why would he commit suicide?"

"The way he behaved after the ice rink surveillance operation was in contrast to his behavior when it came to the Sint- Jansplein crime scene and his suggestion that Katja and Roxie take another look," Chandler said.

Roxie looked at him. "You think he set us up?"

"He knew we would be involved in the interrogations, and only one officer was securing the site."

Hoog punched a fist into his hand in anger. "You're right. But maybe he didn't know what Marsha had planned."

"He must've known it wasn't gonna be a good thing," Duke said.

"When Pieters became chief who did he take over from, and how?" Chandler asked.

"Chief De Klerk. It was a tragic accident. He was burned to death, along with his wife and child, when their house caught fire. There was evidence it was deliberate, someone poured gas through the mail slot. But they never found the people responsible." No sooner had Hoog uttered the words than the coincidence hit him.

"They had him murdered. Maybe he didn't want to go on being in their pay. He could have been about to blow their whole operation apart."

"No wonder Pieters was so angry when we brought Blades in. He knew they would blame him, threaten his wife and children. But when he realized what she had planned for Roxie and me, he couldn't live with it," Katja said.

They sat there in the truck as the significance of the situation sunk in. Their moment of reflection was shattered when the door was flung open. Ward stood in the doorway, wide-eyed and out of breath. "The relic of the Holy Blood—it's been stolen!"

# SEVENTY-SIX

THEY STOOD STARING up at the tabernacle on the altar. The marble angels looked mutely on. Behind them, crime scene technicians took pictures and prints. Hoog watched them at work. Calm, methodical, going through the motions, and yet he knew, it was all ultimately pointless. It was long gone. The Belfort operation had been a sideshow to the main event. The theft of the priceless relic.

Father Saul was beside himself with remorse. He'd had to confess that the relic had been left out overnight in readiness for the photo shoot, and not locked in the safe as usual. The insurance was null and void.

Hoog looked around the church before turning to Katja.

"Why do you think it was stolen?"

Katja's mind had been sifting through the many possibilities all morning, and though there was no proof, it all pointed toward Marsha. "It's all conjecture, but the evidence they found in Louisiana showed Blackburn and Marsha were focusing on blood in their search for immortality. What's to say that this isn't another component of their experiments?"

"I suppose there's logic in that," Hoog said. "Adding the blood of someone who came back from the dead to spice up your immortality drug of choice."

Katja rubbed the bruising on her wrists. "None of this is going to cut any ice with the commissioner."

Hoog had to agree. The loss of the relic could very quickly turn into a public relations disaster if it weren't recovered. And soon.

There had been high-level discussions with the mayor and the chief commissioner, along with officials of the tourist board. They all agreed that those responsible for the relic's theft must be tracked down and brought to justice, and the priceless reliquary recovered. It was decided that they could conceal the loss of the relic for a short amount of time by claiming it was being renovated and restored to its original condition. But if they hadn't found it by Ascension Day when the procession of the Holy Blood was due to start, then the game was up. The city would have to admit to the world that one of the most precious relics on the planet had been stolen from right under their noses.

The effect on the tourist trade would be devastating. The commissioner had made it very plain that money was no object. They'd monitored every port, train station, and airport, and come up empty-handed. Marsha and Brandt Van Zwart had vanished into thin air.

And then a couple of days later they caught a break. Wim had set up a facial recognition algorithm using Marsha and Brandt Van Zwart as the reference. Employing some dubious data breaching techniques, which the commissioner had sanctioned, he launched a swarm of Algo Bots to scan the internet for any trace of them. With the enormous amount of social media sources and the unrelenting posting of selfies, it was only a matter of time before they were found.

Hoog got a call from Wim at the university the next morning. He'd found something. Hoog picked up Katja, and they drove over to the university where Chandler and Duke were waiting with Roxie.

They were all clustered around a large screen looking at a still from a Facebook account.

Wim looked at Hoog. "Recognize this?"

Hoog knew it well. He'd spent an amazing week there with Katja when they were still in the first flush of their relationship and remembered a trip by gondola to see the many tourist sights on offer.

"Venice, that's the Bridge of Sighs," Hoog said.

The bridge stretched over the Rio Di Palazzo and was made of white limestone with windows of stone bars. It connected the new prison to the interrogation rooms in the Doges Palace, designed by Antonio Contino, and built in 1600. It was probably one of the most recognized tourist spots in the world. The picture was a selfie of a young couple on a gondola with the bridge behind them. But it was the gondola in the background that had their full attention. Because inside it, smiling in the sunshine were Marsha and Brandt Van Zwart.

"At least we now know she actually exists," Duke said. "And that she was behind everything," Hoog said. "So, what's Brandt Van Zwart's connection with her?" Roxie asked.

Katja looked at the picture. "Whatever it is, I have a feeling it goes back a long, long, way."

Chandler smiled. "And I have a feeling I'm going to need to renew my passport."

# SEVENTY-SEVEN

MARI FELL BACK onto the bed. Her face glowing with pleasure in the light from the bedside lamp. Ward rolled off her.

"My God, what's got into you?" she asked.

Ward had come home to tell her the news. He'd been promoted to the rank of Detective, effective immediately. He looked at her with a smile.

"I hope that's not a complaint?"

Mari shook her head. Ward's lovemaking had reached a new peak. They hadn't made love like that since their dating days.

"Not at all, and nice to enjoy ourselves before we have to worry about the baby."

Ward nodded. He'd surprised himself. Since learning of the promotion, he'd been energized. Despite the loss of the chief and the theft of the Holy Relic, he felt as if he could handle anything life threw at him. With the success of the drug raid at the ice rink and his near-death experience in the catacombs, Ward's profile had been elevated amongst his peers. Word had come down from his superiors up at the Coiseaukaai station that he should be rewarded for his efforts. With the extra workload brought on by the theft of the relic and the uncertainty surrounding Pieters death, his promotion to detective had become a necessity. He looked over at Mari's smiling face. The increase in salary the job brought with it was also welcome. With a child on the way, it was one less thing to worry about.

"I'm glad you're happy," Ward said. He rolled over onto his elbow. Stroking her cheek with his fingers.

Mari smiled. "As long as they give you some time off when the baby arrives."

"I'm sure they will. That's quite a few months away, and I'm sure we'll have closed the case by then."

"I hope so. It was awful what happened to Pieters. Did you have any idea he was having problems?"

Ward shook his head. "He'd been a bit up and down recently, but nothing serious enough that we were worried about him."

Mari sat up. "Maybe he was just good at hiding it?" Ward thought about this.

Mari was right. Along with his newfound optimism for life and increased sex drive, had come a certainty that Pieters had been involved in something illegal and dangerous. He initially had his suspicions when he went over the cold cases and found the drug pushing cases that hadn't been followed up. Then there was the case against the owner of The Pelican, suspected of supplying drugs from his premises. A case that Pieters had shut down claiming insufficient evidence.

"Maybe he was," he said. "Anyway, this is our evening, let's not ruin it with work." He leaned over and kissed her. "Now, where was I?" Mari looked at him with surprise. "Again?" she asked. He smiled. "If you insist."

# SEVENTY-EIGHT

THE BELFORT CLOCK face flared gold in the setting sun, the ice rink glowing pink in its dying rays. Dua Lipa pulsed from the sound system. Duke, Chandler, and Roxie leaned against the side of the ice rink sipping beers.

Hoog turned to Chandler. "So, do you think you would be able to stand Venice for a while?"

"If they can afford us."

Hoog laughed. "That's not an issue. The relic is priceless on many levels. The loss to the tourist industry alone, considering how many come over to visit the Basilica and take part in the procession of the Holy Blood, is millions."

Chandler thought about this and winked at Roxie. "Maybe I will join you. Until I get tired of canals."

Duke gave a deep belly laugh and shook his head. "Canals my ass."

Hoog clapped Chandler on the shoulder. "Be glad to have you along." He took a sip of his rum-laced chocolate and turned back to Katja. "Know what I'm going to say?"

Katja looked at him. "Let me guess. They're playing our song?"

Hoog shrugged. "Nothing gets by you, does it?"

Katja pushed off from the side of the rink and shouted back to him. "Depends how fast you skate."

Hoog finished his drink and followed her onto the ice. He soon caught up. Reaching out to join hands as they swept around the rink as Dua Lipa's *Be the One* reached its chorus.

293

Look out for the next
Duke Lanoix and Chandler Travis thriller:

# VENICE BLOOD

# ABOUT THE AUTHOR

Mike Donald worked for the BBC as a sound mixer, wrote for comedy sketch shows, and developed up sitcom ideas. He also worked as a script analyst for a gap finance company and has written many award-winning screenplays. Mike lives in Oxford with his wife, and a power-hungry Terrier named Bonny May Donald. Bruges Blood is the sequel to Louisiana Blood, the 2019 #1 best seller in mystery, thriller and suspense on Inkshares.com and 1st in the Mill City Press author awards 2018. The prequel, Louisiana Blood is available on Amazon.com, Amazon.co.uk, and Barnes and Noble online.

# AKNOWLEDGMENTS

As ever I'd like to thank the small army of believers that helped to get this book published. My ever-faithful Beta readers, Peter Ryan, author of the amazing *Sync City*, available on Amazon.com, and Rebecca Ortese, audio narrator extraordinaire, and author of multiple titles available on Amazon.com. Also, a huge shout out to the editing and design team at Story Perfect Editing Services. They are responsible for the amazing cover design for Louisiana Blood, which won an award, as well as the fabulous Bruges Blood artwork. Particular thanks must also go to my hardworking editor at Ink Slingers, Cheryl Murphy, along with an extra big thank you for the immaculate proofreading and formatting by Margaret and Craig at Story Perfect. And finally, a massive thanks to my incredible wife Dorrie, for supporting me during the birth of Louisiana Blood and Bruges Blood. I am forever grateful for the time granted to me to fulfil my ambitions.

Printed in Great Britain
by Amazon

85855196R00174